MAFIOSA PRINCESS BECOMING THE PRINCE

LIZA MALLOY

CHAPTER 1

Part I- Summer Time

Giada

"Your turn, Gia. Two truths and a lie," Elise prompted.

I gazed around the circle at my friends—all classmates from the elite Rhode Island boarding school I'd attended since sophomore year. School had dismissed for summer break just in time for my birthday, but Luca was stuck in Italy for the entire summer.

Instead of spending my birthday lonely and wondering what Luca was up to, I'd invited my closest friends to my family's Connecticut home for an extended sleepover. We'd already lounged poolside until our arms tanned, binged on pizza, and snacks, and gossiped through viewings of two Tom Holland movies. Now we were sprawled out in my bedroom, playing a revealing round of each of our favorite sleepover games.

I thought hard about which truths would stump my friends, then debated the best order to deliver my statements. My friends had all divulged their wildest truths, so the bar was high. Impos-

"

sibly high, really. My life was boring by comparison. My friends had all experienced so much more than me.

I took a deep breath. "I hate butterflies. I have three brothers. And I'm a virgin."

Both Brinley and Harlow leaned forward and frowned.

"I think you switched it, Gia and gave us two lies and one truth. Unless... do your parents have some love-child I don't know about?" Elise finally said.

I giggled. "Nope that was the lie. I definitely only have two brothers."

She and Delaney exchanged a look. "Um, okay but the whole virgin thing?"

"I told you I'm waiting till marriage." I said with a casual shoulder lift.

"We're supposed to believe you and Luca didn't... after prom?"

I shook my head.

Prom had been amazing. Magical, really. Luca wearing a suit was hands down the hottest sight I would ever see. I'd felt like a princess in my dress, and we enjoyed the perfect night together. If I hadn't already been incredibly in love with Luca, I would've been by the end of the night. We had a blast at dinner with Luca's fellow upper-class friends before the dance, and then at the dance itself, Luca's attention was focused entirely on me. He danced with me, staring into my eyes and smiling at me. Even when we took a break between songs, Luca remained fixated on me.

When we returned to campus after the dance, we'd immediately snuck away from the dorm to makeout on the football field. And even though Luca was a tad obsessive about his clothes, he hadn't hesitated to spread his designer suit jacket over the turf so the night dew wouldn't dampen my dress.

Luca was the absolute dream boyfriend. He was an amazing kisser, and from the way my entire body tingled with excitement every time his tongue brushed my lips, I was certain I'd enjoy doing more than just kissing Luca. I also didn't doubt Luca would be good at anything else we tried. He'd take care of me, make me feel safe, and wouldn't even blab to anyone afterwards.

So really, if I were going to have sex with someone before marriage, I absolutely would've done it with Luca right then.

But I wasn't going to do that. I may not be a perfect Catholic, but I certainly planned to abide by that one straight-forward rule.

And Luca understood.

My friends, on the other hand, clearly did not. And I had no interest in explaining my adherence to this one traditional rule to a gaggle of teenage girls…especially when they seemed determined to remind me my boyfriend was on an entirely different continent at the moment, one where according to my friends, no one had any morals.

So instead of dwelling on my nonexistent sex life, I opted to distract everyone, myself included.

"Who's up for a night swim?" I asked, a devious smile on my face.

The girls all shrieked and scurried to locate dry suits.

Luca

The first week in Italy wasn't bad at all. Alessio and I flew over together, so for the first time ever, the flight wasn't torture. Even though we were trapped in a tight space with a bunch of strangers, the flight didn't feel much different than when we spent a weekend just lounging around Alessio's house, watching movies and playing video games. I only napped for about an hour or two, but we had enough soda during the last hour of the flight to leave us feeling refreshed as we landed.

A driver met us at the airport and drove us to my parents' place in Rome. I hadn't grown up in that house, so it had never felt like home to me. The house was beautiful, if not cozy, and emitted old-world vibes, from the furnishings to the architectural touches. The home wrapped around a central courtyard, which was great in the winter but miserable in summer. Without any hope of a breeze, the humidity overpowered the courtyard on balmier days.

Still, the home was well-equipped, with five spacious bedrooms, two large seating rooms, a dining room, a kitchen, and an office. Alessio and I each had our own room, but we'd share a bathroom. No big deal. Down the hall, my papà's right hand man, Tony, occupied a guest room, and my papà was in the master bedroom.

My mother was down at the house in Palermo. As far as I could tell, she tended to spend as little time as possible in the same house as my papà.

I didn't blame her.

I had to admit it felt good to be back in Italy. I gave Alessio the tour, finishing right as my papà returned. He greeted me warmly and then turned to Alessio.

I tensed, not knowing how the reunion between them would go. The last time Alessio and my papà seen each other in person, my papà had nearly killed my friend, so I would understand if there were some hard feelings.

"Benvenuto signore Rizzo," my papà said in Italian. "Welcome to our home and welcome to my family. We are so pleased you have decided to join us this summer. I hope you feel comfortable here."

Alessio nodded, accepting my papà's outstretched hand. "Thanks for letting me stay here. It's a nice place."

"Let me know if there's anything we can do to make your stay more comfortable," my papà said, eliciting a chuckle from me since it sounded like something they'd say at a Holiday Inn.

Alessio nodded, then my papà started out.

"Get some rest this afternoon, boys. We will meet tomorrow in my office. Eleven am."

Alessio turned to me and I shrugged. "You could nap if you're tired," I said.

"Yeah, we drank enough caffeine to never sleep again, amico. We might as well go exploring."

"Alright, you're leading the tour, though. I grew up Palermo, so I don't know my way around here," I said.

We visited some of Alessio's old haunts, then caught an early dinner and drinks before heading home. We were both in bed by eight pm local time. Despite the early turn-in time, it was still close to ten when I awoke.

I dragged myself out of bed, pounded on Alessio's door to make sure he was awake, then showered. My papà was all business at our morning meeting, having brought in his whole local team to meet with us. Mostly, he got updates from each guy on how everything they'd been working on was going. None of it made total sense to me, and I felt like I'd walked in on the second half of a really dull movie or something. But it was also nice to hear that most of the stuff sounded like legit business matters, and not just a bunch of raping and pillaging, or whatever criminals like my papà probably did.

Around one pm, Alessio and I went to lunch with my papà and Iacopo and Lodovico. It was an even mix of business and casual talk, which was awkward. The rest of the afternoon, Alessio and I were to work with Lodovico. We mostly just followed him around to different businesses where he chatted with the owners, collected envelopes, then left. Seemed pretty basic.

The rest of the week followed a similar pattern. In a few more days though, we'd be heading to Sicily. I couldn't wait.

CHAPTER 2

Giada

The sleepover didn't end after one night. A few girls went home, but several of my suitemates stayed for a second night. Exhausted from our previous night of debauchery, we enjoyed a more low-key experience. We napped by the pool, then binged on takeout sushi. We gave each other manicures and pedicures, then smeared blue mud masks all over our faces so we looked like Smurfs. After a few rounds of Truth or Dare, we were all exhausted from the past two nights and fell asleep at a semi-reasonable hour.

On the third night, it was just my roommate, Elise, and me. We'd both enjoyed another poolside nap during the day, so we had plenty of energy by evening. My brother Matteo and one of his friends joined us for a movie, and I'd just started wondering how long it would be until Elise hit on my brother, when my phone rang. It was exactly midnight, which seemed late for a call. I wasn't surprised when I saw that it was Luca. Although, six am seemed awfully early for him.

"It's Luca," I whispered to Elise, excusing myself from the room as I answered.

"Buon compleanno, amore mio," he said, his voice more refreshing than a glass of water in the dessert. *Happy birthday, my love.*

I breathed a laugh. It was officially my birthday. "Thank you. Isn't it six o'clock in the morning for you?"

"It is, but I wanted to be the first one to wish you a happy birthday."

I actually swooned. "I miss you," I said. And I did. I'd barely thought of him the past few days thanks to the chaos of the sleepover, but now, hearing his voice, the longing hit me hard. I wanted to see Luca and touch him. I wanted to hear his voice up close, in person.

"What are you up to tonight?"

I told him about the sleepover, then asked how he was doing. We didn't talk for very long, in part because I wanted him to be able to fall back asleep and in part because I worried about leaving Elise alone with my brother for too long.

When I returned to the living room, the movie was almost over. I plopped down beside Elise, tugging half of her blanket back over my lap and reaching for another handful of popcorn.

"Who was that?" Matteo asked.

"Her boyfriend," Elise replied in a singsong voice.

I felt my cheeks blush. I really didn't discuss my relationship with Luca with my brothers. I hadn't chatted about boys with them much in general, but it seemed even more awkward with Luca since my brothers were sort of friends with him.

"Luca?" My brother furrowed his brows. "Luca called you?"

I nodded then pretended to focus on the movie.

"Isn't it the middle of the night there?"

"Early morning," I said.

Matteo stared at me, making zero effort to hide his surprise.

"Wow. I didn't know you guys were on international-calling basis."

I shrugged. "It is my birthday," I said, then snatched the remote from Elise, cranking up the volume until he took the hint. When the movie ended, Elise and I both retreated to my room.

"Sorry I mentioned Luca in front of your brother," she said. "I just figured he knew things were so serious with you guys."

"It's okay. He does know, but it's just weird. My brothers are way too protective anyway so we don't really talk about dating. And with Luca, I don't know. We were all friends as kids and then the past couple years we hadn't seen much of him, and now it feels like Luca is more mine where he used to be more my brothers' friend, if that makes any sense."

"I get it," she said, even though I was certain she didn't.

"I've sort of played down how serious it all is with Matteo and Angelo, made it seem like Luca and I are more like good friends."

Elise nodded. "So how's your man doing?" she asked.

"He's good. He wanted to be the first one to wish me a happy birthday, so he set his alarm."

"Aww. That is like the sweetest thing ever." Elise clasped her hand over her chest and toppled backwards onto my bed in a swoon. She picked up the framed photo of Luca and me from my nightstand and smiled, holding it out for me to see. Obviously, I already had every detail memorized. It wasn't one of the professional photos from prom, although those had turned out great too, but it was my favorite picture of us. We'd been trying to take pictures with all of our friends and Luca kept making me laugh, so someone had snapped a shot while he was grinning at me and I was laughing. I loved how a simple picture captured the adoration in his eyes when he looked at me and the over-the-top joy I felt whenever we were together.

"You guys are seriously the cutest couple ever," she said. "You must miss him a ton."

I did, although it had been only a week since he'd left. I

wondered if it would get easier the longer we'd been apart, or if I'd feel this way until we were together again. I hoped it was the former, because I was already sick of feeling incomplete.

"You're going to see him this summer though, right?"

I nodded. My family was spending three weeks in Italy, as we did most summers. I wasn't positive how much of that time would be in Palermo with Luca but I hoped most of it. Occasionally my parents dragged me up to Rome. While it was a tad cooler there, it felt infinitely hotter without the ocean breeze of Sicily. Plus, I already knew Luca would be in Palermo when we were there.

"God, I bet the sex will be fantastic after a month apart," Elise continued. "That expression of 'absence makes the heart grow fonder' doesn't really capture the full picture if you catch my drift."

I giggled at her implication but shook my head. I'd told her before that I wasn't going to sleep with Luca—or anyone—but I guessed she figured I'd changed my mind.

"Waiting till marriage, remember?"

Her jaw dropped. "Seriously? I thought you were just saying that so the other girls wouldn't think you were slutty."

I quirked a brow. Given what I knew about the other girls' dating history, I'd have to sleep with a lot more guys than just Luca to qualify as slutty in their eyes.

"So that's still the plan, waiting till marriage?"

I nodded.

"And Luca's okay with that?"

"Yeah. I mean, he might try to marry me the second I'm eighteen, but…"

Elise's face contorted into a grimace. "You couldn't possibly marry someone you haven't had sex with. What if the sex is bad?"

I almost pointed out that picking a spouse based solely off of good sex wasn't a solid plan either, but I didn't. Elise had a point.

I didn't believe in divorce, so whomever I married was it for me. I wanted 'it' to be good.

"He's an amazing kisser. We have great chemistry. And everything else we do is perfect. I'm sure it'll be the same with sex," I finally said.

"Yeah, you're probably right. But if it were me, I'd be worried about spending all summer apart if my guy hadn't been getting any lately though," she said. Then her eyes widened as if she just realized what she'd implied. She turned to me, shaking her head. "I just mean in my own life. There's no way Luca would ever cheat on you."

Her panic level almost made me laugh, so I just smiled and told her it was okay. But I did sort of share her concern. "If he's not willing to wait for me, he's not the right guy for me," I said.

But I really hoped he was.

Luca

Alessio and I rode the train down to Naples, then we caught the ferry to Palermo. Not the most efficient way to get there, but we had fun.

"You always travel like this? Alessio asked, nudging my side.

I shrugged sheepishly, then stepped back. My life was pretty fucking awesome, when I actually thought about it. I was basically on an all-expenses-paid summer vacation with my best friend.

"Let's get some drinks," I said, grinning. "My treat."

When the ferry docked in Palermo, a driver was waiting. This guy managed to make it to my family home, where my mother was staying, in roughly half the time the drive usually took. My mom greeted us both and pretended to be excited to see me, but then informed us we were actually staying at an apartment down the coast. I wasn't eager to test my luck in the car with Mr. Racecar driver again, but he'd already tossed our bags back into the vehicle.

This drive was short, probably around five kilometers total, and I definitely had no complaints when we saw the place we'd be staying. The apartment was right on the beach, with killer views. There was only one bedroom, but that room had two separate beds. Also the fact that we'd be staying there alone was huge. My papà had been a surprisingly good host up in Rome, but freedom was always better.

Alessio and I spent our days shadowing different guys that worked for my papà. We had a decent amount of free time to do whatever we wanted, and we took advantage of every minute. I still had friends in Palermo, and they quickly welcomed Alessio into our circle. We were old enough for the clubs in Italy, so when we wanted to party, we had plenty of options.

I missed Giada. I did, really.

Back at school, she'd actually become my best friend. So without her, it was weird, even with Alessio by my side. I missed talking to Giada, missed her perpetually upbeat attitude, and missed her melodic giggle. And I definitely missed kissing her. Giada had the softest lips and she always tasted like candy. God, she even smelled like candy.

But just because I missed Giada didn't mean I was about to sit around all day pining over a girl who was thousands of miles away while I was in Italy with plenty of girls here. We still talked on the phone, and we'd been counting down the days till the end of July, when she was coming to Palermo with her entire family. I wasn't sure how that would go, me reuniting with Giada while my papà and hers both watched, but I was excited to see her.

I thought she'd be impressed with the progress I'd made that summer. She'd never commented on my lack of maturity, but I sensed she wanted an independent guy. And living in an apartment without parents and working, albeit for an illegal enterprise, I felt like a real adult. I honestly couldn't imagine what it was going to be like, returning to school and going back to the prison of a dorm where they treated us like babies. At least Seniors had some extra privileges and could leave campus pretty much whenever.

Giada's family was arriving the next afternoon. I went with Lodovico and Iacopo to pick them up, and then we were taking them to where her family was staying down the beach. Although her father traveled to the region a couple times a year, they didn't own anything here. I wondered if my papà had arranged them to rent a place so close to our house, but I wasn't going to ask, less he think I considered it a favor to me. Besides, Alessio and I weren't staying at the family home, anyway.

CHAPTER 3

Giada

The rest of my birthday was amazing. My entire family —like all fifty people— came to the house to celebrate right as Elisa was leaving. I relished the attention. One of my favorite aspects of my birthday was always that my family treated it like it was a big deal, almost like Christmas.

But once my birthday was over, all I could do was count down the days until my family traveled to Italy. I tried to stay busy, spending time shopping with my mom, gossiping with my aunts while they cooked, and met up with Elise a few times. Still, time crept along.

By the time we were in the air on our way to Palermo, I was tingling with excitement. The plane circled the runway for an eternity, then once it finally did land, the crew forced us to stay in our seats forever. My parents had already told us they were taking a separate car, stopping to visit Grandma before joining us at the villa where we'd be staying. My mom caught my eye and informed me that Luca would be escorting my brothers and me, as if I didn't already know that was the plan.

When we had finally collected our bags and walked outdoors, I peered around, eagerly awaiting the best welcome hug ever.

I didn't notice him at first. I was so distracted by the beauty of the view ahead of me, where the bold cerulean water met the pure white sands, and all of it reflected in the matching contrast of the white buildings dotting the vivid blue sky.

My eyes registered a dark haired Italian man, wearing thick dark sunglasses, khaki shorts, and a long sleeved white button down shirt, with the sleeves rolled partway up his forearms. But as he spoke the language I still didn't speak, I turned away to stare at the landscape again. That man had to be at least in his twenties. And boring. When Luca arrived, I'd know.

"Hey, Luca!" Matteo shouted just then. Angelo waved too, albeit in a much more reserved way than Matteo. I followed their line of sight, surprised that the guy I'd seen earlier was walking towards us. Two other men, both also wearing suits, flanked him.

As he neared us, I confirmed it was, in fact, Luca. I couldn't see through the dark lenses of his glasses, but I suspected he was looking at me, even as he approached my brothers. He hugged them each, performing the perfunctory kiss on each cheek, then followed up with a handshake and a shoulder pat. It was a picture-perfect, friendly Italian greeting.

I waited for my turn, nervous that there would be other changes since his outward appearance had matured so much. But as soon as Luca neared me, I breathed in his familiar scent and relished the familiar tingling of my skin. His hands gripped my biceps as he kissed one cheek, then the other.

"I missed you," he whispered, lingering on the second cheek.

I tightened my stomach, wondering if he'd kiss me for real despite my brothers' presence. I desperately wanted him to do it, but was equally terrified.

After a moment, Luca released me, his lips curling up into a crooked grin as he gazed at me.

Then, he patted me on the shoulder like I was one of the guys before turning back to my brothers.

What the heck?

The four of us rode in the back of a SUV with the two men who'd accompanied Luca riding in the front. He and my brothers made animated, casual conversation the entire time. After a few minutes, I felt Luca's fingers lightly graze mine.

"You're quiet today, Princess," he said.

"She didn't shut up the whole flight," Matteo said with a chuckle. "Probably tired now,"

"Flying is exhausting," I said.

We arrived at our destination sooner than I'd hoped, and my brothers eagerly climbed out.

"We'll talk later," Luca promised, raising my hand to his lips and placing a chaste kiss on my palm.

That night, we were meeting Luca's family for dinner, but thanks to a terrible seating chart, which put me at the furthest seat at the table from Luca, we didn't get to talk until after dessert was served. Then, thankfully, Luca approached my dad.

"Mr. Conti, may I borrow your daughter for a bit? I thought we might walk down by the water. I can return her to your villa in an hour."

My father answered him in Italian, but I assumed based on his nod that he'd agreed. Then, he snapped. Like, actually snapped his fingers together. "Giada," he called, gesturing for me to go with Luca.

I made no attempt to hide my eye roll.

"It was a pleasure seeing you, my darling," Mr. Marino said as I walked by.

Luca reached for my hand, but I casually swung it away, simply walking beside him until we were outside.

"God, I thought that meal would never end," he groaned. "All evening the only thing I've been able to think about is kissing your soft, sweet lips."

I stopped, ready to do just that. But Luca shook his head.

"Come on, we can talk in private, but we need to go further. Too many eyes and ears here," he said, nodding back to two men who appeared to be standing guard outside the residence.

This time, I let him take my hand.

We walked for a good five minutes before we reached the beach, then Luca kicked off his shoes. I smiled to see that he was sockless, which was such an Italian thing to do. He rolled up his pants, then raised an eyebrow to me and reached for my ankle.

I let him unfasten my sandals and slip them off my feet one at a time.

"The beach is rocky," he cautioned, "But we can walk up here," he led me to a thin sliver of soft sand and then turned to face me. "You're even more gorgeous than I remember."

I bit my lip, tempted to lecture him about ignoring me all night and not protesting that dumb seating chart. But Luca launched into the apology before I had a chance.

"I'm sorry. I wanted to talk to you, to touch you, but with both of our families there... I figured the less I even looked at you, the easier it would be for me to focus. Your beauty is distracting."

I snorted. "That is possibly the most Italian thing you've ever said to me."

His expression was sheepish, but sincere. I supposed I had pulled out all the stops that night. My thin sundress was cut at an angle that emphasized my legs, especially when paired with the high-heeled strappy sandals. My hair fell across my shoulders in loose waves like I knew Luca loved, and I'd chosen a delicate necklace that would draw his eyes to my chest without seeming too obvious.

"You look older than I remember," I said.

"Well, we both are, right?"

"Happy birthday," I said.

"You too," he replied. "Can I kiss you?"

His hand already rested on my cheek, softly stroking my skin in a soothing circular pattern.

I nodded, leaning forward.

The moment our lips met, relief flooded me. He was the same Luca after all. He tasted the same, he smelled the same, and thankfully, he kissed the same. I really would've worried if he seemed like he'd been getting a lot of practice. We kissed for what felt like only a matter of minutes before he pulled away, breathless, and shook his head.

"Did I mention I missed you?" he asked.

I nodded and leaned in for more kissing.

"Baby, I promised your father I'd get you home in an hour. Men like him don't like tardiness."

"It hasn't been…" I began, but then I saw Luca's watch. *Crap.* We'd been making out for forty-five minutes. We hadn't even begun to catch up or talk about our summers.

"We will see each other again tomorrow," he said. "Ti prometto. Then we will talk, okay?"

I groaned, but he simply laughed and kissed me again.

He grabbed our shoes then walked me down the beach a ways further, then deposited me at my door. "Sweet dreams, my princess," he said.

Luca

The moment I reached the apartment, I burst through the door, eager to tell Alessio everything about my evening. The silence which greeted me served as a cruel reminder that I couldn't tell him. For the time being, I was alone. Alessio was spending the next two weeks visiting with his grandparents in Naples.

I dropped to the couch, dragged a hand through my hair, then grinned. Kissing Giada had been fucking amazing. In the time we'd been apart, I'd almost convinced myself that she wasn't any different from other girls. But the moment I saw her, it all came back to me.

I couldn't pinpoint what it was about her, but Giada was like a drug and I couldn't get enough. Everything, from her big, bold eyes to her sassy pout drew me in and once I was close? God, even her smell after a trans-Atlantic flight was tantalizing. After spending the next two weeks with her, surviving the rest of the summer without her was going to be torture.

I stripped out of my clothes, showered off the salty sea air and remnants of sand between my toes, then sprawled out on top of my duvet. I scrolled through emails until a wave of drowsiness washed over me, and then I switched off the light, eager to see what the next day would bring.

CHAPTER 4

Giada

Thanks to the time difference, I was still comatose when a thunderous pounding shook me awake. I rubbed my eyes, uncertain how I still felt as if I hadn't slept at all when the clock claimed it was nearly half past ten.

"Giada," Matteo's voice drifted through the door to my tiny bedroom. He spoke my name almost like a question, making me wonder how my timid brother could have knocked with such ferocity to jolt me out of sleep so abruptly.

A moment later, my question was answered as I heard my older brother's voice.

"This is ridiculous, just open the fucking door and chuck something at her," he growled.

"That's rude, and what if she like, sleeps naked or something?"

"Eww," Angelo replied.

I rolled my eyes. "I'm awake!" I shouted. "And I'm wearing pajamas, you idiots."

"Mom says we're leaving to visit grandma at eleven. Don't be late," Angelo called back.

I groaned, but dragged myself out of bed. At least I could partake in lots of Italy's fine coffee.

We spent the entire afternoon and evening with my grandma, much to my chagrin. Of course I'd realized the purpose of the trip was to visit with her and the rest of my Italian family, but I hadn't anticipated those visits to take all day.

I texted Luca an apology, and he replied that it was fine, and that he was busy doing odd jobs for his dad.

The next day was slightly better, with my mom and I accompanying my grandma to mass, followed by lunch with the family. I was released from the family obligations after dinner. Luca and I met up for gelato, but it still wasn't enough. Two weeks in Italy would never be enough if I only got an hour with him each day. Fortunately, Matteo told me we had the next few days free.

I called Luca to tell him the good news.

"Ciao tesoro," came his greeting.

My cheeks flushed at the unexpected compliment. *Hi, treasure.* "How would you feel about spending the next three days with your favorite person in the country?"

Luca didn't answer for a moment, so I thought he was about to make a joke about someone else being his favorite, but when he replied, his tone was solemn.

"I'm sorry, Giada, but I'm busy tomorrow. And I have a meeting Friday, but after that I could—"

"Cancel your plans!" I shrieked, sounding a tad whinier than I'd intended. "What could possibly be more important?"

"I've got some stuff for my papà."

"What are you doing?"

Luca's hesitation was more telling than his eventual answer.

"Errands."

I blew out a sigh. If I wasn't important enough for him to carve out some time for me after I flew a whole day just to be with him, well, whatever. "Fine. Have fun," I snapped, hanging up.

Luca

I hated blowing off Giada, but I couldn't share details of my work with her. My papà would kill me. But I also wasn't dumb enough to think anything about my situation with Giada was "fine," despite what she said. I thought about sending flowers to her villa, but I didn't want to embarrass her in front of her parents. My ideas for grand gestures were pretty limited with her entire family right there, though.

I stared at my calendar, then finally found the solution. I could fit in a late lunch with Giada the next day, give her a whole list of fun ways to spend her afternoon, and then see her again Friday after my meeting. I called her back, apologized for being a jerk, and told her I'd cancelled some stuff. She didn't question my choice of restaurant, which I'd picked solely for its location and not, as I told her, for its world-famous pastas, but she did wonder why we had to eat so late.

"I could move up the reservations if you want," I bluffed, "But it'll be less crowded later. I thought it would be more romantic if I can actually hear you without having to shout over the crowd."

She sighed, and I knew I'd convinced her.

When we met up the next day, Giada was in good spirits. Time in the sun had deepened the bronze glow to her skin and made her look even more gorgeous than usual, and she wore another one of her sundresses that drove me crazy. I wasn't sure how Giada managed to take such an innocent outfit and turn it into something so arousing, but she did.

Giada talked for the majority of our lunch, which was fine by me. I loved hearing her voice, and I didn't have much to say anyway. She asked about my summer, but I offered the generic version, saying only that I was working for my papà. What else would I tell her—that I'd joined the mafia and spent my days trailing his goons and watching them shake down people for money they owed? No thanks. Giada would never talk to me again if I told her that.

I couldn't even tell Giada what I did in my free time. I hadn't exactly cheated on her, but I knew she wouldn't approve of the ways Alessio and I spent our off-duty hours. We partied—a lot. I drank, danced with other girls, and sometimes even made out with them. I hadn't gone farther than that, hadn't even wanted to, really. But there had definitely been some topless girls at the last party Alessio and I attended before he took off to visit his grandparents, and I hadn't exactly turned my head.

Whatever.

None of that mattered now, and once I returned to school in Rhode Island, life could return to normal. I'd have an entire year to pretend I was a regular high schooler with a typical future ahead of me. Giada and I could enjoy our innocence together, and then I'd go off an accept my fate.

I paid the bill and then walked out of the café, gripping Giada's hand tightly. As I leaned in for the goodbye kiss, I noticed a man just behind Giada staring at us. He lifted up his sunglasses, and I sighed. It was Iacopo. He tapped his watch, then nodded to the man next to him, Tomasso.

"What's wrong?" Giada mumbled, her voice soft like when she first woke in the morning.

"Nothing, but I have to go."

"No." She said it without pleading or whining, as if saying it that way could make it true.

I dipped my head in the direction of the guys. "They work for my papà. They're waiting on me." I pressed my palm against her cheek and she tilted her face against my skin, giving me the false sense of compliance.

"I flew all the way out here to see you and you're always busy," she pouted.

Her family would've dragged her to Italy regardless of my

presence in the country, but this wasn't the time to bring that up. "Mi dispiace," I said instead, apologizing.

"Do you want to go with them, or would you rather spend the day with me?" she asked, straightening her head and pulling her entire frame to attention.

"Amore, you know I'd rather be with you, but…"

She pressed a finger to my lips and glanced around us furtively. "No buts."

Before I could ask what she was looking for, she gripped my hand and jerked me firmly in the opposite direction of the guys.

"Run!" she urged, leading me down a nearby street.

I didn't have time to think as Giada practically dragged me down the steep concrete stairs. We dodged clumps of people exiting and I futilely called "scusi" over and over.

I turned as we reached the bottom of the steps, dismayed to see Iacopo and Tomasso were actually following us. Giada swore under her breath, presumably noticing the same thing I had. Then, she skidded to a stop. The bus heading southeast had just departed, so I tugged Giada across the street toward the northwest bus.

The hiss of the brakes as the bus rolled to a stop told me we were out of time. I leapt up the stairs then reached to grab Giada and tugged her aboard. Her laughter echoed down the aisle as I paid our fare then followed her to the back of the crowded bus. I panted, catching my breath, then pulled her back against my chest, wrapping my arms around her and resting my chin on her head as we peered out the window. I offered a demure wave at Tomasso and Iacopo, who reached the bus right as we chugged along to the next stop.

Giada craned her head to face me and grinned. "I can't believe we just did that."

All I could do was laugh. Sure, my papà would be pissed. He might literally kill me. But at the moment, I didn't care. With

Giada in my arms, nothing could tamper my happiness. I was indestructible.

Giada

*L*uca seemed uneasy at first, but he quickly relaxed as our bus journeyed along. We hopped off four stops later and eventually wound up in a quiet neighborhood. Luca squeezed my hand and led me across a street and down a narrow, sloping alley. I balanced along the edge of the curb like I was a tightrope walker, delighted at Luca's willingness to slow down with me.

"Gaahh. This is just so gorgeous!" I squealed, stopping abruptly.

His eyebrows dipped but then he stepped back and gazed around us, presumably finally appreciating, or at least noticing, all the charm of the city he'd known his whole life. The alley was hidden between two quintessentially Italian buildings—massive structures with fading mauve paint and delightful miniature wrought iron balconies outside every few windows.

"You're gorgeous," he finally replied, his tongue stumbling over the letters and drawing it out.

"Why is your accent so much more noticeable here than back home?"

"Questa è mi casa," he retorted. "This is my home. Well, not my house, but my country. This is where I feel more…comfortable."

I nodded. That made sense. No matter how many times my family went to Italy, I didn't think I'd ever stop feeling like a tourist. Maybe if I spoke the language it would be different, but I doubted it. Back at school, there were lots of international students, but even if there hadn't been, Luca still would've fit in.

He never seemed like an outsider, and most of the time his accent was no more noticeable than the difference between a Boston or Wisconsin accent.

Luca snapped my out of my thoughts by ruffling my hair, then kissing the top of my head. "Come. We have more adventures."

He led me to the Covenant of the Capuchini Friars, a gorgeous Gothic church complex, and the church of Santa Maria della Pace. The whole place had been restored in the Baroque style and the effect incredible.

As soon as the thick doors shut behind us, my head angled back like I was a puppet on a string. The entire place was majestic, but the ceiling was absolutely breathtaking. There were dramatic paintings portraying almost theatrical religious scenes, typical of the baroque period, and then ornately detailed architectural features above all of the arches.

I must have stared, slack jawed, for a good five minutes, before the deep rumble of Luca's chuckle snapped me out of my stupor.

"But on the outside, it just…" I shook my head instead of finishing the sentence to avoid insulting the gorgeous structure. The exterior wasn't necessarily ugly or boring, but certainly unassuming. Nothing on the outside suggested the grandeur to be found inside. "Could you imagine worshiping in such a beautiful place?"

His eyes scanned the room then landed on his watch. "I think we could. In…two hours maybe?"

It was clear from his tone that he had no interest in staying for mass, and as much as I'd love to spend more time in the basilica, I wouldn't understand any of the service anyway.

"No, we don't have to stay. But um, would you be terribly bored if I just sat down for a few minutes?" I thrust my hand into my bag and my fingers were instantly drawn to the rosary in the side pocket. By the time Luca nodded his agreement, I was already rolling a smooth bead between my fingers.

He led me to a pew, then sat beside me.

I held the rosary beads up for him to see. "I was going to, um…" I began, suddenly feeling shy. "I could say the prayers out loud?"

"Up to you," he mumbled.

I began, painfully aware of his eyes on me for the first several minutes. But by the time I reached the Doxology, I was calm. It was impossible to feel anything but complete inner peace while reciting the rosary, which was precisely why I loved it so much. I noticed when Luca stood, and approached a man on the opposite side of the room, but it didn't disturb me. When I finished the final prayer, I stood and joined them.

The man smiled and spoke to me in Italian, but instead of translating, Luca simply replied to the man for me, rubbing my shoulder as he spoke. After a moment, the man left us and Luca turned to face me, his grin widening.

"Samuele said the catacombs are open."

I started to ask who Samuele was, but guessed the answer to that right as I stumbled on the next noun in that sentence. "Catacombs," I repeated.

"Yes, like…the graves?"

I shuddered at the thought, then nodded eagerly. I wasn't about to pass up something as cool as hidden burial grounds under a gorgeous basilica, not when I had my hunky boyfriend at my side to keep me safe.

The narrow staircase leading down to the underground tunnels began as wooden steps, then gave way to stone. As we reached the bottom level, I briefly considered what would happen if a fire took out the wooden structure, trapping us in the hidden cemetery. The temperature dropped substantially by the time we reached the first tunnel, but Luca's arm tightened around my shoulder before I registered the chill.

CHAPTER 5

Luca

I'd switched my phone off the moment we had evaded Iacopo and Tomasso but the men could still find me if they really wanted to. Giada's phone surely had GPS, and if my papà were desperate enough, he could ask her father to track her. Or, he could call her and ask to speak to me. Thus far, he'd presumably done neither.

When we finished exploring the covenant, Giada spotted a waterfront café for dinner. The food was cheap, but delicious. I savored every flavorful bite like a man on death row enjoying his last meal. Sneaking away with Giada was invigorating, and we both laughed more than we had in a long time. As we stood to leave, a floral vendor gave Giada a bold purple bougainvillea bloom.

Too happy to even be annoyed at the vendor's presumptiveness, I handed him a few folded bills, but he simply shook his head.

"Gratis," he said, explaining he wasn't charging us because a girl "così bella"—that beautiful—needed a flower.

Giada thanked him in Italian, then huddled close to me so I could translate as we walked out. A sizeable crowd had filled the streets by now, and as a man bumped me, I jumped. I turned, fully expecting it to be one of my papà's men, ready to take me back to some abandoned building for a beating.

The stranger apologized for running into me and hurried along his way, but I still felt tense.

Giada reached for my hand and squeezed until I peered down at her. "We can get back now if you want. I didn't mean to stress you out. I just wanted to kidnap you for a few hours."

"You can kidnap me any time you want," I said. I reached into my pocket for my phone. "I feel like I should check my messages though, just in case." That way, I could at least gauge my papà's current fury level. Two or three messages probably meant I'd be sore for a few days to a week; five, and I'd probably be dead.

I swallowed the lump in my throat while waiting for my phone to power on. To my surprise, there was only one message. It was a text from Tomasso. He'd written in Italian, but Giada eyed me expectantly so I translated it aloud.

"I covered for you. Just be home by morning and no one will ask questions. You owe me."

"Wow. Nice," she said. "Maybe we should get him a souvenir to thank him." She gestured to a ceramics shop as we passed and I laughed out loud.

"Pretty sure that is not the sort of thing he thinks he's owed," I mumbled. "Where to next?"

Before she could reply, there was a clap of thunder. Umbrellas popped up all around us just as the pitter patter of large, cold drops began pelting the pavement. I shrugged out of my jacket and hoisted it over our heads, then nodded for Giada to follow me. We jogged a few yards until we reached the closest tram station.

I stood behind her beneath the small shelter, and she leaned against me, tilting her head up to smile at me.

I sniffed her hair and smiled, surprised that she still smelled like strawberry shampoo and not like the flower or city rain.

"Are you smelling me?" she asked, her tone incredulous.

In lieu of answering, I buried my nose in her hair, shaking my face back and forth until she howled with laughter. I tried to recall a moment when I'd last been that happy, and I came up blank. It was like finally everything was perfect in my world.

Giada turned to her phone, furiously scrolling for something, then smiled. "Is this nearby?" she held up an address. I peered around the corner, then nodded and pointed in the right direction.

"Want to make a run for it?" I asked.

Giada grinned and dashed out from under the awning right away, getting a good half block away before I even started. She shrieked as she ran, then stopped abruptly. When I spotted her shoe alone on the cobblestone, I couldn't help but laugh. I bent down and grabbed the shoe, then caught up to Giada. She balanced with a hand on my back while I slid the shoe back on her foot, then she took off again, tugging me behind her.

As we turned the corner, she lost her shoe again, and this time, I simply picked up Giada. I couldn't move as quickly with her in my arms, but I didn't mind. The rain had mostly stopped anyway. When we reached the destination, I set Giada on her feet before realizing where she'd led me.

Somehow, my precocious American girlfriend had found a salsa club in Italy.

"I don't dance salsa," I protested, adding "And I'm sure there's a dress code," but she'd already pressed through the entrance.

Giada batted her eyes at the guy manning the entrance and he smiled politely.

"Venti euro," he said to me, correctly assuming I'd be the one paying. I did, and we were on the dance floor before I'd even adjusted to the lighting.

"Why is there a salsa club in Palermo?" I mused as Giada

grabbed a table. A waitress appeared while we were still getting settled, so I ordered us both a limoncello. I caught the panicked look in Giada's eyes, but as I predicted, the waitress didn't ask to see our ID.

"I thought the drinking age was eighteen here," she said.

"That's why I ordered. I'm old enough," I teased.

She didn't protest when the drinks arrived, but she did blink repeatedly after downing her first sip.

"Stronger than you remember?" I asked.

"I'm not sure I ever had this before."

"I figured you'd like the sweetness."

"What was the drink I had at your dad's before dinner that time?" she asked. "That was good, and definitely not this strong."

"Aperol spritz. That's a before-dinner drink. This is for after."

"So many rules in Italy! Explain again why I can't have a cappuccino after lunch?"

I cringed at the thought of such a misstep, and she laughed too hard for me to explain.

The moment we finished our drinks, Giada dragged me onto the dance floor, despite my protests. We were both predictably awful at salsa dancing, particularly in comparison to the other patrons, who all seemed like professionals to me. With Giada though, I didn't mind looking like a fool. Having the most gorgeous dancing partner ensured no one would judge me negatively for anything, and besides, she was fun.

After we struggled through a few songs, one of the older, more experienced-looking ladies offered to give Giada some pointers. She eagerly agreed, so I returned to the table for another drink. Watching Giada attempt to follow the more complex moves, laughing at her every misstep, brought a wide smile to my face. I was so enthralled by her that I didn't notice the man at the table next to me looking in my direction.

When our eyes met, he smiled. "That is your girlfriend? Or

wife?" he asked, adding, "I heard you speaking English earlier, so I hope you don't mind the language."

"Girlfriend. I'm only eighteen."

"The two of you remind me of my wife and myself, when we were younger. Only in our case, she's the Italian and I'm the American."

I smiled politely, but then I realized his wife was the woman trying to teach Giada proper salsa technique. "Ahh, that's nice. Do you live here?"

"We do now, but the first fifteen years of our marriage we were in the States."

I'd never before considered remaining in the States full time after graduation, but as I pictured a life with Giada, I was certain I'd live anywhere as long as it meant I could have her.

Suddenly, my chest tightened at the realization that I could never have Giada, not with the life my papà had planned for me. Giada was the fantasy. My reality was lonelier, darker.

No sooner had that thought crossed my mind, Giada gazed over at me, grinning widely. I couldn't help but smile, even knowing our relationship was doomed.

"Well, I'll let you get back to your dance partner," the man said. "You make a beautiful couple. There's nothing like young love."

I nodded politely before scooting off my seat to join Giada.

Giada

Neither Luca or I mastered the art of the salsa. We paused for another drink, then I slipped off my shoes. When we returned to the dance floor for our final round, I perched my feet on top of Luca's, letting him lead me around the floor like a child. I felt so ridiculously safe all wrapped up in his arms. I suspected his parents were probably mad that he'd blown off his work, figured mine were probably pissed I'd missed curfew by this point. And I knew we'd both be in trouble.

But I just couldn't bring myself to care. Every moment with Luca felt like a present and I didn't want to waste it.

"It's late," Luca finally said, tugging me towards the door.

"We're already in trouble. What's another hour?" I asked.

His lips quirked into a sly smile. "We aren't in trouble. Tomasso covered for me. And I texted Matteo and asked him to cover for you. But that doesn't mean we can stay out all night. I don't even know what excuse he gave your parents."

"Wait, you did what?"

Luca beamed proudly, then repeated what he'd said. I followed him outside and called Matteo. After a quick call with my brother confirmed he'd told my parents I was already asleep in bed, Luca and I made our way down to the beach. The sand was still damp from the earlier rain, making it much more amenable for a casual stroll.

A few lights signaled the presence of boats out on the water, but for the most part, the shore was dark. Behind us, homes were dark, but lamps lit up the corners of each street.

"It's already two am. What are the chances of us getting mauled by a bear or stabbed by a pickpocket if we just wander the streets until sunrise?" I asked.

Luca wrinkled his eyebrows then relaxed his face. "I'm pretty confident neither of those will happen. But I'm less certain that you won't freeze or get grounded by your parents if they realize you're not really in bed."

"Let me worry about that," I replied.

We walked a bit further and then Luca plopped down in the sand. I contemplated whether the sand would stain my skirt then sat anyway. I didn't understand why Luca pouted until he scooted back, positioning his legs on either side of my hips. I leaned against him and he roped his arms around me, clasping his fingers over my chest.

"Now at least you won't freeze," he promised.

I settled back against him, sighing happily. The current was calm, with the lapping of the waves against the shore softly creating the backdrop for what I already knew would be one of my happiest memories. There was hardly a breeze, so I didn't think we'd freeze either, although the temperature had dropped from the sweltering temperatures of earlier.

"I'm glad you kidnapped me tonight," Luca said after a long silence.

I smiled. "Me too. I've missed you this summer. I've really felt the distance more than I expected."

"I know what you mean," he said.

His words surprised me, and I thought about how little he'd actually revealed about his summer. I tried to think of a way to phrase my next question so that he'd actually answer, but then by the time I had a chance to ask, I realized his breathing had slowed and I wondered if he was asleep.

"Luca?"

"Si?"

I breathed a laugh, then proceeded with my question. "Do you like working for your dad?"

He tensed beneath me. "No."

I frowned. "Are you still going to work for him after graduation?"

"Yes."

"Because you feel like you have to?"

"Yes."

I considered his series of one word answers. I appreciated the honesty, but felt there was something still lacking. "Is…everything okay? I mean, with you and your dad, and whatever work you do with him?"

Luca hesitated and this time, his answer was quieter, less certain. "Yes."

I bit my lip. "Would you tell me if it wasn't?"

He whispered his answer straight into my ear, then added the response to my next question, the one I hadn't even yet asked. "No. Because I love you too much. I don't want you to worry about me. I can handle it. I need you to trust me on that, okay?"

I nodded. Above everyone else in my life, I trusted Luca.

CHAPTER 6

Luca

I snuck Giada back into her villa just after dawn, then met up with her family for dinner later that evening. Matteo barely made eye contact with me, but since I only had one more day with Giada, I didn't worry about him. Giada and I spent our last Italian day together at the beach.

I could still taste her salty lips on my tongue a week later, when I was stuck taking shooting lessons from Tomasso. Apparently, when he said I'd owed him, he meant I'd have to hang out with him for an entire day rather than do him some actual favor. It was weird, to say the least. He took me to breakfast, where he forced me to listen to an hour of fatherly advice on my dating and academic life. Then, we'd run errands all morning. After lunch, we went to some creepy deserted woodsy area where we worked on target practice.

I could tell Tomasso was impressed with how much I'd improved since my last lesson with him back in the States, but the second were in the car, he launched into another lecture.

"Look, you've gotta work on your reflexes."

"My reflexes are great. I nearly hit every shot in there."

"That's not what I mean," he said, shifting the car into gear. "Your papà mentioned what happened a couple weeks ago, when you were out with Lodovico and Iacopo."

I cringed and felt sick all over again. The whole thing was stupid. We'd gone on some errand and Iacopo had asked me to hold the gun. When the guy started to run, Lodovico told me to shoot him. I hadn't, and then by the time Iacopo got his gun back, they had to chase the guy just to shoot him in the foot.

I swore under my breath. "Everything turned out fine. I didn't even know they told him."

"They tell him everything. That's sort of the deal," he said with a click of his tongue. "And you might not think you have anything to prove, but—"

"You don't think I have anything to prove?" I interrupted. "Bullshit. Everyone is watching me just waiting for any sign of weakness. They don't think I deserve it, that I earned it. They don't think I'm anything like my papà."

Tomasso cast me a sideways glance then nodded. "Then prove them they're wrong."

Obviously, that was my plan. Except, there was a problem. "What if I don't want to?"

Tomasso merged onto the highway before answering. "You don't have to be anything like *him*, Luca. But you do have to be strong, fearless, and decisive. You can't keep looking for reasons to give people a second chance. And you can't wait around for someone else to do your dirty work."

I didn't have a response for that.

"There's a reason your papà has you working with Iacopo and Lodovico. They don't hesitate. They do what has to be done without pause."

I snorted. That was an understatement. They were the embodiment of the expression 'shoot now, ask questions later.'

"There's mercy in that decisiveness, Luca. They may not be

sparing people in the way you want them to, but they're not making them wait, either. They aren't playing mind games or getting their hopes up. Their methods are effective, and they're not cruel." He turned to me. "You could do worse."

I sighed. At this point in my life, I felt like that was pretty much my personal campaign slogan...*Vote Luca Marino. You could do worse.*

I thanked Tomasso for the ride, then finished packing up my stuff. Alessio and I were flying to New York at the crack of dawn the next morning. We'd have less than a week to get our shit together back home before returning to campus for fall classes.

I couldn't wait to be back in Rhode Island, back in my fairy tale life with my princess. But I also worried that maybe I needed a little more than a week to detox from the life I'd been living if I didn't want my reality to leech into my fantasy world.

Giada

*A*fter Italy, the last few weeks of summer flew by.

During the flight home, I survived a super awkward conversation with Matteo where he basically interrogated me about what all Luca and I had done during the night he'd covered for us. I told him the truth, but I got the impression he didn't believe me.

Back home, I divided my time evenly between back-to-school shopping, outings with friends, and lounging poolside. I got into the habit of talking with Luca first thing in the morning each day, which was around lunch time for him but generally before he started doing much work. He seemed just as excited as me to return to campus for what I already knew was going to be the best year ever.

The last week before moving back to the dorm, I was overwhelmed with stuff to do. Despite all my shopping, I still needed a few practical things. Plus I had a dentist appointment, my annual checkup with the doctor, a hair appointment, and really needed to get in to the spa to get my brows done before school pictures.

"We can get our nails done after your doctor's appointment," my mom said, her tone casual.

I watched, unease trickling into my chest as she began to inspect the photos above my desk. Most were candids I'd snapped, but there were several of Luca and I, too. I remembered Elise was the photographer for those.

"Nails sounds good," I said, eager to distract my mom. She was way too focused on the pictures of Luca for my tastes. "Maybe some shopping too? I could use a new swimsuit." I needed to get a bikini wax too, but I probably wouldn't mention that one to my mom.

My mom reached for a picture of me wearing a bikini. Luca stood beside me in a pair of swim trunks and an unbuttoned short-sleeved shirt. My hand rest against his bare stomach, my fingers hidden by the sides of his shirt. I was staring at the camera smiling, but Luca's nose was buried in my hair. It looked like he was smelling me but I suspected he was actually kissing my head. He was terrible at simply smiling for pictures while looking at the camera.

"You need to get birth control when you're at the doctor today. I can't believe we've put it off this long," she said.

My abs tightened and my jaw dropped. I'd known nothing good could come out of the razor-sharp focus she'd showed the pictures, but hadn't expected that.

"Mom, I don't need to be on birth control. I promise," I shot her a look that I thought conveyed my awareness of what activities required birth control and my assurances that I wasn't engaged in any such behaviors.

She rolled her eyes, apparently having interpreted my look

differently. "Really, Giada?" She waved the picture of me and Luca.

I snatched it out of her hand and placed it back on my desk. "We aren't doing anything in that picture. We were at the beach, with a whole group of friends."

"Giada, you and I both know this is long overdue. You're at boarding school. It's not like we can be there babysitting you."

"I don't need a babysitter and besides, the school has pretty strict rules. Guys aren't even allowed in the girls' dorms."

She ignored me and continued. "You have a boyfriend now, not to mention one who is so much older, I just need you to be safe. In another year you'll be heading off to college, and you have your whole life ahead of you. The last thing you need is to get knocked up in high school and—"

"Mom!" I interrupted again. "I'm not having sex. And I'm not going to. I'm waiting until marriage, so…back off."

Her lips pressed into a firm line. She stared at me until I felt like my skin was on fire. "You honestly expect me to believe that your eighteen-year-old boyfriend is totally fine with abstinence?"

I gritted my teeth together. "I don't care what you believe, but I'm telling you the truth. I am not having sex with anyone until I'm married. So for you to force me to take drugs…"

"Fine." She held up her hands in defeat. "No birth control. But if you change your mind, I don't even need to know. You can get the prescription from your doctor on your own. But the pill doesn't protect against STDS, so you still need—"

"Mom!"

She relented and backed out of my room. I slammed the door and flopped back onto my bed, taking the picture with me. Only one more week until I'd actually see him again in person. I traced my finger along his abs in the picture, smiling at the memory of his taut, warm skin.

Suddenly, a week felt way too long to wait.

CHAPTER 7

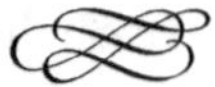

Part II- Luca's Senior Year

Giada

The first week back at school was everything I'd anticipated and more. Elise and I upgraded our dorm room décor so we could fool ourselves into thinking we were splitting a fashionable Upper East Side Manhattan apartment. I got all of the classes I wanted—including a fashion design elective that hadn't even existed as of the last year. Best of all, Harlow and Delaney planned a huge beach bash for the first weekend back.

By some miracle, Luca even agreed to wear a colorful floral lei at the party. I'd gone early with Elise to help set up, but I spotted Luca the moment he arrived. He hadn't exactly dressed for the Hawaiian theme, but he looked hot in the khaki shorts and short-sleeved, white button-down shirt. And once I draped the lei around his neck, we coordinated perfectly. I'd bought a pale, aqua floral wrap skirt and top specifically for the party. Since blush and peach flowers already adorned the outfit, I'd stuck a matching flower in my hair instead of wearing a lei around my neck.

I fielded probably twenty separate compliments on my dress in the first hour alone, and even Elise made a comment about how she was starting to get jealous.

"I could just take it off if that'll make you feel better," I retorted.

"That would make me feel better," Luca chimed in.

I felt my cheeks flush, but Elise burst out laughing. She tugged me onto the dance floor for "Girls Just Want to Have Fun." We kept dancing until I noticed Luca break away from his friends and start eying me. I turned to tell Elise where I was going, but she just nodded and waved me off.

I figured Luca was more likely looking for a makeout session than a dance partner, but I was game either way. I'd almost reached him when Blair stepped in front of me.

I stopped so abruptly that sand kicked up over my sandal. "Hey," I said, a fake smile plastered to my face. If she seriously thought I'd forgotten what a witch she'd been to me the year before, she had another thing coming. But I could pretend to be nice, at least. "Having fun?"

"Totally. You?"

"Yep. I was just headed over to Luca, though."

Blair glanced over at Luca, who had started to approach us. "Cool. Well, have fun."

I opened my mouth to tell her the same when she dramatically faked a fall, splattering her bright red drink all over the top half of my outfit.

"Oh shit. Giada, I'm so sorry. That's like, totally going to leave a stain. Ugh. And that was such a cute dress." Blair smirked.

I clenched my abs, feeling heat race through my entire body. I'd never before wanted so badly to strangle another human. I felt Luca's hand on my hip, almost as if he sensed me about to turn to violence.

"Gosh Blair," I began through gritted teeth. "No worries. Because actually, it's not a dress. It's a wrap skirt and the top is totally separate." I glanced down at the top, seeing the punch bloom into wider stains as it soaked into the fabric. I reached behind my back, quickly tugging the knot securing the top in place. "It makes a great swim suit cover up too, doesn't it?" I asked, keeping my tone demure and locking my eyes on hers as I raised my brows and let the top flit to the ground.

Several guys whistled and Luca's fingers tightened along my now-bare waist. After I moment, I broke eye contact with Blair and turned to my ever-growing crowd of admirers. "Maybe we should all go for a swim later?"

The guys and girls cheered in response to that. Blair slinked off, defeated, and I exhaled, trying to dispel all of my anger.

"Tell me that's your bikini top," Luca said, his eyes wide like he was about to go crazy.

"Of course it is, babe," I replied, kissing him softly on the lips. "Could you do me a huge favor and just rinse this in the ocean though? I don't want the stain to set and the skirt is too long for me to go out very far."

Luca took the top from my outstretched hand, still staring skeptically at my chest. Once he was out of earshot, Elise grabbed my arm and we both burst out laughing.

"Oh my God, that was amazing," she said. "How do you think so fast under pressure? The look on Blair's face was priceless!"

I had to agree with that. "Even if she ruined the top, it'll be worth it just to have seen her when the guys whistled."

Elise grinned. "Well, you do look totally hot, but you and I both know that is just a bra."

I shrugged. She wasn't wrong, but thankfully the bra had a

thin layer of padding and a solid white color that easily passed for a bikini. As long as I didn't get it wet, no one would know the difference.

"Can I borrow your roommate for a minute?" Luca asked Elise when he returned.

She winked at me, then stepped away.

"Your top is drying by the picnic table," he said.

"Thank you," I replied, roping my arms around his neck and stepping close.

"I thought I might have to step in and defend you against Blair. And then I thought I might need to protect her from you. But then what you did..." Luca paused and shook his head. "You are constantly amazing me, Giada." His fingers worked their way around my back and I savored the moment, memorizing the sparkle of his big brown eyes and the curve of his full smile. He slowly leaned closer, and when I couldn't wait any longer, I rose to my toes and closed the distance between our lips.

I could've kissed Luca for hours, and being at the crowded party where everyone was either dancing or drinking or making out, no one else really cared what we were doing anyway. Besides, it was relatively dark and felt somewhat private. Still, there was curfew, so I couldn't stay out all night, no matter how good I felt to be wrapped up in my boyfriend's arms.

Luca was the one to end our kiss. He squeezed my hips, then swatted his palm against my butt. I shrieked, even though it hadn't even stung. "You've got to go," he said.

I groaned, but walked back to Elise, stumbling like the girls who'd had too much of the punch. Unlike them though, I was only drunk off of Luca.

Luca

he first week of classes was uneventful, which stupidly, I took as a good sign. My classes seemed tolerable so far, Gavin and I still got along, and Alessio and Marcus seemed to still be an item—despite not having spoken the entire summer. I divided my evenings between my friends and Giada, and somehow managed to feel like a completely normal American high schooler. It helped that my papà agreed it was important for me to focus on my studies, so I'd only be working one weekend a month.

Unfortunately, he needed a favor the Sunday morning after my first full week of school. I supposed I should've been grateful that I hadn't known about it in advance. I'd enjoyed a Friday night date with Giada—a cliched dinner and a movie, spent Saturday swimming and eating at the beach with Giada and a ton of our classmates, then played paintball with some of the guys Saturday night. Had I been dreading the job for my papà all weekend, I wouldn't have had nearly as much fun, especially if I'd known what we were doing.

Apparently, some guy cheated my papà and Tony out of money Saturday night. Iacopo and Lodovico were supposed to go deal with him Sunday morning, but Lodovico came down with a nasty bout of food poisoning. According to Iacopo, the dude couldn't get off the pot without fear of shitting his pants and was puking in a bucket every few minutes on top of that.

Still, I wasn't sure why I was the next person on the backup list, especially in light of how pissed of my papà apparently was. His phone call woke me from a dead slumber at eight am, and he told me to be ready in fifteen minutes. I was barely dressed by the time Iacopo texted that he was outside my dorm.

The guy's apartment was over a half hour away, so I was thankful when we stopped for coffee and food. Iacopo didn't tell me much about what we were doing or why, just that the guy cheated my papà and needed to learn a lesson. We were visiting him at his home, when he was supposed to be alone, and my job was to make sure he didn't move while Iacopo talked to him.

"How do I do that?" I asked.

Iacopo reached into the glove compartment, then dropped a gun onto my lap.

I picked it up and clicked open the barrel.

"It's loaded," Iacopo said, his tone displaying insult as I confirmed what his words said. "And there's obviously no silencer, so try not to kill him. I'd rather not have to explain that."

I opened my mouth to ask more questions, but Iacopo swerved the car into the curb and parked it. He jammed another gun into the back of his pants, then checked his watch, almost as if he were bored.

"I have lunch plans back in the city, Luca. So we need to be efficient. Can you handle that?"

I nodded, and followed him to the door.

Iacopo knocked once. After a beat, I heard a rustling noise inside.

"Open up, Marty. This will be a lot worse if you dick around with us. Right now we're just here to talk. But if you play games with us, Mr. Marino might take a different approach."

A moment later, the door opened a crack. A pale, skinny, middle-aged man poked his head out. He looked like he hadn't slept in days, and terror filled his eyes.

"Look, I didn't mean to—" he began.

Before he finished his sentence, Iacopo had kicked the door open.

The man scrambled and reached for a gun.

"Luca!" Iacopo shouted.

I trained my gun on him, realizing by the time I'd aimed that Iacopo had already pinned the guy with his own gun. My hands trembled around the cool metal, but Iacopo looked confident and steady.

"Drop the fucking gun, Marty. I don't have time for this shit."

Marty hesitated.

"If you want us to shoot you, we can shoot you. But I'd rather leave you be so you can figure out a way to get Mr. Marino his money. How does that sound?"

Marty's eyes darted back and forth from me to Iacopo. After a moment, he slowly wedged his gun back into his jeans. Iacopo followed suit and re-holstered his weapon as well, but I kept mine out.

Marty frowned.

"Don't you worry about the kid. He's in training, you know? That's Salvatore's boy. Handsome, isn't he?"

Marty didn't move.

Iacopo pointed to the table. "Sit down. Hands on the table where I can see them."

Marty complied.

Iacopo discussed the details of how much money my papà thought Marty had stolen, and how soon he'd need it repaid. I tried to focus on my hands, willing them to stay steady. I imagined I was at school, listening to a boring lecture, or even sitting through a convocation about college applications. Nothing to be nervous about, just normal boring shit.

I'd almost convinced myself of that fact when Iacopo shifted.

"Okay, I'm glad you agree to the terms, but here's the thing. Mr. Marino really doesn't like thieves. He's old world like that, and you know in the old world how they punished thieves?"

Marty shook his head so fast it almost looked like a twitch.

"Luca?" Iacopo asked.

I wasn't even completely sure what the question was, let alone the answer.

"Seriously? Neither of you have any guesses?" Iacopo rolled his eyes. "Pretty sure it's biblical so maybe you need to spend your Sundays in church."

"No, no, no," Marty mumbled, starting to pull back from the table.

Iacopo stepped forward and slammed his hand over Marty's. "Hold still!" he shouted. "Luca, shoot him if he moves."

"In Biblical times, they'd take the whole hand. But I'd rather not kill you," Iacopo said, pulling a switchblade from his pocket. Marty's eyes widened and his pale face took on a greenish hue.

Before I could even process what was happening, Iacopo slammed the blade down across Marty's hand. Blood spurted across the room and Marty wailed.

My arm holding the gun lowered and I felt my breakfast rise up in my throat. I pressed my arm to my nose, trying to block the overwhelming coppery stench of blood. My ears began to ring, which almost seemed like a blessing as it blocked out Marty's crying.

Iacopo gazed around the room then handed Marty his phone. "You should call the paramedics. Tell em you had a cooking accident. They can probably reattach those if you find the fingers."

I gagged and the full contents of my stomach pushed up, but I held back as Iacopo glared at me.

"We'll get out of your hair now, but let that be a lesson to you," Iacopo said, casually wiping the blade of his knife on a kitchen towel before wrapping the towel around Marty's hand. The man sat at the table, whimpering and shaking. I could barely tell how many of his fingers had been cut, what with the quantity of blood pooling around his hand. But from the splatters across the table, floor, and cabinets, I'd guess that at least three had been maimed.

Iacopo started towards the door, but a sickening crunch sounded from under his shoe. He froze, then lifted his foot slowly. "Well, shit. That'll be harder to explain, but they can probably still fix it. You should call now though, before you pass out." He paused, then turned to me. "Luca, dial 911 on his phone."

I did as I was told, taking small breaths through my mouth so as not to puke everywhere. When the operator answered, I gazed to Iacopo for further instruction, but he simply shook his head. I set the phone by Marty. He was conscious, but maybe in shock.

Then, I grabbed a knife from the butcher's block by the sink and moved to the fridge. I didn't see anything like carrots that would be obvious items for chopping, so instead I grabbed a bag of takeout.

Iacopo shrugged, so I dropped the knife in the pool of blood, plopped the bag next to it, then delicately stepped over the splatters of blood and made my way out of the apartment. Once we neared the curb where we'd parked, the remote unlocked the car with a beep. I reached for the handle, eager to hide in the safety of the car, but Iacopo stopped me.

"Wait!" he said. He gestured to my shirt. "You've got some..."

I gazed down to where he'd gestured, immediately seeing the gloppy bright red streak on my shirt. I turned my head and puked all over the side of the street. I hurled until my stomach was completely empty, and then I started to stand, caught another glimpse of my shirt, and began to dry heave for another full minute.

A hand patted my back. "Come on kid. Time to go," Iacopo said.

I glanced up, wiping my mouth on the back of my hand. He thrust a wad of paper towel in my direction, which I accepted. I dabbed at my mouth, then my shirt, but it didn't help with my shirt.

"Here," Iacopo said, offering me a white sleeveless shirt. "Change quick and put yours in the bag. We need to go."

I did as he said, and a minute later, we were in the car. I didn't say a word the rest of the drive back to my dorm. When he pulled into the curved entrance to drop me off, Iacopo gestured to the bag holding my soiled shirt.

"What do you want me to do with that?" he asked.

I shrugged. "I don't care. Burn it."

Iacopo rolled his eyes. "Teens today. So dramatic," he mumbled. He shifted the car into Park, grabbed the bag, and dumped it into the trash can beside the walkway leading to my dorm. "Study hard, kid!" he called after me.

I barely made it inside before I vomited again.

CHAPTER 8

Giada

*L*uca hadn't responded to either of my messages that morning, so after a late lunch with Elise, I called him. I'd even picked up an extra bagel for him while we were out in case he'd slept through lunch.

"Hey," he croaked, picking up on the third ring.

"Hi. Did I wake you?"

"No, I was just…"

I waited for over a minute for him to finish his sentence. When he finally spoke again, all he said was that he was already up.

"Are you sick? You sound awful. Elise and I went to the deli for lunch. I grabbed you a bagel if you want it."

"No, I'm not sick. Or hungry. I'm just in a shitty mood."

"Did something happen?" I tried to think of what could have possibly happened since I'd seen him the day before.

"I'm just stuck in my head. I'll be fine tomorrow. I don't want to drag you down too. Let's just talk tomorrow."

"Hang on," I said. "If you're really having a bad day, you shouldn't be alone. We should go out and I'll cheer you up."

He hesitated. "What did you have in mind?"

"Uh, well, I was going to go to church at four, but I could do something else."

"I thought you went in the mornings."

"I overslept," I admitted.

"Oh. Well, I don't think I'm in a good headspace for church."

I was about to reiterate that I understood and we could do something else, but then I decided to be honest. "I know you don't love going to church, but when I'm in a bad mood, sometimes it's the only thing that perks me up. It might be just what you need."

Luca cleared his throat and I could almost picture him rubbing the thin layer of stubble on his chin. "Yeah, I don't think so, Giada, but you should go. I'll be fine."

"We could do something else instead. Retail therapy?"

That at least made him chuckle.

"I had a crazy dream last night," I said after a pause.

"Oh?"

"Not that kind of a dream," I said, feeling myself blush. "I, um, I dreamt that I put a bunch of laxatives in Blair's morning smoothie and she spent all day sprinting out of class to the bath-room." I giggled at the memory of the vivid dream.

"Now that might cheer me up," Luca said. "Say the word and I'll spike the drink."

"Thanks but no thanks," I said. "Call me if you change your mind and want to hand out, okay? It doesn't have to be church. But it might surprise you and take your mind off whatever is bothering you."

I hung up, touched up my nails, then finished my homework. I didn't expect to hear from Luca, so I'd picked one of my more conservative outfits for church. When he called and said he'd meet me at the campus chapel, it was too late for me to change.

Luca looked like he'd showered and dressed up, but I could tell there was something wrong under the surface. Luca fidgeted and peered around the chapel as if expecting an explosion or something. He was adorable when nervous, but I hated seeing him so uncomfortable, especially in a place that soothed me by its very nature. I brushed my fingers against his and he startled, then relaxed, gripping my hand tightly.

"You always this jumpy in churches?" I asked.

"It's been a while," he admitted with a shrug, still glancing over his shoulder uneasily.

I nodded my head towards the next pew. "There's room."

He started down the row, maintaining his clutch of my hand. When we sat, he pulled our hands onto his thigh. His eyes were focused ahead, on the altar, but the way he continued chewing his lip told me he was still nervous.

I extricated my hand from his tight grip, spurring him to turn to me. I brushed my fingers across his cheek. "Church is supposed to be comforting, not stressful," I told him.

He wrinkled his nose. "I don't belong here."

I didn't have a response for that. "I'm glad you came with me," I whispered instead, right as the priest invited everyone to stand.

By the end of the service, Luca had relaxed considerably, but there was no denying he was eager to leave. He grabbed my hand and practically dragged me back down the aisle. Once we were outside, he tilted his head up to face the sky, inhaling slowly.

I pulled my phone out of my purse and clicked on the weather app. After confirming Monday would be gorgeous, I worked out a plan.

"Uh oh, why are you smiling like that?" he asked.

"Why are you gazing at the heavens like you're surprised you didn't get struck by lightning during that service?" I was teasing and didn't expect an answer, but Luca replied anyway.

"I'm not the kind of person who goes to church every week."

"You're Catholic. You belong in that church just as much as anyone."

He dropped his gaze to me. "I'm not a good person Giada."

My heart broke a little seeing how serious he was when he said that. "You are an amazing person Luca. Just because you occasionally think about doing bad things doesn't make you a bad person." I paused. "Besides, it's not like you actually did anything to Blair. You just offered."

Luca opened his mouth as if to speak, then shut it. He roped his arm around my shoulder, pulling my close, and kissed the top of my head. Somehow, he'd managed to grow another inch or two over the summer and I had not. He seemed to appreciate looming a full foot above me much more than I did.

"You are way too tense for a teenager," I finally said.

"Si," he agreed, resting his chin over my head.

"We need to have some fun. Remind you that being a kid is supposed to be fun, not stressful."

"Fun?" he pulled back enough to show me his quizzical expression.

I nodded. "I already promised Elise I'd do hair masks with her tonight, but I don't have anything important going on tomorrow and the weather looks perfect."

"Perfect for…?"

"The beach! Just the two of us though. Leave all that school drama at school."

His grin widened. "A beach day sounds promising. But Giada, are you forgetting something?"

I shrugged. I probably was.

"Classes. We have school tomorrow."

"Oh. Yeah, I know. I figured we could…opt out."

"Opt out. Like ditch?"

"Sure."

"You want to skip a full day of school and go to the beach," he recapped, his eyes filled with disbelief.

"Mmm hmm."

Luca clicked his tongue. "Giada Francesca, you naughty girl."

"Is that a yes?"

"Of course it's a yes. When have I ever turned down the chance to break the rules?"

I giggled and we walked to his car. He held open my door for me then walked around. He started the engine, then paused, turning to me.

"How come you're okay skipping school but not getting back at Blair?"

"What do you mean?" I asked, not seeing a connection between the two.

"You follow the rules. But skipping school is against the rules. And I've seen you drink, miss curfew…"

"Okay, okay," I interrupted before he could list all of my infractions. "I get it. I'm not perfect. What's your point?"

"Your conscience seems pretty clear. How do you decide what rules you break?"

"First off, my conscience is clear because I go to confession, which you could do too if you weren't so stubborn."

"Pass."

"And as for the rest, I'm not cherry picking. I follow the rules that matter."

"Who's to say which ones matter?"

I could tell from his tone that Luca thought he'd stumped me, but there was an easy answer to that question. "God."

"God," he repeated.

"Yes. The Bible goes on and on about being a good person and not hurting other people. It doesn't say anything about underage drinking or school attendance. I have no moral qualms about breaking man's rules, but I'd like to stay on good terms with God."

He frowned and I realized what I'd said. "I don't mean you're not a good person if you've hurt someone else. I mean, fighting isn't great obviously but it's also not the sort of thing that'll damn you to hell if that's what you're thinking. And besides, that was ages ago, and…"

His hand clapped down over mine, shutting me up. "Giada, it's fine. I know what you mean. So…beach tomorrow?"

"Yes please."

Luca

I called Tomasso after church. I figured Iacopo would've already told everyone about me hurling all over the sidewalk and maybe Tomasso would take pity on me and get me out of school the next day. As it turned out, Iacopo hadn't mentioned anything about our outing to him or, as far as he knew, anyone, but he still agreed to cover for me. Next, I asked Alessio if his sister would call and pretend to be Giada's mom.

Once I got both of us successfully called out of school, I tried to go to bed. But every time I closed my eyes, I saw the look on Marty's face when he saw Iacopo's switchblade. I heard the shriek the moment the metal sliced into his skin. I smelled the coppery twang of the blood as it spurted across the room. And the more I tried not to think about it, the more vivid all of the memories became. By midnight, I swear I could feel the blood splattering on my shirt, could taste it as it pooled across the table.

I ran to the bathroom sometime after one am, hurled, then somehow fell into a blissfully dreamless sleep.

Alessio called in the morning on his way to school, waking me. I should've been up anyway, needed to at least go to breakfast and head towards first period before blowing off the rest of my classes if I wanted my excuse to look legit. I'd told him what had happened—I had to, really. I wasn't sure how I'd survive if I hadn't been able to tell anyone. Alessio wouldn't have thought it was a big deal if he'd been there in my place. In his mind, the guy deserved what he got. Alessio was probably the type of son my papà needed, or at least the kind he wanted. But he was also a good enough friend to realize it had been rough for me.

"I looked online, and they can totally reattach fingers," he said after the typical niceties. "Happens more than you'd think with cooking."

"Oh," I said, too groggy to formulate a better response.

"Look, and don't stress the puking. If he hadn't told Tomasso, I bet he won't tell anyone. For all he knows, your sausage and egg sandwich just didn't sit right."

"Thanks." I dragged myself out of bed, noticed Gavin was already gone. I switched the call to speaker to free up my hands and began getting dressed. I'd showered the night before, and I'd planned to wear my swim trunks under a pair of school-approved shorts so I could change once we arrived. "I couldn't sleep last night though. I kept thinking about it, just seeing his face and hearing the scream."

"Stay busy today. You just need a distraction."

"I told Giada I'd ditch class with her. We're going to the beach."

"That sounds distracting. Think you'll finally get lucky?"

"No." I confirmed I had cash in my wallet, then slipped into my shoes. "And normally, she's the perfect distraction, but it's hard to be around her when all I can think about is the shitty stuff I do when I'm not with her. It's like the worse of a human I am, the better she becomes."

"The yin to your yang?"

"I don't think that's what that means," I said.

"Eh. Whatever. You balance each other out. I still think finding some chick who'd fuck your brains out would be a better distraction today, but whatever you decide, have fun. I gotta go now."

I sighed and was about to end the call when Alessio spoke up.

"Luca? Don't be so hard on yourself. *Non sei rotto.*"

He hung up, leaving his words repeating in my ears. *You're not broken*, he'd told me.

An hour later when I met Giada in the parking lot, I was having serious doubts about the plan. I couldn't even blink without picturing stupid Marty. And the more I thought about it, the angrier I got. I was pissed at my papà for forcing me into this life, at Iacopo for doing what he did, at Marty for trying to steal, and even at Lodovico for bailing on the errand to start with. I felt like hitting a punching bag for a few hours, not frolicking at the beach with my girlfriend.

But when Giada skipped up to my car, a shy smile on her glowing face, I couldn't tell her that. The moment we pulled past the gate for the school, Giada cranked up the music. While I'd been dodging flashbacks of my Sunday from hell, she'd apparently curated the perfect beach playlist. She blasted the music, danced around like my Audi was a nightclub, and even rolled down her window a few inches to let her hair blow in the breeze.

We stopped at the grocery to pick up snacks and sandwiches for a picnic, and Giada was unusually touchy-feely. Rather than hold my hand, she clutched my bicep in both hands, drastically hampering how fast either of us could walk.

"Afraid I'll run away and leave you at the supermarket?" I teased.

She wrinkled her nose in that adorable fake scowl of hers. "I just like touching you. And it's not like you need both hands to shop anyway."

I quirked a brow.

"Okay, well, you still seem a little grumpy so I thought I'd cheer you up. And studies show it's impossible to be grumpy when the most beautiful girl in the world is touching you."

"Most beautiful in the world, huh?" I teased.

By the time we reached the beach, Giada had doubled down her efforts to cheer me up. She set up a small portable speaker to continue her upbeat playlist, then swayed to the music as she stripped off her street clothes. I swallowed hard at the sight of her in her turquoise paisley bikini. Her toned skin was still tanned golden from the peak of summer, and the swirling shades of blue reminded me of our time together in Palermo alongside the Mediterranean.

My mouth went dry. Suddenly, all I could think about was touching Giada. As my eyes locked on the curved golden clasp between her breasts, I couldn't even remember what Marty looked like, let alone how he sounded when Iacopo hurt him. I stepped closer, inhaling the delicious scent of her vanilla and strawberry lotion.

"Why do you always smell good enough to eat?" I asked.

Giada licked her lips, then parted them as if to answer. But before she could speak, I kissed her, roping an arm around her lower back. Her skin was already warm and the way she felt pressed against me made my heart race.

When I finally released her, I unbuttoned my shirt and shucked my shorts. It wasn't a particularly hot day, so we both lounged on the blanket, talking and kissing. After lunch, Giada tried to talk me into doing karaoke—just the two of us. I agreed on the condition that she go for a swim with me.

The moment the frigid Atlantic water hit her skin, Giada shrieked. For a split second, my mind flitted back to the day before, to the last shriek I'd heard. But then Giada splashed me, and I tugged her into my arms, kissing her salty lips until all I could think about was Alessio's comment about sex being the best distraction.

I didn't doubt he was right. If merely kissing Giada made me feel this good, I could only imagine how amazing the sex would be. God, sex with Giada would probably heal all my trauma and solve all my problems.

Everything about her contrasted so starkly with everything else in my life. Giada was goodness, joy, and innocence. She alone was my savior.

I couldn't help but wonder what that meant I was to her.

CHAPTER 9

Giada

When my brother, Matteo, called an hour after I got back from the beach with Luca, I panicked. I was certain my parents had heard I'd ditched school and he wanted to warn me.

But instead, he just wanted to take me out for pizza before he left for college the next week. I agreed, and two days later, I found myself seated across from my favorite brother at the only semi-decent pizzeria near campus. We made small talk while we looked over the menu and waited for our food, but by the time the pizza arrived, we apparently delved into deeper topics.

"So are you and Luca still, um..." my brother paused awkwardly, shoving a massive bite of pizza in his mouth.

"Attending the same school? Taking the same art class? Are we what?" I asked, smirking.

He blew out a sigh, clearly not eager to say it. "Are you still dating?"

I smiled, victorious at having forced him to spell it out. "Why wouldn't we be?"

"I don't know. You spent the summer in different countries."

"Lots of people have long distance relationships."

He wiped his mouth on a napkin before shaking red pepper flakes onto his next slice. "Yes, but you are in high school."

I raised my shoulders.

"So that's a yes?"

"Yes. We are still dating. Does that bother you?" I had time to eat half a slice of pizza before he answered.

"I don't know. I always liked Luca, and I know you guys were close when we were all kids, but…"

"But what?"

"We aren't kids anymore. And he seems a lot older than you."

Luca and Matteo were both eighteen, but I didn't bother pointing that out. And I wasn't sure what my brother meant. He hadn't said that Luca *was* older but that he *seemed* older. That seemed more a knock on my maturity than a commentary on Luca's birthday.

"He's probably my best friend," I said. I felt like Elise should fill that role, and she did, somewhat. But Luca was the one that I could spend every moment with and never get tired of him. Luca was the one that I felt comfortable sharing every single thing with.

Matteo stared at me for a moment, his expression unreadable. "So he's nice to you?"

I dropped my pizza on my plate and glared dryly at my brother. "Yes, he's nice to me. I just finished saying he's my best friend. Do you think I just have really low standards?"

He sighed and shook his head. "I don't know. Dad's basically planning your wedding already, but Angelo hates that you're with Luca. And I think mom's more on Angelo's side here."

I nearly laughed at his comment about my dad, but the rest of his statement drew more of my attention. "Mom is never on Angelo's side," I began. Although, she had never really liked Luca since the time we'd gotten busted missing curfew together. "What is Angelo's problem?"

Matteo shrugged and reached for the last slice of pizza. He offered it to me, but I shook my head, stuffed. He'd already eaten five slices but apparently possessed that magical bottomless stomach so common amongst teenage boys.

"Angelo doesn't trust Luca. He says he's rough around the edges."

I could see that about Luca. It was part of what made him so endearing though.

"He really doesn't like Luca's father," Matteo continued. "He doesn't think you should get involved with their family."

"Luca doesn't like his father either," I admitted, reaching for my soda. "He actually told me his father doesn't love him."

"But he's an only child," Matteo said.

"Right? That's what I told him. The only way your parents don't love you is if they have siblings to love and they can blame you for your grandparent's death."

Matteo's brows dipped. "Giada, no one blames you."

I shook my head. "Sure. That's why I'm at boarding school and you're living at home with the other favorite child. Anyway, that's not the point. What does Angelo have against Luca's father? And why does he hate him so much when dad doesn't?"

"I honestly don't know."

"Hmm, well, seems like a moot point anyway. The only times I've even seen Salvatore Marino are when dad and Angelo are with us."

That seemed to reassure Matteo. I thought we were about to move on to a different, less awkward topic, but then he made a sour face.

"I just want to make sure that you're not… I mean, just because your boyfriend is eighteen doesn't mean you are. You don't need to do…adult things just to be with him."

"Oh Lord," I said, hiding my face in my palms.

"I'm serious, Giada. "Don't let him talk you into anything you don't want to do."

At that, I laughed. "Have you ever successfully talked me into anything?"

He considered that. "Well, no, but Luca might be more persuasive."

I rolled my eyes. "I am impervious to pressure from other people. I believe you once called me the most stubborn person alive and I promise, I haven't changed that much at school. Now can we talk about something else?"

He grinned and quickly agreed.

Luca

The longer I went without seeing my papà or running errands for him, the better I felt. And spending most of my free time with Giada certainly didn't hurt, either. She was with her brother Wednesday, but I thought her family had all gone home by the time I took her out on Thursday. We'd eaten dinner on campus with friends, then headed out for dessert, decaf coffee, and a walk around town.

By the time we returned to campus, we had just enough time for a short makeout session. I knew we'd never stop kissing if we started in the privacy of my car, so we stepped out of the car. I shut the door, then nudged Giada back against the car door.

I settled against Giada, cupping her cheek in my palm as our mouths pressed together, our tongues tangling around each other. She tasted like coffee and cream, and it was a thousand times better than the tiramisu we'd just shared. Everything about her kiss was perfect, especially the way I completely lost myself in her. When I kissed Giada, her body completely absorbed me. The outside world melted away and the thing remaining was the sensations of her—her soft sighs, her sweet taste, her vanilla scent, her warm breath on my cheeks, and her damp lips tugging at my own.

It was no wonder we frequently lost track of time while making out. We lost all touch with reality when we were together.

But that night, something abruptly yanked me back into the real world. I was so absorbed in Giada that I didn't even realize an actual person had pulled us apart until his palms slammed into my shoulders, knocking me further back.

Giada yelled something, but I didn't even register her words as my fist was already slamming into his face. It wasn't until I was winding up for my second hit that I even realized who it was that had attacked me.

"Angelo!" Giada hollered, echoing my thought.

I punched her brother again right as someone else grabbed me from behind, pulling me off of him. Angelo gathered his bearings and lunged at me, so I swung again, then kicked at him. He grunted and the guy behind me loosened his grip on me so I swiveled around and took a hit at him. I didn't recognize him, but I didn't care at the moment.

"Luca!" Giada shouted. "Luca, stop it!"

But I couldn't. As Angelo came at me again, I saw red. I would've pummeled him again and again, except Giada flung herself against me, blocking my next hit. I braced myself for an attack from the other guy now that my defenses were down, but instead, I heard another voice yelling.

"Hey! Break it up!" the voice shouted.

I turned in the direction of the voice to see my P.E. teacher and the soccer coach both jogging towards us.

"Shit," I mumbled.

"What is wrong with you, Angelo?" Giada asked, dropping my hands and turning to her brother. He ignored her, frozen where he stood, so she shoved him.

"Hey!" Mr. Simmonds called as they came to a stop beside us. "What is going on?"

The four of us just stood there, staring at the teachers.

"You two, inside now. Straight to the office," Mr. Simmonds said, pointing at Giada and me. "And who are you? Do you even go here?"

Angelo glared at him with ice in his eyes.

"That's my brother and cousin. They're a little late for family visiting day, apparently," Giada said. "They started it."

"If you're not students here, you need to leave right now or I'm calling the cops," Mr. Simmonds said. "And consider yourselves banned from campus until further notice."

Angelo maintained his glare for another moment, then dropped his gaze and nodded for the other guy to follow him. "You stay away from my sister," he said, getting up in my face one last time before heading to his car. He'd parked roughly ten yards from my car, so I wondered how we hadn't heard them approach. But then again, we'd been distracted.

I replied under my breath and in Italian, but Giada still shot me a disapproving stare.

"Office. Now," Mr. Simmonds repeated, nudging me in that direction.

Giada reached for my hand and pulled me in that direction. Mr. Simmonds joined us but the soccer coach waited until Angelo had completely left the campus before joining. Since it was after hours, I figured we wouldn't have to meet with Mr. Andrews until the morning, but I was wrong. Apparently, he worked late some nights.

Mr. Simmonds paraded me into the office and took a seat beside me. Giada wandered in after, closing the door softly after Mr. Andrews asked her to.

"These two were fighting with some boys from off campus," Mr. Simmonds said.

"Giada didn't do anything. She was just standing there," I said.

"It was *my* brother," she said.

Mr. Andrews held up his hands then turned to Mr. Simmonds.

"When we walked up, Luca was fighting with the two other boys. They confirmed they aren't students, and they left."

Mr. Andrews turned to Giada. "You know the boys' names?"

"It's my brother and cousin. I don't know what they were doing here."

He slid a notepad to her. "Write down their names. I'll need to discuss this with your parents. We don't permit visitors who violate our campus rules, so they won't be allowed back."

She began writing. "I can't imagine that'll be an issue. They've never come to visit before."

"And what was the root of this fight?"

"They just attacked Luca for no reason," she said.

Mr. Andrews stared at me then blew out a sigh. He handed me a tissue. "Your knuckles are bleeding. Your story is that was self-defense?"

I glanced down, not even sure how he knew my knuckles were bloody since I'd intentionally kept them out of sight. "Yes," I said. "We were minding our own business."

"So neither of you have any idea what the cause of this fight was?"

Giada and I both remained silent, but then Mr. Simmonds piped up again. "Ms. Conti's brother expressed his displeasure that she is dating Mr. Marino."

Mr. Andrews nodded, his hands drifting to his forehead. "Look, this is an academic institution. We don't have strict rules against dating, but when any student activities start leading to fights, we need to take a step back and consider whether our social activities are interfering with our educational opportunities." He paused, then looked at Giada, then me. "Neither of you need any distractions. Do you understand?"

She nodded immediately, so I did as well, although I really didn't have the slightest clue what we were agreeing to.

"Since you say these boys attacked you, you could file a police report. Is that something you would like to look into, Luca?" he asked.

"No."

"I'm happy to just call the police so we can get a record of what happened, and then—"

"No," I repeated, firmer this time.

"Okay. Well, Giada I will be calling your parents to discuss this, but as you weren't involved in any fighting, you may go. Luca, our school rules are clear that it doesn't matter who starts the fight. Fighting on campus results in an automatic suspension. Given the circumstances of this fight, though, I'll settle for one week of detention and one week of community service. But if you're involved in any additional fights, whether on campus or not, with students or not, there will be no further leniency. You'll be suspended. Understood?"

I nodded.

"And I need to call your parents as well to let them know you were involved in a fight. But given the hour and the fact that I have to be back here for meetings in less than ten hours, I'd like to go home now. I'll call both of your parents in the morning."

He motioned for us to leave, so we did. Mr. Simmonds walked us out, literally escorting us to our individual dorms so we couldn't even say goodnight.

CHAPTER 10

Luca

Surprisingly, my mom was the one who called after Dean Andrews told my parents about the fight. She said she was coming to see me—that day. I'd tried to use my detention as an excuse, but apparently the school decided meeting my mom for an early dinner was more of a punishment than actual detention. I wasn't sure they were wrong.

I was, however, pleasantly surprised to see she actually was alone, aside from her driver.

"Papà couldn't make it?" I asked, climbing into the seat beside my mom and nodding to the driver. Unlike me, my mom actually rode in the backseat when one of Papà's guys chauffeured her around town.

"You know how busy he is, especially right before we leave."

"You're leaving?"

"Rome," she replied, as if it were obvious. I'd assumed they'd leave in October, like usual, but I supposed sooner was better. "And you're flying to spend Thanksgiving break with us."

"But there's no Thanksgiving in Italy."

My mom shot me a look. I suggested a couple of restaurants I thought my mom might like, but a moment later we parked in front of some overpriced café I never would have picked for her.

I climbed out of the car and opened my mom's door, then did the same for the entrance of the café. She paused and inspected my hand, sighing loudly after noting the already fading cuts along my knuckles.

"Those Conti boys are trouble," she mumbled, holding two fingers up to the hostess. The girl looked familiar, but I couldn't tell if she went to my school or was just the right age.

"It was just Angelo and his dumb cousin. Eddie, I think."

"Eddie? What kind of a name is that?"

"Edoardo."

She rolled her eyes, followed the young hostess to a table, shook her head at the table, and pointed to a different table. "I'll take an iced tea with lemon. No ice," she told the hostess. The girl offered a confused smile but turned to me.

"Coke please," I said. I waited until the girl left to point out that she wasn't our actual waitress.

"So? She's getting paid to do a job. She might as well bring our drinks."

I tapped my fingers on the table, willing our drinks to come sooner. My mom busied herself looking at the menu, so I did the same. The place served a bunch of foods old church ladies would enjoy, like chicken salad sandwiches and egg salad croissants and a bunch of other concoctions using too much mayonnaise. My mom ordered some fuji apple salad with grilled chicken and I went with a club sandwich and a cup of soup.

"No mayo," I said, not releasing my grip on the menu until the waitress acknowledged my statement.

Mom waited until we were alone to launch into the lecture I'd been anticipating.

"I understand the fight wasn't your fault, but I just assumed this thing with you and Giada was over. You had your fun over summer."

I tilted my glass to my lips and slowly sipped my soda, wondering if I could drain the entire cup before my mom figured out I wasn't going to respond. She only let me down about half of it before continuing.

"I wish you'd date some other girls."

"Mamma, be nice."

"It's not that I don't like her. She seems… fine."

"Ma…" I'd hoped my tone would caution her from continuing, but it didn't.

"She doesn't speak Italian. And she's spoiled." She held up her hand to stop me from interrupting. "I'm not saying that as a criticism, but it's a fact. I see the way you look at her and it worries me. You two will never work out in the long term because you're both too accustomed to getting your own way. You're basically the same person. What you need is to be with someone different from you, someone who compliments your weaknesses and balances you out."

That actually made me chuckle. "Giada is nothing like me. Trust me. You are worrying for nothing."

She narrowed her eyes at me, but I kept talking before she could say anything else.

"Also, if you don't want me meeting spoiled girls, maybe you shouldn't send me to an expensive boarding school. Giada is not the only principessa on campus."

"I'm only saying you should think about your future. Girls like her get attached early. And for all you know, she'll try to trap you into staying with her by—"

"Mamma!" I interrupted.

My mom stopped talking, but cast me a look that said she still thought she was right. I was not about to get into a discussion of sex with my mom, but I also wouldn't let her trash talk the girl who wouldn't even let me touch her boobs after nearly a year of dating.

"You don't need to worry. Can we talk about something else?"

The waitress brought our food and my mom agreed to change the subject.

As she dropped me back of at campus, I asked again about their upcoming trip and who all was coming. By the time I walked into my dorm, I was already formulating a plan. My house would be empty all weekend long and it would be a pity to waste that opportunity. I waved to my mom, then hurried inside to call Giada and invite her to Staten Island for the weekend.

Giada

I hadn't hesitated when Luca asked me to spend the weekend with him. I felt like I should've at least pretended to consider it, but the second he said there'd be separate bedrooms and zero expectations, I was sold.

Luca led me into the house through the garage in the back. He typed a ridiculously long code into the small box beside the door, then waited while it buzzed and then opened. We were standing in the mudroom, though the hooks and cubbies were all empty but one. Luca shrugged his duffle bag off his shoulder then reached for mine, setting both on the bench. He typed another code into an alarm box, then motioned for me to follow him into the kitchen.

"There's another alarm I need to disarm in my papa's study. Make yourself at home," he said, scurrying off down the hall.

I gazed around the room, smiling. Though Luca didn't talk about his parents much, when he did, he always gave the impression they were cold. But the kitchen told a different story. Despite the crisp modern cabinetry and appliances, the room oozed warmth. Bold golden accents filled the room, and various nods to their Italian heritage were scattered throughout. On a wall beside the refrigerator, a large photo frame contained a collection of Luca's school portraits over the year. There was one spot left, for his senior picture, I assumed.

"Oh God, don't look at that," he said, dragging me away from the wall. "Do you want something to drink or you want the tour or…" he leaned in and planted his lips on mine before finishing his sentence.

A moment later, a loud noise startled us apart. "Is someone else here?" I asked, trying not to panic.

Before he could answer, a man rounded the corner behind me. Another one entered the room from a different door, past Luca. It was obvious from their demeanor they weren't robbers.

"What are you guys doing here?" Luca asked, frowning.

"I could ask you the same thing," the guy behind me said, his accent even thicker than Luca's. "Who's this?" His hand reached towards me. In retrospect, he may have just been going to move my hair off my shoulder or something, but all I saw was a hand moving towards my chest and I reacted, slapping his stubbled face.

His eyes filled with annoyance and he grabbed my wrist, hard. Luca lunged forward and grabbed me, freeing my hand, just as the other guy spoke. I couldn't decipher anything he said except for Giada Conti. I supposed that meant he was introducing me.

"Mi dispiace," the creepy, younger one said.

"English," I snapped.

"Sorry," he translated.

"Giada, this is Lodovico and Pietro."

"Nice to meet you," said the older one, Lodovico.

"My parents are out of town, so why are you guys here?" Luca asked.

"Ahh were you expecting the house to yourselves?" The men both laughed. "Your father never leaves the property unattended."

Lodovico stepped closer, then switched to Italian. He spoke quickly, addressing his words only to Luca. After a few sentences, he paused, then laughed before continuing. I gazed at Luca for some hint as to what they were saying, and his jaw was tightly shut but his cheeks had turned bright red. He flipped his middle finger at the men but said nothing as they continued.

"Some might say it's rude to speak in another language in front of someone who doesn't understand that language," I interrupted, still annoyed.

I'd expected the two men to apologize, but instead they both grinned. Pietro patted Luca on the arm. "Have fun translating that," he said as they sauntered out.

Luca blew out a sigh and rubbed his neck.

"What was that all about?"

"They said we're fine to stay here but that my papà asked them to keep an eye on the place." He paused, probably sensing my discomfort with their presence. "We won't see them again."

I swallowed the lump in my throat, not terribly eager to share a house with those two. "Who are they?"

"Uhh, uncles?" Luca shrugged. "They work for my dad. Lodovico's here a lot. Pietro is his son."

"So your cousin?"

"Well, not literally, but you know how that goes."

I was intimately familiar with big families full of relatives with no biological connection, so that was reassuring at least. "What were they teasing you about?"

His cheeks flushed again. "You."

"What?"

"No, not like that. I um, I don't bring girls back here often. Or, like ever. So they were joking about me finally getting a girlfriend. And then Lodovico said something about how he might need to check with my papà about whether I'm allowed to have girls in my room or what the rules are."

"Are you?"

Luca chuckled. "I have no idea. I assume yes, because my parents really don't have strict rules on that sort of thing."

"So are they telling your parents I'm here?"

"I don't know. I'm sure they'll at least mention I'm here. Don't worry either way."

I frowned. "What if your father calls my parents?"

"He won't. Pietro was right about that."

"About what?"

"He made a comment about how my papà would be thrilled if I knocked you up. He was joking, but my papà really loves us being together so I'm not so sure he's wrong." Luca paused. "Anyway, can I give you the tour?"

I smoothed a hand over the knot in my stomach and nodded.

CHAPTER 11

Luca

We spent the afternoon in the backyard, talking and kissing. Later, we ordered dinner and then snuggled together on the couch and watched movies.

I thought for sure Giada was going to insist I drive her back to school after our run in with Pietro and Lodovico. But it actually ended up having the opposite effect. She agreed to stay, but didn't want to sleep in her own room, even after I assured her they'd actually left for the night.

We kept all of Giada's stuff in the guestroom. After she changed into her pajamas—a paper thin pair of white lace shorts and a lavender tank top with the same flower pattern as the shorts—we shut the guestroom door and snuck into my room together. I didn't think Ludovico or Pietro cared where she slept, but then at least they'd be confused if they returned.

"Cute pjs," I said. I was completely serious, but she wrinkled her nose as if I'd been teasing.

"What do you wear to bed?" she asked.

"Nothing," I replied with a wink.

Giada scowled.

I rummaged around in my drawer and pulled out a pair of my more conservative boxers. The material was thicker so it would be a little less obvious when I was thinking about the girl in bed beside me.

Crap. Just thinking about thinking about it was enough to set me off. I'd never actually had a girl in my childhood bed overnight. It was going to be a long night stretched out next to her and trying to think about anything except how close to naked she was. I started to turn away, but decided it was pointless. There was no way I'd successfully hide my arousal the entire night so I might as well just distract her.

I stepped closer, cupping her cheeks in my hands and kissed her. Giada's response was filled with uncertainty, but she gradually warmed to me, leaning in and resting her hands on my biceps. I ended the kiss before I gave in to the urge to tackle Giada onto my bed and full on make out with her till she realized how stupid her whole abstinence thing was. I flipped down the covers of my bed and walked around to the side to climb in, carefully arranging the blanket over my lap.

I gazed up to see Giada still standing at the foot of the bed, her teeth working her bottom lip. "I won't bite," I said, patting the bed beside me. "Promise." It was a big bed, queen size, in American terms, so Giada could easily spend the entire night without even touching me. But that is not what she did. After staring at me for another moment, she followed me into the bed. She crawled under the covers, then inched closer and closer, until she was right beside me. I lifted my arm, making a space for her head to rest on my chest. No sooner did I adjust to the soft tickle of her breath on my bare chest and her hair tickling my arm than she splayed her palm across my belly.

My entire body tensed, and then I spent the next several minutes trying to gradually relax so as not to be terribly obvious. She'd touched my bare stomach before, lots of times when we were swimming. But then we were in public. And upright. Being in my bed was oh so different, and my body knew it.

Suddenly, the silence became more awkward than any of the things I could think of to say. "So, this won't cause you some guilt complex, will it?"

"Hmm?" Giada rotated her body closer to me so she could face me. Now instead of her side pressing against me, it was nearly on top of me.

"Sleeping next to me. That's not...forbidden in your ethical code?"

"I don't think so."

That seemed odd. "Why not? How's it any different from sex?"

Her laughter filled the room, disarming me so that I didn't stiffen when she rolled fully on top of me, resting her head flat on my chest. "I hope it's different in a lot of ways, but I guess I wouldn't know."

I saw her point. "Yeah, good point. So it doesn't have anything to do with your parents?"

She considered that for a moment. "Well, my parents were pretty clear on the no sex before marriage thing with me and my brothers, but I'm sure neither of them listened. And I'm positive my parents wouldn't approve of this little sleepover, no matter how well we behave." Giada paused, lightly tracing her fingers along my arm in a way that sent shivers down my spine. "Besides, there's a lot of things I do that they don't approve of."

"But they like me," I reminded her.

"They do," she agreed. "Or at least my dad does. But if he saw you now…"

We both laughed and I kissed the top of her head.

"So if it's not because of your parents, what made you decide to wait? The church?" I asked.

"Yes, that's a big part of it. But I guess also, it just seems more romantic this way. Maybe I'm naïve, but I think sex should mean something, that it'll be better if I actually love the person I'm doing it with. And I want it to be something special I share with my husband. Like, I know by the time I'm married I'll have dated and kissed and danced with a bunch of other guys and had so many other experiences—outside the bedroom—without my husband, so wouldn't it be great to have something I only experience with him?"

I thought about it, and it did seem more romantic. "Yeah, I could see that. What if you don't meet your husband till you're like thirty though? Are you gonna wait that long?"

"God I hope not," she said with a laugh.

That made me smile, until another question came to me. "What if your future husband didn't wait? Like, what if he's already been with other women before you even start dating?"

"I don't know."

"Is that a dealbreaker?"

"No." Giada paused. "It seems like maybe one of us should know what we're doing. It's not like I could change what he has done in the past anyway."

Despite the fact that she was stretched out on top of me, the conversation felt easier because of the lack of eye contact. It was as though we were both able to be more honest because we were close, but not too intimately focused.

"I know you were with Emily, Luca," she said suddenly.

I cringed. *Stupid Emily.* I'd literally only messed around with her to get my mind of Giada and now it was biting me in the ass. "I didn't have sex with Emily. We did other stuff, but never…"

She quietly processed my confession for a moment. "But you're still not… a virgin."

"No," I said, praying she wouldn't ask more. I didn't want to lie to Giada, but nothing could make me admit to her that I'd slept with a stripper.

"Your first time…was it…anyone I know?"

"No."

"Have you…done that with anyone else at school?"

"No."

She sounded relieved. I didn't blame her. "I thought Italians tended to wait longer than Americans. Is that just a myth?"

Truthfully, a lot of Italians did seem to wait till they were older. In part I figured it was the heavy influence of the Catholic Church and in part the closer family structure. Obviously I was lacking that part. "I must have hung out in the wrong crowds," I admitted.

She giggled.

"So I'm not out of the running yet?" I asked, hoping she'd know what I meant. She did.

"I wouldn't be dating you if you were." Then she paused. "Well, maybe I would actually. It seems silly to only date boys I might want to marry. My mom said the whole point of dating is to figure out what you want in a partner. Of course, Elise says the whole point is to have fun."

"Can't you do both?"

"I guess so."

"I could tell you what you want, if you haven't already figured that out," I offered.

"Oh yeah? Go for it."

I thought for a moment. "You want someone who makes you laugh. Someone who feeds you…" I paused and she giggled so hard that it rattled my chest. "Someone who spoils you and takes care of you, but who also keeps you on your toes. You definitely don't want someone boring. You want someone who understands your family, loves to travel, and has the money to take you around the world."

"Are you calling me a gold digger?"

Yes. "No, but…am I wrong?"

Giada laughed again. "Not so far."

"You also want someone tall, dark, and handsome, preferably with a sexy accent. Someone who doesn't just appreciate your love of fashion but shares it." I paused again before saying the other thing that struck me. "And you want someone who wants you infinitely more than you want him."

Giada was quiet for several breaths. When she finally spoke, her voice was softer. "You don't really think that, do you?"

I wanted to tell her the truth, that I liked her so much it hurt sometime. That she was the first girl I would actually consider dating without the hope of any sex till marriage. I wanted to tell her that having her in my bed, in my house, made me wish more than anything that somehow that would be our future, that someday we wouldn't just be playing house for the weekend. I wanted to tell her that possibility was the only thing that kept me going some days when I was stuck doing my papà's bidding. But I didn't want to scare her off.

"I'm here, Luca. I'm breaking all the rules for you. You have to know that means something."

"Not *all* the rules," I reminded her.

She thwacked my chest with her finger.

We kept talking until eventually we both fell asleep.

Giada

I drifted off at some point while Luca and I were talking. I wouldn't have thought it possible, but it was actually really comfortable to lay on top of him. He'd wrapped his arms around my waist, holding me in place, and I realized I felt safer than I had in a long time. Not that I felt unsafe usually, but this was different. There wasn't a doubt in my mind that Luca would protect me against anything and everything, without me even asking.

When I woke, I was still sprawled across his chest. By some miracle, I hadn't drooled all over him, but I didn't trust myself to keep that up. I'd need to move, but I wanted to relish the security of the position a little longer. I thought about what he'd said, his description of what I wanted in a man. Obviously, he'd been describing himself, but as he listed each characteristic, I realized he was right. Those were all of the things I wanted—or maybe needed—in a lifelong partner.

I wasn't naïve enough to think Luca and I would last forever, but I also wasn't jaded enough to completely dismiss the possibility. The world was filled with people who married their high school sweethearts. Who was to say we couldn't be among those lucky few?

Luca seemed to still be asleep, so I slowly inched off of him, pausing once I was on my side facing him, my leg still over his. His breathing remained even and calm, so I continued shifting into a more comfortable position. I rolled away from him, trying not to steal the covers. I held my breath, as if that would somehow ensure he didn't wake.

Just when I thought I'd succeeded, Luca moved. He rolled towards me, his chest pressing into my back as his arm swung over my waist. He didn't budge for a minute after that, so I assumed maybe he'd turned in his sleep. But then he kissed the back of my head and squeezed me tighter. My heart clutched at the thought that maybe, just maybe I could feel this safe and this loved every night as an adult, with Luca holding me just like he was now. Crazier things had happened, right?

I placed my hand over his against my waist, then relaxed against him, gradually drifting back to sleep.

CHAPTER 12

Luca

J'd woken before Giada, headed to the bathroom to relieve some of the pressure that had accumulated after spending a night with her mostly-naked body curled against mine, then crawled back into bed beside her just in time for her to wake. I made breakfast while she showered and dressed, and then we made our plans for the day while we ate.

I was going to take Giada into the city and show her around. She'd grown up near New York, but hadn't ever really explored it. Right as we finished eating, Lodovico showed up and insisted on driving us.

Giada excused herself to go dry and style her hair, leaving me alone to argue with Lodovico.

"We don't need a chaperone. I know how to drive," I said.

"Oh? When is the last time you drove in the city?"

I opened my mouth to answer, with a lie, of course, since I didn't think I'd ever technically driven within the city bounds, but he kept going.

"And where do you plan to park? You'll have to walk miles to get anywhere you want to go after you park. Is she going to walk in those shoes?" He gestured to the patio where Giada was finishing up a phone call. She wore a short skirt and high heeled shoes with straps that wrapped up her calves. Very fashionable, equally impractical.

"Fine. If it's okay with her, you can drive. But no following us around like a babysitter."

Lodovico saluted me like I was his captain. I rolled my eyes and went to ask Giada. Not surprisingly, she was fine with him driving. I didn't know why she wouldn't be, since she, too, spent her days being chauffeured around by an older Italian man. Although, the guy who drove her lately didn't seem that old. Maybe her brother's age.

Wandering around Manhattan with Giada by my side was even better than walking around campus with her. I loved having the world see that she was mine. The jealousy in other guys' faces made my day.

It didn't hurt that Giada was even more affectionate than usual. If I wrapped my arm around her waist, she'd rest her head against my arm while we walked. If I reached for her hand, she'd clutch my fingers tightly and lift them to her lips to kiss them every few minutes. And when we stopped at the crosswalk, Giada rest her hand against my stomach as though she was claiming me. Feeling her hand there reminded me of the night, of having her in my bed all night long.

I bit back a groan then tried to focus on the present. Giada had been talking about wanting me to see the campus of Columbia. "So what's so special about Columbia?"

"It's gorgeous," she began. "And it's right in the middle of everything but not so in the middle that my father won't let me go."

"I guess that answers my next question," I replied. NYU seemed much more her style, but I had to wonder…if her father wasn't comfortable with NYU, would Columbia really be much better? "What are you going to study?"

She shrugged. "No clue. My mom thinks I'd like art history. Or maybe something literature related. Or just art? Angelo says I should do philosophy, since I spend so much time daydreaming. I think he's just messing with me though. Or maybe sociology? I like helping people."

I squeezed her hand. I didn't doubt she could do whatever she put her mind to. Giada was smart. Most people underestimated her. I loved her enthusiasm about the future, too, although I'd be lying if I said I didn't have a tiny pang of jealousy. My papà had made it abundantly clear that I was not attending a university, either in the U.S. or in Italy. He wanted me to take some business and economics type classes, but that was it. I wasn't sad about not getting to spend more time in a classroom, but Italy had some gorgeous universities. I'd be missing out on a lot of experiences on the campus. And even if I had decided not to go on my own, at least then the decision would've been mine.

"Maybe you'll fall in love with Columbia and want to go, too," Giada said, skipping ahead of me then stopping directly in front of me. She clasped both of my hands in hers and smiled, her brown eyes twinkling.

"I'm not sure that's in the cards for me," I said, ending the discussion by tugging her hands until we were closer and then kissing her. She kissed me back for over a minute, which I hadn't expected in the middle of a busy sidewalk. When she did end the kiss though, I had another question for her.

"Will you take Italian at the university?"

She made a face. "I tried to learn when I was younger. I'm awful at foreign languages."

"For me? I'd love for you to actually understand all the sweet nothings I plan to whisper in your ear when you finally do sleep with me."

Her grimace turned to a smile, and then she blushed. "Yes, Luca. For you, I will learn."

We'd just made it to the next corner, right by the deli where I wanted to take her to lunch, when I heard my name. I turned around to see a tall man in his early thirties approaching us.

"Luca Marino? Is that you?" he asked.

I nodded tentatively.

"I'm an acquaintance of your father. I've been trying to reach him but I hear he's out of the country. You didn't go with him?"

"Obviously not. What's your name?"

"Alan. Here, let me get you my card. So when is your father coming back?"

"I don't know," I replied, growing increasingly suspicious as he rummaged in his pocket. I dropped Giada's hand so I'd have my own hands free if I needed them, but it's not like I could do anything. I had a switchblade in my pocket but I sure couldn't pull that out on a busy street.

"Who's your friend?" Alan smiled at Giada right as I glanced down at the card he handed me. *Shit.* He was FBI.

"Giada Conti," she said sweetly. I cringed, wishing I'd stopped her before she answered.

The cop looked from Giada to me then back to her and then chuckled. "Oh that's great. The next generation, teaming up already. How old are you now? The last time I saw anything about you, you were just a kid. Where have you been?"

"Boarding school," Giada said, skipping his first question. I reached for her hand again, squeezing it hard enough to get her to look at me so I could send her my best "shut up" signal.

"We've got to go," I said.

"Yeah, I won't keep you. Hey, uh, but what part of Italy is your dad in now? Naples? I thought you used to have a place in Palermo."

"Come on," I mumbled to Giada, tugging her along.

"Nice to meet you!" she called out, her tone overly friendly.

We walked into the diner, and I waited until we got our menus to excuse myself to go call Lodovico.

We stayed in the rest of the day, spending most of our time kissing. I took a long shower before bed, picturing the gorgeous girl waiting for me in my bed while relieving the tension that had built since earlier that morning. When I finally emerged from the bathroom, Giada had changed into her skimpy nightgown, but she was eying me uneasily.

For a moment, I thought she must have guessed what I'd been doing behind closed doors, but then she spoke.

"I want to ask you something but I'm going to sound like a complete hypocrite," she said. "And you can tell me no. I won't hold it against you."

I frowned, fairly certain I was incapable of telling her no, especially when she looked like the sex goddess of my dreams. But instead I just nodded.

"Okay, so, I haven't changed my mind. I'm not having sex before marriage," she continued. "And I still think there's some other stuff that probably counts as sex and is therefore off the table for now, but…"

My heart skipped a beat and my brain latched onto her use of the phrase "for now." I felt an eternity pass while I waited for her to finish her sentiment.

Giada's cheeks burned bright red, and as my eyes trailed down her body, I realized her chest was flushed too. My attention returned to her face as she licked her lips.

"I was just wondering if maybe you would um touch me," she finally said. "Like just above the waist, and with no expectation of—"

I launched myself across the room and welded our lips together before she could finish talking. There'd been a day the last spring where I'd briefly touched Giada's breasts, but then it was seconds before I found Alessio after he'd been beaten. Giada and I had never talked about what we'd done, and I'd gotten the impression that she was comfortable with me touching the sides of her breasts but probably not her nipples. Now it seemed like maybe she was giving me the green light.

I sat on the bed beside her and lifted her onto my lap, keeping enough distance between us so that she wouldn't feel that I was already rock hard and assume I misinterpreted what she said. I kept my hands on her waist until I felt her relax against me. Then, I slowly moved my hands up her body. I squeezed her breasts, relishing every bit of the sensation. They filled my palms perfectly, and even through the thin fabric of her gown, I could feel the warmth of her smooth skin.

I sucked Giada's lower lip into my mouth as I raked my thumbs across her nipples. She inhaled sharply and her mouth went limp for a moment, but then she resumed kissing me back. I moved my thumbs again, this time noting that her nipples were hardening under my touch, transforming into little pebbles. I kissed Giada's neck, sucking her delicate skin and imagining my lips were slightly lower on her body, replacing my hands.

My breathing had grown ragged, but so had hers. And Giada had scooted further onto my lap, so there was no way she wasn't feeling my latest erection pressing against her. But she didn't seem to mind.

Quite the opposite, really. She kissed me more freely, like when she'd chugged some of the spiked punch at a party, and she seemed to be squirming against me, almost leaning into my touch. After another minute, a soft moan escaped her lips. Her body tensed and then she cried out again. It took a second for me to realize what had happened.

I could've died in that moment and felt complete. As it was, the sounds Giada made when she came would be burned into my brain until the day I died. Her quiet, breathy moan was without a doubt the most beautiful sound I'd ever hear, and I knew I'd do everything I could to get her to make those noises more often.

"Oh my God," Giada panted, pulling back from the kiss. Her

head was ducked so I couldn't see her expression, but I suspected she was embarrassed. "I didn't—"

I pressed my lips to the top of her head. "If we could do that like every day, that would be awesome," I said.

She slowly gazed up. "Luca, I didn't even…I mean, you didn't get—"

"I had the most fun I've had all weekend just now, and that's saying a lot," I interrupted. "I don't need anything else."

"Really?" Skepticism filled her eyes.

"Really. That was awesome. I think we should do that again."

Giada laughed, still blushing, then bit her lip. "I love you," she said.

"Ti amo," I replied.

She smiled, crawled off my lap, and made her way towards the bathroom. I figured she'd just need a minute, so I told her I was going to go check that the house was all locked up. I'd already done that, but I needed to take care of my own release… for the third time that day…before laying down beside her to sleep.

Giada

The next weekend, Enzo came to pick up me and Elise. She was coming home with me to shop for homecoming dresses. We'd attempted to find some near campus, but had failed miserably.

The drive was over two hours, but since Elise and I had barely talked all week thanks to both of us being super busy, the time passed quickly. I wanted to tell her about my weekend with Luca, but I'd warned her in advance not to say anything in front of Enzo that would reveal I'd been at Luca's house. I wasn't sure how much he'd rat out to my parents and I definitely didn't want them knowing I'd been alone overnight with my boyfriend.

So, I narrated all of the appropriate details from our weekend, omitting where we'd been. Right after I finished telling her the part about the weird guy that talked to us outside the diner and how Luca later told me the guy was a cop, Elise had to pee. Enzo pulled over at a rest area, and we all climbed out of the car. Enzo and I stayed beside the car, just stretching out legs, while Elise ran in. Once she'd disappeared into the cinder-block building, Enzo turned to me.

"Giada, you know you can never say anything to the cops, right?"

I turned to Enzo, trying to decipher the meaning behind his scrunched up expression combined with those words. "About what?"

"About anything. Ever. If anyone even remotely connected to the police ever asks you a question about anything at all, you have to say nothing. Has anyone ever told you that?"

I shook my head, certain based on his disappointing stare that I had not answered correctly. "So you were eavesdropping on my conversation with Elise?"

"The one where you said an FBI agent questioned you and Luca? Yeah, I was."

"I didn't know he was an FBI agent," I pointed out. "And it didn't seem like it mattered."

"I know. And I'm just telling you for the future. Even if the question they ask sounds innocent, like if they ask where you were and it's a date when you know you were in class. Or what the weather was the last time you went out with Luca. Or even what your full name is." He paused until I made eye contact with him. "You say nothing. Even if they act like you have to answer, and that there will be consequences if you don't. You still say nothing. You ask for a lawyer or you call your dad. That is it."

"Why would the cops ever want to question me?"

"I don't know that they would, but I get the impression trouble sometimes follows Luca. And besides, sometimes they try to stir stuff up with the kids of successful business owners. Or maybe they don't like Italians. It could be anything."

"Okay, but it seems like telling the truth would be the easiest way to end any witch hunt."

Enzo shook his head. "That's not for you to decide. If that's the case, your dad will sort it out. But you don't have access to the big picture, so you just can't say anything. No one is asking you to lie. Just stay quiet."

I blew out a sigh. Silence was not my strong suit. Still, now that I had confirmation that Enzo was listening to every word I said, I let Elise talk the rest of our drive back to Connecticut. That night though, when I was sure Elise and I were alone, I asked her what I'd been wanting to know all week.

"So, when you're with a guy, have you ever, um, climaxed without actually doing…" I paused, not even sure how to finish my sentence.

Elise rolled towards me in the bed and I was so grateful we'd already turned off the light since I knew my face would be beet red. "Are you saying Luca gave you an orgasm?"

I hesitated, then answered. "Yeah."

"Oh my God. Tell me everything. Wait, this happened last week? At his place? And I'm just now hearing about it?"

"It's been a busy week. We both had that English paper due, and—"

"OMG, Giada. Losing your virginity is more important than a damn essay!"

"That's just it. I didn't lose anything. He didn't even touch me there. We weren't even naked."

"Okay then I'm confused."

"We were making out and he was paying a lot of attention to my boobs."

"Of course. Guys are obsessed with boobs. And you have fantastic ones, so of course Luca loves touching them."

I quirked a brow at her compliment, but decided to let it go. "Yeah, well I guess I love him touching them too, because it was like every single touch I felt much, much lower. Like, he wasn't touching me there, but it totally felt like he was."

"And you're sure it was an orgasm?"

"Pretty sure. I mean, he's done stuff before that felt good, but this was like, I don't know, I felt like I was on this roller coaster and it was just out of control and I couldn't have stopped even if I wanted to and then all of a sudden there was this burst of pleasure and it was like—"

"Okay, yeah, that was an orgasm. You can stop now before you make me jealous."

"So is that weird that it happened just from what we were doing?"

"No, I don't know. Maybe he's just really good at that. Or maybe you just really needed the release. I wouldn't question it. But if the boy makes you see stars from that, why aren't you letting him do more?"

I sighed. "You know why."

"And you know I think that's dumb, but even so, there's a whole lot more than just putting the P in the V, you know?"

"I know, but—"

"Think about it, Giada. You say you're following the Bible, but the Bible's whole thing is about procreation, right? So anything that can't get you pregnant doesn't count."

"I'm not sure—"

"So let the boy work those magic fingers on other parts of your body or, you could really treat yourself and see what he can do with his mouth," she said, interrupting me yet again.

I dragged my pillow over my face. "I really want to take your advice."

"It's good advice," she said.

"That's exactly what the devil himself would say," I retorted, only half joking.

CHAPTER 13

Luca

Homecoming weekend was alarmingly normal. Alessio's school had their homecoming festivities the same weekend, so I didn't see him, and with my papà and most of his cronies in Italy, I didn't hear from them, either. The game itself was a blast, and our team won. After, Giada told me she'd been thinking about what we'd done at my house and she wanted to try it again—or maybe something else—after the dance.

So of course, I could think of nothing but sex the entire night. Giada didn't help matters with her dress selection. She wore a short, fitted, sequined magenta dress, with a tiny cutout just below her chest. The gown was tasteful enough to be appropriate for our school event, but clingy enough to reveal every aspect of her perfect body. We spent the night dancing and laughing, then headed out to an afterparty.

The guy hosting the party was a local who attended our school, and his parents were out of town. We'd never been close friends, but I was grateful for the invite since the location meant Giada and I would have our pick of private bedrooms to fool around in. I was so eager to see what she meant by the "something else" that I could've left the dance after the first song, but I was determined to be a gentleman. I grabbed us both a drink at the party and made small talk with some classmates while Giada sipped hers. I figured the alcohol would relax her no matter what happened next, but luckily, she seemed just as eager as I was for some alone time.

We'd been at the party less than an hour when she tugged me by the hand towards the stairs.

Giada

*L*uca and I found an empty room and he locked the door behind us. Neither of us hesitated to start making out. I'd already decided that I wanted to return the favor tonight. I wasn't exactly sure how, but I was determined not to leave this room until I'd given Luca an orgasm. I believed him the week before when he said he'd enjoyed touching me, but I also knew what I felt, and it was way better than anything he could've experienced from just kissing me.

After a few minutes of kissing, I stepped back a little. I slid my hand down over the front of his shirt, paused at his belt, then kept going, skimming my hand lower. I'd touched his pants before, but always on his butt. This felt infinitely more intimate, touching the front of his pants. I froze, my hand on the prize, as he sucked in a sharp breath and pulled away from the kiss, tilting his forehead against mine.

"Is that...okay?" I asked, stroking upwards, then back down. His dick was already rock hard and sticking straight up, straining against the confines of the suit pants and belt.

Luca moaned and mumbled something indecipherable in Italian, so I kept going, encouraged by his ragged breathing and the flittering of his eyelids. But after a moment, his hand slipped off my back and gripped my fingers. He gazed at me, his eyelids hooded.

"I want to touch you," he said, his voice barely a whisper.

I wanted that too, but now was his turn. I opened my mouth to explain, but he cut me off.

"Not that," he interrupted, misinterpreting my hesitation. "Only my hand, I promise. I want you to feel the way you make me feel. You can stop me at any time."

Luca's eyes focused on mine and I felt like I would melt. I supposed I managed a slight nod, then he tugged me back to the edge of the bed. He kissed me, cupping my jaw in his hand, and guided me onto the bed with him. He shifted us until I was on my back with one knee bent and he was stretched out on his side, hovering over my straight leg. He kissed me more, then paused, smiling down at me. "You're so beautiful, Giada. I could spend an eternity dancing with you."

I opened my mouth to tell him I felt the same, but his hand had drifted to my mid-thigh, and no words came out. His fingers stroked my bare skin, first giving a light massage to my thigh, then inching his way upwards. Luca's attention was on his hand, so I took the opportunity to watch him. His breathing was still heavy and fast, but I could tell he was concentrating, too. He moved slowly, pausing just to the side of my thin, silky thong, and then his fingers snuck under the fabric.

"Oh God," I breathed as he stroked my bare flesh. I suddenly felt too vulnerable, and too far from him, so I tugged on his shoulder, bringing his face to mine.

His fingers paused but only for a moment, and it wasn't long after he began touching me again that an intense heat began building deep in my core. Just when the feeling grew too strong and I was certain I'd explode, all the pressure erupted into ripple after ripple of pleasure. In an instant, I understood exactly why most people didn't wait until marriage for sex.

"Oh my God," I repeated, my voice still barely a whisper.

Luca breathed a laugh and slowly untangled his hand from my clothes. He smiled at me, so I sat up, pressing my lips to his again. As soon as I felt like myself again, I reached for his lap again, now more eager than before to return the favor. Though I hadn't been with a guy before, I wasn't an idiot. I knew what would happen. So I unfastened his belt, using both hands to unbutton his suit pants.

"You don't have to…"

"I want to, but you might need to show me what you like," I said, suddenly unsure of myself again.

His chuckle sounded like a low rumble, deep in his throat. "Baby, I like you. You could just look at me and that would be enough."

I tugged on his briefs, unsure if I should just reach my hand beneath the material like he did for me or if I should help him undress. He lifted his hips, deciding the matter for me as he lowered his clothes just to his upper thighs. Before I could get a good look at him, he turned, and tugged several tissues from the box on the nightstand. It was then that I stole a glance.

I felt my eyes widen at the sight, and instantly I felt even more breathless. I shouldn't have been surprised. I'd felt it through his clothes before, but somehow, seeing it fully uncovered, standing at attention, I lost all train of thought.

"Giada," he whispered, nudging my eyes back to his before capturing my mouth in a kiss. I focused on his lips for a moment, until I'd fully relaxed, then I boldly reached my hand forward. His skin felt warm and smooth, and since I didn't exactly know what I was doing, I simply stroked him out of curiosity, letting my fingers explore the base, then move upwards.

Luca's breathing sped up, and after another minute, his hand found mine. He wrapped his hand over mine, then guided my hand up and then down his length. Apparently convinced I was a quick learner, his hand moved, letting me to work independently as he pressed his fingers softly against the side of my throat. Every part of me tingled with anticipation as I kept going, probably enjoying this as much as he was, if not more.

Luca shifted his hand again, this time reaching for the strap of my dress then wandering lower to caress my breast. Now, I was certain I was enjoying this more than he was. And all of it was making me want him to repeat what he'd done earlier.

Just as I was completely focused on myself and the way my own overly sensitive body was reacting to his touch, Luca grunted and nudged my hand out of the way, pressing the tissues over his lap. His lips left mine, but he held my head close. After a moment, I became aware that the room was silent aside from both of our heavy breathing. Outside the room, loud bass music thumped and voices mixed above each other.

Luca mumbled something in Italian, then presumably translated. "What am I going to do with you?"

I smiled sheepishly, then glanced at his lap. "I'm guessing this is one of those things where I'll get better with practice," I said.

He laughed. "As long as I'm involved, you can practice whenever you want, but that was perfect." He dropped the tissues into the trash and tugged his pants up, fastening his belt before I even registered what was happening.

"Well, I'm sure…" I began.

Luca's finger pressed to my lips before I could finish my thought. 'I swear Giada, if you're about to say another woman's name or compare yourself in any way…"

"I love you," I said instead.

He flashed me his best lopsided grin, then reached for my hand. "Me too. But we should probably get out of here before people start to think we're up to something inappropriate."

CHAPTER 14

Luca

The week after homecoming, I totally understood the expression walking on sunshine. Life was good. Not even a pop quiz in Physics could drag me down. My roommate Grant even called me out for whistling in the shower. I was riding high all the way until Friday, when my papà called and let me know Alessio and I needed to head home for the weekend to help Iacopo and Lodovico with some errands.

We left right after class on Friday, which meant I didn't get to spend any time with Giada. Alessio and I made the most of the lengthy drive, and tried to have a good time that night. But Lodovico had already told me my papà expected me to help with some punishments the next day. Mostly, we'd just be collecting debts, but there was one guy who'd been late. I was supposed to teach him a lesson.

"Why can't I do it?" Alessio asked. "I never get to do the fun jobs." He kept his tone light, as if he legit wanted to do it and wasn't just trying to save me from a task we all knew I couldn't stomach. But Lodovico wasn't buying it.

"The boss was specific. Luca is doing it," he said. "But it's your call what exactly you do. You don't have to cut off any fingers or shoot anyone. You can be as creative as you want."

"As lenient as you want," Alessio said.

Iacopo rolled his eyes. "I wouldn't be too lenient or your papà won't think you've learned much at all. The punishment should fit the crime."

"And, here's a pro tip. Don't hurl on site," Lodovico added.

I sighed, then retreated to the theater room with Alessio to watch movies until we were too tired to stay awake longer. Once I was in my bed, all I could think about was the last time I'd been in that bed—with Giada. I typed out a quick text to her.

"Being in my bed is lonely without you," I wrote, adding a picture of myself pouting. I didn't expect her to reply this late, but she did.

"Miss you too. Sweet dreams," she said. A moment later, a fuzzy picture of her sleepy face came through.

I fell asleep smiling despite myself.

The next morning, I skipped breakfast just in case my stomach didn't cooperate with the assignment. I binged on the coffee, and let Alessio's presence distract me.

"You know what he wants you to do, Luca. Just do it and get it over with," Alessio said.

He made it sound so simple, like it was a one-time thing. And maybe it was. Maybe once I tortured someone once, the next time wouldn't bother me as much. Maybe, it would become second nature eventually.

"If you don't do it, someone else will," he reminded me.

That was true. I also recalled what Tomasso had told me. There was mercy in decisiveness.

"I've got your back," he added.

"I know. Just…let me do it."

After an hour of driving around with them, collecting debts and making threats, I started to think all my panic had been for nothing. But then we reached the final stop for the evening. It was a small shop that sold secondhand sporting goods.

"What does this guy need protection for?" Alessio asked, squinting at the unassuming façade of the shop.

"The guy sells more drugs than yoga mats. We've been keeping the cops and the competition off his back for years, but lately he keeps pushing back. He's getting cocky and I'm fed up."

"I also hear he's a dick in his personal life," Iacopo added. "He called your papà last month when the cops dragged him into custody for knocking his girl down a flight of stairs. Seemed to think we'd have some way to help him out of that mess."

"Why are we still helping him then?" I interrupted. "Wouldn't it make more sense to just cut ties?"

"Seems we're moving in that direction, but for now, he's still got money." Lodovico killed the lights as the car pulled into a spot. "You two head in the front and we'll come around the back," he said to Alessio and I.

We nodded and hopped out. As we pressed in the front door, I instantly noticed the security camera. I flashed a look to Alessio, making sure he was aware too. If one of us forgot to grab the tape, the other wouldn't.

"We are actually closing in just a minute," a man said. "Something I can help you with real fast?"

"You owe his dad money," Alessio said, sauntering right up to the counter.

The man looked up abruptly, his calm, cool demeanor changing in an instant.

"I d…d…don't know what you're talking about."

"He told us to collect your regular payment, plus an extra five hundred for calling him late one night."

"He didn't even do anything. He left me to rot in the jail overnight."

"You're a slimeball who beats women. Why would someone help you with that?" I retorted.

"Business has been slow. I don't have the money yet, but I'll get it!" he raised his voice at the end as Alessio located a baseball bat. He swung it into the security camera and then dropped it casually by his side.

The bat was a cliché, but effective, weapon. I opted to be more original. I grabbed a fifteen pound hand weight from a display near the counter and dropped it over the display case adjacent to the cash register. Alessio snickered as glass shattered everywhere.

"Oops," I mumbled.

"Let's go see about that money," Alessio said. "Care to join us in the back room?"

The man froze. "I'll give you what I've got, but…"

Alessio lifted the bat near the man's head. He flinched and closed his eyes.

"Walk," I told him.

He led to the back room, with me following closely. Alessio opened the back door to let Lodovico and Iacopo join us.

"Everything okay?" they asked.

I shrugged. "He was just about to pay us in full."

"I don't have it yet. Business has been slow, and…" the guy had turned his stare to Lodovico and Iacopo, assuming they were the ones to be worried about. Alessio offered me the baseball bat and I started to reach for it, then came up with a better idea. I flipped open my switchblade and pulled the guy against me. I pressed the blade against his throat, so determined to hold him in place that I actually nicked the skin.

He let out a shriek.

"You have one week, and the price has gone up another ten percent. Can you handle that, or should we kill you now?"

Iacopo showed the slightest hint of a smile, but neither Lodovico or Alessio displayed any hint of emotion at all. Apparently, I was surrounded by sociopaths.

"Yeah, yes, I can. It's fine. I will figure it out. I promise," the man stammered.

I loosened the blade away from his neck, then paused. I tightened my grip on the back of his head, then with all my strength, forced his head downward, into the edge of the half wall by the back room. There was a grotesque cracking sound as his jaw slammed into the concrete, and blood spurted in every direction.

"That was for your girlfriend," I whispered. "Don't fucking hit women, you coward," I released my hold on him and he crumpled to the floor.

Lodovico nudged something with his toe and I grimaced as I saw what it was. A tooth.

We grabbed lunch before finishing our errands, then Alessio and I spent the evening at the club. All my papà's guys seemed to think we were celebrating. The consensus was that I'd done well. Apparently, I'd proven myself and then some.

Somehow, that wasn't reassuring. We headed back to Rhode Island the next morning and I still felt sick about it all.

Giada

*L*uca didn't return to campus until Sunday afternoon. I asked if he wanted to meet up for dinner, but he said he was tired, so I went out with friends instead.

On Monday, I tracked him down after second period. I had his schedule memorized, so it wasn't hard to find him, but I hadn't anticipated it being quite so easy to surprise him. He was looking down at his phone or something so I managed to get my hands all the way around him to cover his eyes.

Before I could even say "guess who," he dropped his phone and roughly knocked my arm out of the way. His expression was fierce as he turned towards me, but then in an instant, it softened.

"Shit! Giada, I didn't..." he shook his head and blew out a stressed sigh.

I bent to grab his phone, which was miraculously unscathed despite his refusal to use a functional protective case. "Jumpy, are we?"

"I'm sorry," he mumbled, frowning.

I rose to my tip toes and leaned in, but made him bridge the final two inches between us to kiss me.

He did, but only briefly.

"I have to get to class now. Lunch?"

Luca nodded.

"I'll try not to be so sneaky this time," I teased.

Luca was quiet at lunch, which was so unlike him, especially after a weekend away. I wasn't that hungry anyway, so I cleaned up my stuff and nodded for him to follow me into the hall.

"Everything okay?" I asked when we were alone.

"Just great," he mumbled, his expression conveying the opposite of his words.

"O-kay. You just didn't say a whole lot back there."

"Well, I didn't really have a strong opinion about Ansley's stupid dress color. Why was she even talking about it?"

"I mean, it's prom. It's kind of a big deal."

"It's a dance. And it's four months away. She seriously doesn't have anything more important to worry about?"

His eyes darted from side to side like he was searching for something. I knew I could take the bait and argue more, but I just wanted him to calm down. I roped my arms around him and squeezed tightly. He fidgeted against me for a moment, resisting my comfort. I could sense the exact moment he relented, his hard body relaxing against me. He dropped his forehead to my shoulder, then after another minute, reached his arms around me, returning the hug.

I could've held him for hours, but we had class. And probably an audience by this point. Besides, what I really wanted was answers. What happened when he went home for the weekend? Why was he always so...off-kilter when he returned?

But I knew better than to push and ask him directly.

"I missed you this weekend," I whispered.

Luca pulled back enough to gaze into my eyes, his gaze so intent that I felt like he was looking through me, reading my mind.

"Why are you so good?" he asked.

I wiggled my eyebrows suggestively. "Would you prefer I be bad?"

He dropped his hands from my waist and giggled. "Ti amo," he said. "But we've both got to get to class."

I smiled as Luca pressed a kiss to the tip of my nose. His fingers grazed mine and then he turned to leave.

"Hey Luca," I said before he was out of earshot. "Just so you know, there's only three months until prom. And I have high expectations, so don't act like I didn't warn you," I teased.

He tapped his forehead as though making a mental note of the information.

CHAPTER 15

Luca

I slept like shit Monday night, waking every couple hours from nightmares filled with visions of blood spurting everywhere. Somehow, my memories had mixed my wrongdoings, so now I was the one chopping off fingers and not just smashing jaws. My victims were always faceless, but I'd watch myself as if on a movie screen, moving through a room like the villain in a bad action movie. I'd slice one guy's fingers, then break his friend's nose. When I left a room, I'd wipe my bloodied hands on my shirt to clean them off.

Each time I awoke, I was sweaty and panting and I'd reach for my hands, squinting in the darkness as if searching for a hint of the blood I knew I'd find. The guilt was crushing me, and I couldn't even figure out why. Neither of the men I'd hurt were innocent. I hadn't even been the one to hurt one of them. But I still couldn't shake the feeling that I was the bad guy.

I couldn't confide in Giada, or anyone else on campus, for that matter. And Alessio didn't seem to share my guilt complex. He did, however, try to make me feel better. He reminded me we

"

weren't messing with innocent guys. Anyone we hurt had whatever we did—or far worse— coming to them. If we didn't take action, someone else would—and chances are, they'd be far less lenient than I was.

Still, I couldn't ignore the dread building in the pit of my stomach. I knew this was only the beginning. The things I was doing now were bad, but they would only get worse. The stakes would only get higher over time, and the breaks in between the demands that I act like a monster would get shorter and shorter.

I wasn't sure I could live that way but, then again, I didn't exactly have a choice.

Giada

When I met Luca the next day after class, I could tell he was grumpy before I even spoke to him. His hands were balled into fists, his posture looked stiff, and a scowl stood where his mischievous grin should have been. I wasn't surprised, since this was par for the course when he returned from a visit home, but I had hoped today would be the exception.

Normally, I was a pro at cheering up Luca. Or at least distracting him. But today I was tired and overly stressed myself. Midterm grades were back and none of mine had gone as well as I'd hoped. Elise and Delaney were arguing, Blair still hated my guts, and one of my nails had ripped nearly down to the middle. I just wanted to snuggle with my boyfriend and have him tell me everything would be okay. I didn't have it in me to be his cheerleader, yet again.

I sighed and plastered a smile to my face as I approached. "Hey hot stuff," I cooed.

Luca offered me the fakest of grins and pulled me into a cool embrace. He pressed his lips against the side of my head before releasing me. "Where to?"

"I really need to study," I said, wrinkling my nose in anticipation of his protests. "My grades are awful and I have to get perfect scores on everything between now and finals. We could go to the lawn though. It's a nice day."

Luca gazed across the quad towards the open area we all uncreatively referred to as the lawn, then nodded. He gripped my hand and we started in that direction. "How was your weekend?"

I debated offering some generic answer like I normally would when I sensed his weekend had sucked, but I really needed to vent, and there was literally no one else I could complain about these problems to. So, I started telling him all about the drama between Elise and Delaney.

It wasn't like I thought their drama would bring about the end of the world. I knew neither would murder the other, start a world war, or somehow ruin my chances of getting into college. But I lived with those girls. Their moods and their behavior seriously impacted every second of my life in the dorm. So I thought Luca might care. Or at least feign sympathy.

He didn't.

"Gee, sounds rough. However did you survive?" Luca replied in a cool, mocking tone when I finished explaining how Elise dragged me out of the dining hall before I even finished eating on Sunday.

I turned to Luca, taken aback by his harsh response. He caught my expression and his own features softened.

"Sorry. Continue."

"No, it's fine. I'll just vent about it to the other friend I have who doesn't live in the same dorm. Oh wait, that's no one." I stomped off towards the tree we usually sat beneath when studying on the lawn. "You know, not all of us get the privilege of having these big important problems that we get to unload on everyone around us after every visit with family. Some of us just want someone to listen every once in a while to our mundane shit, okay?"

Luca dragged his hand through his hair. "I said I was sorry. You can keep talking," he mumbled.

I flung my hands in the air. "No, I can't. You already made it clear you don't care at all what I'm talking about."

"Well, I'm sorry if I'm having trouble taking all the girl drama seriously when other people are dealing with actual problems."

I rolled my eyes. "Right, because you are the only person who is allowed to have issues with your dad. Nobody else here has any hurt feelings at all about being sent away to this school or all the shit that went down right before." I squeezed my eyes shut, trying to block out the now distant memories of the fateful day when I watched two men shoot my grandpa.

Luca dropped his backpack by his feet. "You think your father is like mine but he's not. At least he doesn't treat you the same way mine treats me. You're not another one of his minions to boss around."

"If you want your dad to respect you, be a person worth respecting. Stand up to him. If he tries to go low, you go high."

A sardonic laugh escaped his lips. "Yeah, I'm not sure you'd like how that turns out," Luca said, rolling his eyes.

I reached for his arm, but he jerked away causing my nail to snag his sleeve. "I don't even know what you're talking about Luca. You don't tell me anything."

"Not everything is your business, Giada."

For some reason, that hurt more than the other things he'd said. I crossed my arms over my chest and turned to leave. Then, I thought better of it.

"You know what, Luca? You're right. Maybe it's not my business. But maybe I'm sick of seeing you act like a whiny baby every time you get back from running some errand with your dad or visiting home."

"Whiny baby? Are you fucking kidding me?" Luca swiveled towards me and stepped closer, getting right up in my face.

I wasn't about to back down, but then I felt my feet start to inch away without my brain telling them to. Unfortunately, I bumped into a tree and had nowhere else to go. Luca held his ground, glaring at me. I thought about how, even a day before, I would've loved being this close to Luca. I would've looped my arms around his neck and kissed him until a teacher yelled at us to stop. Now, I knew my heart was thudding for a very different reason.

I wasn't actually scared of Luca. He wouldn't hurt me. But I was very afraid of the person he'd become at the moment. And more than a little concerned about whatever had caused him to act this way.

"At the end of the day, only you know what you're dealing with. I can't fight your demons for you, especially if you don't want to let me in. And that isn't even the point." I paused, hoping a deep inhale would steady my shaky voice. "This is your senior year of high school, Luca. You only get one of those."

"Unless I flunk," he interrupted.

I ignored him and continued. "You choose how you want to remember it. Do you want to focus on the good or the bad? And it's not just that. You also choose how you want to be remembered here at school by your classmates. You are more than the sum of your parts. You aren't just what happens to you. You have free will. You have choices."

"Except I don't."

"Even if you don't feel like you can choose what you do, you still get to choose how you feel about everything you experience."

I paused again, but this time, Luca just stared back at me.

"I'm done trying to cheer you up. I can't save you from yourself." I reached my hand up and shoved Luca back several feet before striding around him. I walked away slowly, hoping against all logic that he'd call after me. He didn't.

CHAPTER 16

Luca

I felt like a dick after the fight with Giada, but I was so messed up that I didn't know what to do. My instincts told me to apologize immediately, but then I reasoned maybe this was for the best. Giada was right about one thing—she couldn't save me from myself. As for the rest, well, she had no idea how truly fucked up I was. She didn't know what I did for my papà and she never would. Was I always just going to come running back to her and expect her to cheer me up?

Even worse, part of me worried I was putting her at risk. I hadn't forgotten my papà's threat. If I didn't do what he said, Giada might suffer. Maybe I was just being selfish. Maybe it was time to cut her loose.

I called Alessio to get his take on it all. As always, he oversimplified everything.

"For starters, you're a complete dick. You're gonna have to eat her out until you have lockjaw to make that up to her," he said, cackling at his own crass joke. "And second of all, no, you're not putting her at risk. Think about it."

I did, and I had no brilliant thoughts worth sharing on the matter.

"Your dad hurts Giada to punish you, and then he's got the whole Conti family on his bad side. Sound like a smart business move? No. But let's say you dump Giada and go out with some other girl. Could your dad mess with her to piss you off? Absolutely."

I considered it and realized Alessio was right. "So you're saying Giada is basically the only girl I can date."

"No, date whoever you want. I'm just saying she's the only girl your dad will never hurt no matter what you do."

"Cazzo," I swore. "I need to apologize."

"Yeah, and maybe buy some jewelry."

I thanked him and hung up, then started brainstorming. I'd need something big to really make it up to Giada. After twenty minutes, I had my plan. First, I texted her a groveling apology, broken down into half a dozen separate messages.

"Giada, baby, did you block my number?"

"I deserve that and a million times worse."

"I was an ass today. I'm sorry."

"I don't know what is wrong with me. You deserve better."

"Everything you said was right."

"I'll do better. Let me make it up to you."

Finally, she replied, asking what I had in mind. I grinned, then replied that it was a secret and she'd have to trust me.

The next weekend, I drove Giada out to my papà's warehouse on the outskirts of town. I hated being there, since that was the place his goons had taken me every time they'd jumped me. But it was the only place I could think of that had a lot that was big and empty enough for what I had planned. And I figured spending the day there with Giada was the best way to form some pleasant associations with the place. I'd run it by Iacopo already so no one would be suspicious if they saw my car circling the place.

She'd only mentioned a hundred or so times how no one in

her family would teach her to drive, so I knew it was something she wanted. And when I overheard her on the phone, begging Lorenzo to teach her, I decided I wanted to be the one to do it.

I pulled into a space in the middle of the parking lot, smiled as I confirmed it was mostly empty. Killing the ignition, I turned to Giada.

"Are we out of gas?" she asked, wrinkling her nose at the sprawling buildings before us. "I'm not going in there."

I leaned across the center and kissed her before answering. "You don't have to go inside. But get out."

She eyed me warily.

"Baby, don't you trust me?"

She climbed out of the car without a second thought. *Wow.* That was flattering.

"What now?" she asked after I exited the vehicle, too.

I motioned for her to come to my side. "Now you drive," I said.

Her eyes lit up and she dashed around the back of the car, leaping onto me. She roped her arms around my neck as I caught her, laughing as her legs wrapped around my waist. "Oh my God, Luca! I love you," she said, planting a huge kiss on my mouth. "Are you serious though? You're actually going to let me drive your car?"

"Si, Tesoro," I replied, laughing at her enthusiasm.

"Isn't it illegal?"

"I'm willing to risk it if you are," I said, adding, "Besides, my papà owns this lot and the warehouse."

She kissed me again before I lowered her to the ground. I handed her the keys and settled into the passenger seat.

"I've literally never sat over here," I said. I pointed to the button that would adjust the seat for her and then waited for her to start the car. When a minute passed and we were still waiting, I turned to face her just as she burst out laughing.

"I have no idea how to start your car, Luca," she admitted, covering her face with her hands.

"Just put your foot on the brake and push this red button," I said, laughing along with her.

"And the brake…that's the one on the right?"

I cringed. "The left. Brake is on the left." I said a mental prayer for my poor car, then fastened my belt and braced myself on the handle above my window.

"Oh stop," she said, swatting me. She got the car going, and I showed her how to shift into Drive. We practiced stopping and starting, and then she bumped into the turn signal so we took it as a sign to practice turns. By the end of the hour, my cheeks were sore from laughing so hard, though I figured my neck might be a little achy the next day from the whiplash.

We paused, leaning against the hood of the car for a lengthy makeout session, before switching back to our correct seats. I'd had a blast teaching her to drive, but even if I hadn't, her method of thanking me would've made it worthwhile anyway. I was about to release her when I noticed someone approaching. I pulled my head away from her quickly, tightening my grip on her.

It was Xavier, the guy I'd beaten up the year before when my papà had dumped me at the warehouse.

"Shit," I mumbled under my breath. "Giada, get in the car."

Not surprisingly, she didn't. "Who's that?" she asked casually.

"He works for my papà. I'm not in the mood to talk with him. We should go. Fast." I nudged her elbow, but she stood firm.

"Buongiorno," Xavier greeted us, smiling in that way that only sociopaths and mobsters seemed to do, with his lips curved all the way up but his eyes remaining unaffected and filled with disdain. He spoke in Italian, asking if my papà knew we were there. I kept my tone casual and replied that he should, as I'd run it by Ludovico. Then I told him we were leaving anyway.

"Giada, let's go," I said.

Xavier's ears perked up as I addressed her in English. Or maybe it was her name that caught his attention.

"Who's your friend?" he asked.

"Not your business," I replied, practically dragging her to her door.

Giada swatted my hand. "Don't be rude, Luca. Giada Conti," she said to Xavier, extending her hand.

He accepted her hand and shook it, smirking at me. I blew out a sigh. Any other girl would be terrified of this thug, but Giada treated him like a charming old friend. And then it struck me why. Her uncles, her father's friends, shoot even her brothers—they all looked just like this. She's grown up around this exact type of man that terrorized the rest of the town, except she'd never learned to fear them because they always worshiped the ground she walked on. They always treated her like the princess.

"Marco's girl," he said.

She smiled and nodded. "Do you know him?"

"Not personally. We've crossed paths a few times." He turned back to me again, clearly bemused by her obliviousness to his evil nature. "Well, you two drive safe."

I dipped my head in a curt nod and he turned to walk away. I released the breath I'd been holding and stepped into the car.

"He seemed nice," she said as I shifted into gear.

"He's not."

She stared pointedly.

"What? He isn't."

"Maybe he would be nicer to you if you weren't rude to him," she replied.

"Or maybe you aren't the best judge of character."

"Excuse me?" Her eyes widened proportionally with her degree of annoyance.

I cringed, wishing I'd kept my mouth shut. Although, maybe it was for the best. Eventually, Giada would need to learn that she couldn't trust everyone.

"Look, you haven't lived the worldliest life. You've been sheltered. You think everyone is a good person and most people aren't."

"Most, huh?" she repeated with an eyeroll.

"Giada, I'm not trying to pick a fight. I'm just saying maybe don't assume you can trust everyone you meet."

"I don't."

"You sure seemed pretty confident that Xavier was a good guy."

She flung her hands in the air. "The only reason I spoke with him is because of you. I trust you, not him."

I rolled to a stop at the red light and turned to face her, resting my palm on her thigh.

"It didn't occur to me you'd introduce me to someone bad," she said.

I blew out a sigh. "I'm sorry. It's my fault for not telling you then."

"Not telling me what?"

I hesitated, unsure how to phrase it. "The guys that work for my papà, a lot of them are not good people," I finally said. "Some of them aren't nice to me and a few of them are dangerous."

"Dangerous?" she repeated, frowning.

"Yes, so if you meet someone who claims to have some connection to me or my family, assume you should keep your distance unless I tell you otherwise."

She was quiet for a moment, then said, "Your dad wouldn't let dangerous people be around you. Are you saying *he* doesn't know what they're like?"

"Tesoro, can you please just trust me on this? Mio papà is not like yours."

Giada

*A*fter the surprise driving lesson, Luca was the perfect boyfriend for the rest of the semester. He helped me with my homework, made flashcards to help me study, and even explained some of the trickier math concepts. Since Luca wasn't planning on going to college, he didn't worry about his own grades. For me, on the other hand, this year felt like the most critical year ever. I was painfully aware that the grades I earned this year were the last ones colleges would see when deciding my future.

When Luca wasn't helping me study, he brought me snacks, offered backrubs, and texted me silly memes to distract me from my stress. Actually, he offered lots of different options for distractions, but most of them seemed less likely to result in better grades on my tests.

"I think you've reached the point where you've studied too much and anything else at this point will just hurt your grade," Luca said, nudging my book shut with his finger. We were in the corner of the library, sprawled out on the floor. He was leaning against the wall, legs stretched out in front of him. I'd been resting my head on Luca's lap, alternating between reading one sentence aloud then closing my eyes and repeating it in hopes of memorizing everything.

The librarians were pretty chill about this sort of arrangement during winter finals. They still maintained absolute silence in the closed-off study rooms, but the open areas surrounding the stacks filled the role the lawn served during warmer times of the year. The week before finals, most students were still upright in study carrels or sofas, but by the time exams actually began, it was like we all lost the energy to sit unassisted. A visitor walking through the library this week might accidentally confuse the building for a shelter following some local environmental disaster like a hurricane or something based off of how many unkempt teens were splayed across the floor.

I'd prefer to study in my room—or Luca's, but the dorm moms had cracked down this semester and it had become impossible to sneak any member of the opposite sex into the dorm, even for innocent purposes like studying. That unfortunately also meant that Luca and I were restricted to public places off campus, random less populous areas of the library, and his car for our makeout sessions. I didn't mind kissing in any of those locations, but I definitely missed some of the other touching we'd started doing.

"I'm serious. It's been proven that endorphins help you solidify memories. And do you know what releases endorphins?" Luca asked.

"Exercise," I replied.

Luca slapped his palm to his forehead. "Sex."

"Luca!" I scolded, glancing furtively around us to see if anyone overheard. Luckily, no one seemed to be paying attention to us.

"Not just sex. Any orgasm," he clarified, leaning closer so he could lower his voice.

His warm breath tickled my forehead and suddenly, I became painfully aware that my face was directly over his crotch. I shifted to sit up, scowling at the bemused smirk on Luca's face.

"It's also great stress relief and proven to help improve quality of sleep," he added.

"If you put this level of research skill into your homework, you'd have straight As," I told him.

"I'm good with Bs. Look, it's up to you. I'm just offering to help you out. Not seeking anything in return." He raised his hands as if to show he was unarmed, but that was the biggest load of BS ever. Luca's greatest weapons were his smile and his eyes, and he used both freely. Even people who were immune to his obvious good looks and his crazy hot body were still susceptible to his charm. He'd just bat those eyes and grin and people would do whatever he wanted.

"Luca, I'm obviously not opposed to you doing that for me, or me reciprocating, for that matter. But I'm not about to do that in the library, and last I checked, we couldn't get into each other's dorms. So unless you have a better plan..."

Luca popped to his feet like a ninja and then extended a hand to help me up. I accepted, then spent a full minute stretching all the muscles that had cramped up while we were studying. We gathered up our stuff and Luca glanced at his phone.

"We have nearly two hours till curfew and thanks to daylight savings time, it's already pitch black. We will have all the privacy we need in my car."

"Luca—"

"Giada, trust me."

I didn't say anything as Luca drove off campus, but I was ninety-nine percent sure his plan would not work. I hated for him to get his hopes up, so I finally spoke up as we started towards a nearby park.

"Babe, I appreciate the thought, but I'm not about to risk being one of those girls who gets caught making out in the back-seat of a car."

"Va bene. We'll stay in the front."

"And I'm not taking off my clothes in a car," I added.

He glanced at me. "Do you know my favorite thing about your uniform?" He didn't pause for me to answer. "The skirt. So convenient."

My eyes dropped to my lap. He had a point. The material was thicker and longer than the stylish schoolgirl skirt you'd see in the fashion magazines, but it was still a skirt. "Okay but the tights are ridiculous. Nothing is getting past them."

"I'm happy to rip them, or you could just take them off while I'm driving. Wedge them in your backpack. Then if anyone happens to find us when we're kissing, that's all they'll see—two fully dressed teens kissing. They'll never know you used to have tights on."

I considered his words, then bent down to unbuckle my shoes

so I could slip off the tights. I caught a glimpse of Luca's smug grin the second I started to shimmy out of my tights, but I said nothing.

"You could toss your bra in the backpack too," he suggested.

"Luca!" I scolded.

He laughed.

A few minutes later, we'd pulled to a stop in the back of a parking lot beneath a burnt out streetlamp. He'd parked so close to the edge of the spot that a tree almost completely blocked the passenger window and part of the front windshield. I gazed around the parking lot and decided it looked safe, but also empty. There were two other cars, but both were parked in the far back row, and therefore likely belonged to employees who would be inside until closing. Any customers who arrived would park by the front.

"Just let me kiss you, Giada," Luca said, unfastening both of our seatbelts and angling himself over me.

He didn't have to tell me twice. His soft lips crashed against mine and by the time his tongue swept through my mouth, I was already regretting my stubbornness at refusing to remove my bra. Luca worked around the obstacle though, as his hand went up my shirt a minute after we began kissing. He caressed me through the thin fabric of my bra at first, but then he yanked the cup downward.

I sucked in a sharp breath as his fingers stroked my bare nipple. Luca froze, peeling his lips away from mine at the hiss, and I clasped my fingers behind his head, nudging his mouth back to me. "Don't stop," I mumbled against his lips.

He complied, but he shifted both of us again a moment later. He reached down and tugged one of my legs over his. I squirmed, finding the new position more awkward for kissing him, but the second his hand reached between my thighs, I realized what he was doing. I let out a shaky breath, suddenly nervous, and Luca pulled away from the kiss yet again.

This time, before I could protest, he licked two of his own fingers, then recaptured my mouth with his own. A moment later, I felt his damp fingers below my skirt on my most sensitive flesh.

I gasped and nearly bit down on Luca's lip and the sudden, intense sensation. He took that opportunity to lick the fingers from his other hand before returning them up my shirt. When his wet finger stroked my nipple in time with his other hand stroking along my slit, a wave of dizziness swept over me.

"Oh my God," I panted. I tried to keep kissing him, but I couldn't concentrate on anything except for the intensely exquisite sensations overtaking my body. Luca pressed his lips to my forehead, holding me in place as I panted and let his fingers play me like an instrument. I was certain I was about to pass out when all of a sudden a sharp electric jolt passed through my body, starting at my core and radiating down all of my limbs.

"Fuck, Luca, oh my God, Luca," I moaned, clutching his arms as if I'd fall off the cliff it he didn't hold tight.

Luca kept touching me until I'd regained the ability to see and breathe and think, at which point I nudged his hands out of the way and let my head sink against my chest.

After a minute, Luca chuckled. "Holy shit, baby. That was the hottest thing ever. I mean, the way you said my name when you—"

I swatted his arm to cut him off.

"Ow!"

I gazed up and noticed the fiery red marks on his bicep. "Jesus, what is that? Did I do that?"

Luca bit back a smug smile. "Yeah. Pretty sure your nails hit the bone. I'm going to have scars for life."

"I am so sorry!"

Luca gripped my chin in his hand. "Giada, stop. I assure you, whatever happens the rest of my life, these will be my absolute favorite scars."

I readjusted my bra, still certain my cheeks were beet-red.

"Also sure that will always be the hottest thing I ever experience. You didn't even touch me and I almost came."

I lifted my eyes to meet his. "We have a few more minutes before we need to head back to campus. I'm not letting you do that and then not returning the favor."

Luca glanced around us uncertainly. "Well, I'm not exactly wearing a skirt, and there's a little more of a mess when I finish."

I reached into my backpack and pulled out a travel size pack of tissues. I tugged several free from the package and handed them to Luca. Then, I reached for his zipper. He grabbed my hand.

"Let me," he said.

He fidgeted with his pants and a moment later, had freed his fully erect penis from his khakis and boxer briefs. I stared at it for a moment, noticing all the lines and squiggles and how red and engorged the tip appeared. I still couldn't even sort of fathom how something so large and hard was supposed to comfortably fit inside a woman's body, but I wasn't about to ask that. Even more perplexing was how just looking at this weird body part was somehow turning me on all over again when I'd just had the most intense release of my life.

"Giada, you don't have to…" Luca began, moving like he was about to put it away.

"No, I was just wondering if maybe I could, um, use my mouth? Like not the whole time, but maybe just for a minute?"

Luca stared at me for so long that I almost wondered if I hadn't actually spoken aloud. Finally, he said, "Umm, yes. You can do whatever you want but I thought you said you weren't doing that until marriage."

"I changed my mind. That's not what that rule meant," I said, quickly adding, "I didn't change my mind about the rest, just that this isn't really sex."

Luca nodded. "Yeah, agreed." He kissed me long and hard,

then stared at me again. "But um, I'm not going to last a whole minute with your mouth on me, so just be ready to move when I nudge you."

I nodded, suddenly feeling super shy. I licked my lips and then leaned forward, shifting closer to the door so I could reach. I wasn't completely sure what to do or what to expect, so I started by simply tracing my tongue around the tip of his penis. The skin was warm, and tasted just like any other part of his body. I swirled my tongue around again, then gazed up, almost surprised to see Luca was watching me.

He offered an encouraging smile, then gathered my hair into a makeshift ponytail in his hand. I wasn't sure if it was to improve his view of me or to keep the hair out of my way, but regardless, I felt emboldened. I wrapped my lips around him and took the first inch or two into my mouth, swirling my tongue around as I went down and back up. I wasn't sure if I was doing the right thing, but Luca's breathing was picking up.

Right as I finally felt like I found my rhythm, Luca tugged gently on my hair, pulling my head backwards and scooting his hand, filled with tissues, over his lap. He grunted, then exhaled into more of a moan. He turned to me and grinned.

"Well, it's official. I'm flunking all of my exams because I won't be able to think about anything except your pretty little mouth screaming my name and sucking my—"

"Luca Thomas!" I shouted even though I was pretty sure he had no intention of finishing his sentence.

"Tomás," he corrected.

"Tomás," I repeated, loving the sound of his middle name when he pronounced it with his sexy native accent.

Luca grinned, fastened himself back into his pants, then dumped the soiled tissues outside his car door.

"Litterbug," I said.

"I'll make up for it next week," he promised, leaning in to kiss me before backing out of the space.

I sighed and relaxed against the seat, realizing Luca had been right about at least one thing. I felt so much less stressed now. I gazed out the window, totally unconcerned with anything, least of all final exams.

After a minute, Luca squeezed my bare thigh. "Not complaining about the view, but you may want to put those tights back on before we get to campus."

I groaned, but took his advice. We made it back to campus with over a half hour to spare before curfew. Luca parked in the same spot he'd occupied before, and we started towards my dorm.

"Why haven't we been doing this every day after studying?" I mused.

Luca laughed and wrapped his arm around my shoulders.

CHAPTER 17

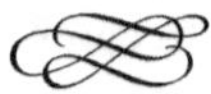

Giada

*D*espite the distractions, I survived finals. I'd managed to secure all As and Bs, and I had instantly shifted into full celebratory holiday mode.

I was spending winter break in Italy with my family, as we did most years. Since Luca and his family were also in Palermo this year, I had zero complaints about the plans. Even better, my parents agreed to let me and Luca stay out overnight "with friends" for New Year's Eve.

We did have some friends in Palermo, although they were more Luca's friends than mine. And they were in fact hosting a party on NYE. But Luca and I were not attending the party. In reality, we'd just headed to a hotel outside of Palermo on our own and celebrated the new year alone in a hotel room.

"I'm surprised my dad let me go overnight, at least without sending one of my brothers or Lorenzo to keep tabs on me," I said, checking out the view from the room.

"He doesn't need them to watch over you when he knows I'm

"

with you," Luca said, standing behind me, roped his arms around by waist, then rest his chin on the top of my head.

I sighed peacefully and relaxed against Luca. I loved when he held me like that. Something about the way we literally fit together reassured me that we were, in fact, a perfect fit. We had to be right.

"Most fathers aren't okay with their teenage daughters spending a night with their boyfriend," I said. "And he isn't so stupid that he thought we'd be with friends the whole time. I mean, maybe he did, but he had to suspect we were sharing a room."

"I dunno, his good little Catholic girl would never do anything ungodly," Luca said, tickling my stomach.

I made a face, but Luca was right. I was a complete hypocrite. I liked to think of myself as somehow more faithful, more obedient to the laws of our religion than most around me, but at the end of the day, I picked and chose what I'd follow just like everyone else. I still knew it was wrong to fool around with Luca and even to share a bed with him, but in my heart, I could justify it. We weren't hurting anyone, so what did it matter? Besides, if God really hadn't wanted me to be with Luca, why had He thrown us into each other's path again and again? Why hadn't He made Luca ugly? Or nerdy? Or a jerk?

And besides, if Luca was the man I was supposed to marry, was it really so horrible to jump ahead a bit?

"Your parents trust you with me because they like seeing us together. You know that. If you had any other boyfriend, your father wouldn't have let you leave the villa tonight. My papà likes us together too."

I had to agree with that, and it reminded me of something else I'd been wondering for a while. "Luca?" I waited for him to answer even though he was still right behind me, wrapped around me like a koala bear on a tree branch.

"Si, Tesoro?"

I blushed and lost my train of thought. Something about him speaking Italian always had that effect on me, like he was just so comfortable with me that he forgot we didn't speak the same language. Except, of course I knew what that meant. He often called me Tesoro, his treasure.

"My dad never told me why he switched me to this school, but he knew you went there. Do you think you're the reason why he transferred me?"

Luca released me and stepped to the side so he could see me. He quirked an eyebrow, then paused to think. "I don't know. Maybe? I wouldn't put it past either of our fathers to try to manipulate us like that. I think they'd both be very content to see us together forever. I'm not mad though."

"No, me neither. Maybe the only time my dad's meddling worked out in my favor."

He leaned in and pressed his lips to my forehead, sending shivers down my spine. Then he wrapped his arms around my waist again, but this time hugging me from the front. I enjoyed the soothing comfort of his grip for a moment before speaking my next thought aloud.

"Where do you see us one year from today?"

He thought about it for a moment, then answered without loosening the embrace. "Right here. We should make this a New Year's tradition."

I smiled at the thought, but it wasn't exactly the answer I wanted. "No, I mean, what happens to us next year, after you graduate?" The question had been looming over us for months now, but this was the first time I'd directly asked it out loud. I already knew he was going to be working for his dad and not going to college. He already knew I had one more year of high school and then planned on four years of college. But we hadn't addressed any of the details.

His arms loosened then dropped. "I have to be in Italy next

year. It's like an apprenticeship, for my family business. But I'll be back a lot. It will be fine."

I didn't love thinking about us being apart the next year, but I did like that he didn't even consider the possibility of us not being a couple anymore. Still, I decided to press my luck.

"What about in five years?"

Luca took his time answering, but I held my breath while he thought.

"Summers in New York and winter here?" he finally said, flashing me that adorably hopeful grin of his.

"Are you asking me?"

"Of course. If you'd rather we spend winter in New York and summer here, I suppose I can be flexible, but that doesn't make much sense…"

"Luca," I interrupted, eager to see his sparkling eyes staring at me again. "You think we'll still be together in five years?"

He reached for my hands without dropping his gaze. "Amore, I don't see any future for myself that you're not a part of."

I swear my heart melted a little. I rose onto my toes and kissed him, pausing only enough to whisper, "I love you Luca Marino."

We spent the next hour kissing, then moved to the tiny shower and kissed and touched each other there until the water ran cold. I was freezing when we toweled off, so we used the in-room coffee machine to make hot cocoa. Luca had already pulled on a pair of thin sweatpants, but when I started to get my pajamas, he shook his head.

"Can I keep you warm instead? I want to try something."

I raised a brow.

"I promise you'll like it."

I snorted at his self-assuredness.

"Lay down," he said.

"My hair is wet."

Luca grabbed a spare towel from the bathroom and lay it

down under my hair. Once I stretched back on the bed, he draped a soft blanket over me. I shivered, and the fabric tickled my bare breasts. Luca grabbed my feet and scooted them upwards, forcing my knees to bend. He then inched one foot to the side and crouched between my feet, smiling.

"Why are you dressed and I'm not?" I asked.

"So you trust me," he replied, shimmying under the blanket and covering my body with his own. "And maybe because I don't trust myself."

I breathed a laugh at his response, then kissed him. While Luca kissed my lips, his hand trailed down the side of my body. After a minute, he shifted lower, kissing my neck, then my collarbone, then the top of my breast, and then—

"Oh my God!" I nearly screamed as his lips closed around my nipple.

Luca laughed against my breast, swirling his tongue around the tip before moving to the other one. My hand drifted to the back of his head, almost as if I were trying to hold him in place. Maybe I was, but when he pulled back, I let him.

"I thought you'd like that," he gloated, "But I wanted to try something else today."

Before I could ask what he meant, he was kissing my stomach and then inching lower. Every muscle in my body stiffened the second I realized where he was headed. I instantly thought of a million reasons to stop him, but as my hands reached down to do so, Luca gripped my wrists and pinned them to my sides.

He kissed the top of my pubic mound, then gently ran his tongue along my slit. At first, it felt weird, and wet. But then he nudged my knees further apart, deepened the pressure with his tongue, and slid one hand up my torso. A jolt of pleasure shot through me as he rolled my nipple between his fingers at the precise moment his tongue stroked my clit. All of my nerve endings were on high alert and I felt every touch so intensely.

I heard myself panting but was too close to my climax to

be self-conscious. My body raced to the peak of pleasure then teetered on the precipice. I was torn between yearning to maintain that feeling for perpetuity, and the certainty that I'd die of a heart attack if the intensity lasted another second. Too soon I was falling, swept up into wave after wave of bliss.

I tugged the blanket over my face, suddenly feeling so naked and vulnerable. Luca settled beside me, but didn't rush me. When I finally inched the blanket down to look at him, he was sipping his hot cocoa and staring at me. He set the mug on the night stand and smiled at me.

"So what's the verdict? Si o no?" he asked.

I could only roll my eyes, shake my head, and pull him towards me for a kiss.

We managed to go another hour without making out, but then started all over again. We spent the next several hours talking, cuddling, then fooling around, and before we finally drifted off, long after midnight, I found myself wondering how married people ever got anything done.

Luca

I awoke to a sweltering weight over me. I opened my eyes slowly, wincing at the sun pouring in through the flimsy curtains. I moved my hand to nudge the blankets off me, then paused. Giada was blanketing my body, not some hotel quilt. There was a thick white duvet on top of her, but I didn't think I could move that without waking her. And it probably wouldn't cool me off much anyway.

I squinted at the clock, surprised that it was only half past ten. Not that that was early, but it wasn't as late as I would've expected to sleep after the late night we'd enjoyed. We'd stayed up past three, drinking, laughing, talking, kissing. Touching. So much touching. And tasting.

Just thinking about it made parts of my body grow very alert.

I laughed silently at the irony of my trying to hold still only to have the one organ I clearly couldn't control spring to attention and wake Giada anyway.

Giada was so beautiful when she slept. She was always attractive, but asleep, there was this extra peacefulness about her. She looked even more innocent, even more refreshing. I could definitely see myself waking up to Giada every morning, and I wasn't sure what to do with that realization. It didn't scare me, oddly enough, but it seemed weird.

Rationally, I believed I shouldn't love another person this much at eighteen. I should be fantasizing about all of my future conquests, like every other eighteen year old boy. The whole point of the next five years was to sleep with as many women as possible, according to every one of my friends. Not to pine over the same girl, no matter how perfect she was.

I'd meant what I'd said to Giada. I really couldn't picture my future without her. Or at least, I didn't want to. But maybe it wouldn't have been so terrible if I'd met her later in life, after we'd both had a chance to live a little first.

Giada's breathing shifted suddenly, and a moment later she stretched across me, the softest of moans escaping her lips. She lifted her head, squinting at me from beneath thick lashes. She yawned, then smiled.

"Well hello there."

I smiled back.

"I trapped you here, didn't I?" she asked, making no attempt to move off of me.

"Not complaining."

She gazed at me for a moment longer, then started to roll to her side. I grabbed her hip and rolled with her, bringing our faces closer together.

"I haven't brushed my teeth yet," she said, but I was already kissing her.

An hour later, we had dressed and packed up our stuff. I'd arranged for late checkout, so we weren't in any major rush, but we did have to get back to our parents at some point that day or they'd suspect we'd lied.

"Shoot. I don't think I have any euros," Giada said, shutting her purse. "Are you supposed to tip housekeeping here?"

I actually wasn't sure, since I hadn't stayed in too many hotels on my own. But my papà always seemed to be leaving cash for everyone he met, so it didn't seem like a bad idea. "Yeah, check my wallet."

I finished zipping my duffel bag right as Giada flipped open my wallet. Four condoms, their small purple foil packets all attached by the perforation, cascaded to the ground. I winced, but there was no point in trying to conceal them. Giada's hand was still on my wallet, but her eyes were squarely on the foil packets.

I gently pried the wallet out of her hands and pulled out a couple euros. "Right, so that should be enough," I said.

Giada bent down and picked up the condoms, pinching one between her fingers and closely inspecting the texture. I didn't know what to say, so I stayed quiet. Finally, she glanced up at me, her eyebrow raised.

"Did you have plans after this?" she asked.

"Giada, no, I…" I started forward and reached for the condoms, but she pulled her hand back.

"I'm kidding," she said.

Oh. Of course she was. "I just wanted to be prepared. Not trying to pressure you."

She sat on the foot of the bed, still clutching the packets like they were some magic bean. "You didn't mention you brought these."

I furrowed my eyebrows. It seemed like mentioning I had

them would constitute pressure and that she should be praising me for keeping quiet. "Would it have mattered?" I finally asked instead.

She shrugged, then finally handed them back to me. "Did you want to do that last night?"

I couldn't help but laugh out loud. "I always want to do that with you."

Her hair flipped down over her eyes. I wedged my wallet into my pocket and crouched down in front of her.

"Baby, come on. Last night was perfect. What I wanted was to spend the first moments of this year with you, and I got to do that. And when you're ready, yeah, I want to do that too, but I can wait." I tucked her hair behind her ear and guided her chin until she was facing me.

"You might be waiting a while," she said.

"I'm okay with that." I pressed my mouth against hers, teasing and prodding softly until she gradually warmed to my touch and parted her lips.

"I'm not mad," she said when she finally broke off the kiss. "I just thought you understood my stance on this."

"I do," I said. "And I'm not trying to pressure you. That's why I didn't even mention I had them." I paused. "But there have been a couple other things you said you'd never do that you ended up changing your mind about. I just wanted to be prepared in case you changed your mind on this."

Giada groaned and flailed back on the bed. "Ugh. I am such a hypocrite."

"You are not."

"I am, too."

"Okay, fine. Let's just do it now and get it over with," I suggested. "Then you can get all that Catholic guilt out at once. You can even combine the confession for what we did last night with what we do this morning."

Her eyes drifted shut and her cheeks flushed. I hoped it was due to the memory of what we'd done the night before because that was now what I was thinking about.

"How come you never have that Catholic guilt?" she asked when she finally sat upright.

I rose to my feet and reached for our bags. I could never explain to Giada the level of guilt I wrangled on the daily, or the type of shit I did to merit it. So instead, I answered with a different truth. "No God could ever make me feel guilt for making you feel good. Only way I'm feeling guilty about the stuff we do in the bedroom is if you're not enjoying it."

Giada narrowed her eyes at me. "I don't think it's normal for you to be so good at all this bedroom stuff at our age. Are you sure you didn't have a few dozen partners before me? Where do you get your skills?"

I kissed the tip of her nose and held open the door to the hotel room for her to exit first. Then, I smirked and said, "Porn."

Her laughter filled the narrow corridor as we walked towards the car.

CHAPTER 18

Giada

Once second semester started, I began to feel like there was a timer counting down every minute I had left to spend with Luca. I knew graduation wasn't the end of the line for us, but it was definitely a big change. We'd never again be students at the same school, and at least for a year, we wouldn't even be residents of the same country most of the time. The more I thought about all the things that would inevitably change, the more I thought about everything I wanted to savor at least once more before everything changed.

But the more I thought about that, the more I got hung up on the one thing we'd never even done once. I did everything I could to distract myself. I went to church more. I volunteered more. I even spent more time with Luca doing the stuff that should've been a perfectly good substitute for the thing we weren't doing.

None of it was working.

My frustration came to a head the first Monday in January. Luca and I had driven off campus for dinner, except as was our custom lately, we spent so long fooling around in his car that we ran out of time to eat anything at a restaurant and ended up just grabbing takeout. We'd gotten more callous in our activities too, still sticking to the front seat but occasionally not waiting until it was completely pitch black outside to launch into our makeout sessions.

And sometimes, like today, I ended up straddling Luca in the driver's seat. Actually, I wasn't completely sure when that had happened. But we were both now in the stage of fixing our hair and hiding the evidence of any improprieties, so I scooted back into my own seat and tried to pretend I was classy.

"You know, according to the Church, it's a sin for us to touch each other like that," I said.

"Everything that's even remotely fun is a sin according to the Church," Luca replied. "Besides, you get a clean slate at confession."

I started to explain that the point of confession was not to give us free reign to sin whenever we wanted, but stopped. That was not the point. "I'm not sure doing any of that stuff is any less of a sin than sex before marriage. And for that matter, even after you're married, sex is still a sin if you're not doing it for procreation, and I don't want that many children, so I'm bound to be sinning at some point."

Luca's eyebrow raised. "I'm not really sure what you're getting at. Or is this just another moral quagmire of yours?"

I worked my bottom lip between my teeth for a moment, garnering the courage to just be blunt. "I don't want to wait until I'm married to have sex," I finally blurted out, staring directly at Luca.

Luca's expression changed instantly, but he didn't speak.

"Say something."

He shook his head slowly, then leaned across the center console and barely brushed his lips to mine. "You should think about it more," he finally said.

"I have. If that's not what you want, then fine. But I don't need you to tell me what I want."

"Okay. Well, I most definitely like that idea of not waiting," he said.

I felt my cheeks tug into a smile. "Okay. So…tomorrow?"

Luca laughed. "No, principessa. You don't want our first time together to be in my car. We'll go somewhere nice."

"Saturday?" That was the next time we could get off campus.

He nodded. "Saturday."

Luca

I suffered through the longest week ever. I was positive Saturday would never come, or if it did, that something would happen to screw up our plans beforehand. Either my papà would phone in an errand, or Giada would get sick, or I'd get detention. And no matter what happened, Giada would then interpret it as a sign, and then we'd never end up having sex.

So to say the feeling of walking into that hotel room with Giada on Saturday was surreal is absolutely an understatement.

I'd expected Giada to be nervous, and she was. I hadn't anticipate being nervous myself though, either. That part didn't make sense. I'd done this before. There wasn't anything too complicated involved in the act itself and, since Giada had no experience, it wasn't like I could disappoint her or not live up to her past.

Despite that, I was nervous. I was nervous she wouldn't like it, nervous it would change the way she felt about me, nervous it would bring us further apart rather than closer together. I took two showers that day, taking matters into my own hands both times, so to speak. I figured that would take the edge of and at least ensure I'd last longer. Half the time when Giada just looked at me, I felt like I'd combust, so it seemed a necessary precaution.

I also checked my wallet about a dozen times to make sure I had protection. After that, all I could do was concentrate on being my normal charming self.

We left campus right after lunch, and we couldn't check into the hotel until three, so we went out for ice cream. Giada looked gorgeous as always, with her lush brown hair cascading over her shoulders and her thick, black lashes shading her big brown eyes, but she was just as nervous as I'd expected.

"This is not gelato," I commented, trying to distract us both.

"No," she agreed.

"I can't find real gelato anywhere here."

She smiled. "What's your favorite flavor back home?"

I considered that for a moment. "Bacio. It's uh chocolate and hazelnut. Or stracciatella."

"Cookies and cream?"

"More like chocolate chip, only much better." I paused. "How do you know gelato flavors but not basic conversational words?"

She shrugged and giggled. "I remember the important stuff."

We reached the hotel right around three, and while I was going to suggest we take a walk or something, Giada clearly didn't want to waste any time. She lifted her sweater up over her head, tossed it over the chair, then smiled shyly.

"Tesoro, we don't…" I began, but she'd already begun unzipping her skirt.

As she let it drop, my jaw followed suit. Giada was wearing lace-trimmed thigh highs, clipped to her black panties with little ribbons connecting it all. It was by far the sexiest image I'd viewed my entire life.

I opened my mouth, but there were no words. I didn't even understand where my sweet, innocent principessa would have found such attire.

"Shopping trip last weekend," she said, clearly reading my mind. "You like?"

"I…I…" I licked my lips, certain I was already drooling.

Giada crooked her finger at me and I obeyed, drinking in one last sight of her before I pulled her against my torso, kissing her. I wasn't surprised that our kisses grew frantic faster than usual, and I certainly wouldn't complain. She worked the buttons on my shirt, then I pulled back to take off my undershirt, too. The kissing resumed as she unfastened my button and carefully lowered my zipper.

I nudged her towards the bed and she lay back, her teeth scraping her bottom lip as she watched me shuck my pants. I ran my hands up along her thighs, feeling her smooth skin beneath the satiny nylons.

"Are you sure, Giada? Because we could…"

The look in her eyes cut me off. "I am sure, Luca. I want this, with you, now."

I nodded, joining her on the bed and resuming the kissing. I licked my fingertips, then played with her breasts exactly how she liked, and when she seemed to grow tired of that, I replaced my hands with my mouth. I knew from prior experience that I could make Giada come just from touching her nipples, but she squirmed against me, clearly eager for more.

"Luca," she whined, tugging on my hair with her fingers.

I gazed up at her, unable to stop smiling.

"Stop stalling," she said, holding out one of the condoms I'd set on the bed beside us.

"It's called foreplay, not stalling," I replied.

Her sheepish grin was adorable. "I know, and I love it, but we do that all the time and today I thought we were—"

I kissed her lips to shush her. "We will, Giada. But I don't want to hurt you."

"You won't."

I wished I shared her confidence. "The longer we do this stuff before, the less likely it is to hurt you, so I'm not stopping now." I paused, then added my other stipulation. "Also, I don't think most girls come the first time, so we need to make sure you come at least once before we—"

"Ugh." She groaned. "You're being ridiculous and taking all the fun out of this. How about you get me ninety percent of the way there and then we can just finish together?"

I brushed a stray hair off her forehead. "Giada, I'm gonna last like five seconds inside you. And then I'll just feel bad if—"

She nudged me to the side. "Okay, new plan. I take care of you now, then we resume this foreplay business and you can get me ninety-eight percent of the way there. And I promise to fake it if it's not gonna happen in time, so no hard feelings either way."

I was sure there was some major problem with her plan, but her lips were already on my cock, so all rational thought had left my brain. By the time we were back on track with the foreplay, I was determined to think about anything other than what was about to happen. I wanted to give myself and Giada as long as possible our first time. As promised, she let me use my mouth and fingers to get her almost to climax, and then she nudged me away.

"Luca, please," she whispered. "I'm ready."

My heart thudded at how hot she looked saying those words. I opened the condom, then poised over her.

"Are you sure?" I asked.

"Yes," she replied, reaching a hand behind my neck and pulling my face to hers, kissing me hard. I positioned my tip at her entrance and inched in just the slightest bit. Giada tensed beneath me, and I pulled back from the kiss.

"I'm fine," she whispered. "Keep going. Just, slow."

I gauged her expression as I pushed in another inch, then again paused. I thrust in the rest of the way, then froze. "You still okay?"

Her eyes flitted open and she smiled. "Yes." Then she kissed me again.

I waited another minute before moving, using the delay to shift my hand between us, stroking her nipple. When I felt her breathing start to pick up, I began to move slowly, shifting in and out as delicately as possible. Being inside Giada was the most incredible feeling I'd ever experienced, but I was so focused on not hurting her that I was actually holding off on my own orgasm better than I would've expected.

I kept stroking her nipple and after another minute, felt Giada moving against me. The pleasure started to ratchet up quickly after that, but just when I grew certain I couldn't hold off another minute, Giada's fingers dug into my hips and she pulled back from our kiss. I concentrated on restraining myself as I came, then pulled out of her and rolled onto my back, pulling her on top of me.

"Holy shit," I breathed.

"I told you so," was all she said before kissing my cheek.

CHAPTER 19

Giada

The next week, I couldn't concentrate on anything. The guilt was overwhelming—crushing, really. I couldn't tell Elise about it because that felt like blabbing about a private moment Luca and I had shared, and I couldn't talk with Luca about it because then he'd feel bad even though I was the one who'd basically forced him to do it in the first place.

So that left one place to confess my sin which, of course, was the place I was supposed to go to confess it in the first place. I absolutely couldn't confess *that* on campus though, so I had to wait until the weekend and then go to the church way out in town.

I'd never before been nervous about confession, but this time, I was practically shaking by the time I sat down in the small booth. The priest greeted me but sounded distracted or bored, and then he quietly listened to me drone on about zoning out during mass, not listening to my parents, and taking a few sips of alcohol outside of communion. He started to dish out my penance, and we said the act of contrition prayer together. I sensed he was about to give me absolution when I finally worked up the nerve to interrupt.

"That isn't all," I blurted out.

"My child, is there something else on your heart?"

I cringed. "Yes. Um, I think I omitted one sin."

"Okay…"

"I know I did. It was intentional. I mean, I purposefully didn't tell you, so that's a sin also."

The priest paused. "What other sin do you have to confess today?"

I took a deep breath. "I, um, well, I had um physical relations with a man who isn't my husband. Like, I don't have a husband. This is the guy who is going to be my husband, so maybe it's not that bad, but…"

"My child, all sin is sin in the eyes of our Heavenly Father. Impure thoughts, impure actions, sexual activity…these are all sins for which you may seek forgiveness, but only if you do, truly seek such forgiveness."

I didn't fully understand, and after a moment, the priest seemed to figure that out.

"Some sins are obvious wrongs. Usually those are sins that hurt someone else. When we commit those sins, we know we've sinned. It's easy to feel remorse." The priest paused. "But that doesn't mean other sins don't have a victim or that they are any less severe. In fact, going in to a sin fully aware that the act is a sin and doing it anyway, that is the precise type of premeditation that lends itself to mortal sin. Knowingly choosing sin is a rejection of God's love and law."

I blew out another sigh. "And I suppose withholding that info during confession isn't great either."

The priest chuckled softly. "No, my child. But it is not altogether unexpected. Sin pulls you away from God. When you sin, you're hurting your relationship with God. You're hurting yourself. And that makes it harder to find your way back to God."

"So what do I do?"

"You pray. You trust your faith to lead you towards better decisions in the future. And you accept God's love and forgiveness."

That sounded deceptively easy.

"But my child, being sorry that something you have done is a sin is different than being sorry for having sinned. Do you understand what I'm saying?"

"Umm."

"I cannot absolve you of a sin when your heart does not truly regret your actions."

I had nothing to say to that. After a moment, the priest handed me a pamphlet.

"Read this, and read the Bible passages referenced. Continue your prayers, and if you need more guidance before your next confession, consult some of the additional websites on the back of the brochure."

I took the pamphlet from him and wedged it into my purse, then made a beeline out of the church so fast I nearly broke my ankle tripping over my strappy heels.

Since my church confession hadn't quelched my guilt, I asked Luca to meet me at our favorite restaurant off campus so we could talk. He looked so handsome and was so sweet that I instantly felt terrible for being weird and having avoided him all week.

I waited until we'd ordered to spill my guts though.

"I have a confession," I began. "I was sort of avoiding you this week."

His horrified expression was infinitely worse than I'd imagined. I reached across the table and squeezed his hand.

"No, don't think that. It's just, well, the Catholic stuff. I was dealing with some guilt this week and I didn't want to unload on you about it since it was my idea in the first place. So I went to church today and I tried to go to confession, but it didn't work."

"It didn't work?"

I nodded.

Luca frowned and sipped his water. "So, you're saying you regret what we did, and—"

No!" I interrupted so loudly that a couple nearby patrons turned to stare. I cringed, then lowered my voice. "I'm saying I *don't* regret what we did. That's the problem. Apparently you can only get absolution for a sin if you regret what you did and don't plan to do it again."

A myriad of expressions crossed Luca's face before he spoke again. "So what I'm hearing is you don't regret what we did and you do want to do it again?"

"Yes. So now I feel terrible. Can you stay focused?"

"Sorry, yeah. So, here's the thing. Jesus tells us we should love people, right? That's all you're doing. These other rules aren't coming from God. Those are man's rules."

"Man's rules?"

Luca nodded. "Yeah. I mean, priests don't even let married people use birth control. You can't tell me God came up with that stuff."

"Well, technically the Church is shifting its position on birth control, but—"

"Not the point. The point is, you can be a good person, and still doing what God wants you to do. That's what matters. Whether you follow these silly man-made rules, that doesn't matter. Those change over time anyway."

I sighed. "That's true."

"You're getting hung up on a rule that a bunch of old-fashioned men came up with. Don't let them shame you. Besides, if we're getting married eventually, it's not even breaking the rule. It's more like a timing technicality."

The waiter brought our food, so we concentrated on eating for a few minutes. Then, Luca spoke again.

"Would it make you feel better if we just didn't do it again?"

I had considered that, and I told him what I'd concluded. "No. I feel like that ship has sailed, you know?"

He chuckled at my analogy.

"But maybe I'd feel better if there were like a sign, so I could tell for sure if I'm doing the right thing," I said.

Luca nodded. He thought for a moment, then said, "Okay, so if lightning strikes the restaurant, we'll know we should not do it again. Otherwise, we are good to go."

I bit back a smile. "That seems a tad specific, but you've got the idea."

Luca pulled out his phone and checked the weather app. "Forecast shows sunny skies till Thursday."

I smiled.

Luca

The next morning, Giada texted that she was dying. She missed breakfast, so I tried calling her on my way to class, but she didn't answer. A minute later, she texted that her throat was too swollen to talk. She was headed to the clinic.

After my first class, I got another update from Giada. She had a 103-degree temperature and a diagnosis of strep throat. I cringed. I texted her to feel better and to call me after a nap.

She called me at lunch. She sounded terrible.

"Do you have to quarantine in the clinic?" I asked.

"No, they started me on antibiotics. They moved Elise into the common room and told the other girls to stay away. I guess I'm only contagious for the next twenty four hours so they'll come clean the room tomorrow afternoon and then she can return in the evening."

"So what you're saying is you're all alone in your room for the next twenty-four hours," I repeated, my tone light.

"Yes, alone and feeling like death!" Giada snapped.

"I was only teasing. I'm sorry you feel bad. I'm glad you got the good drugs so you feel better soon though."

"Me too. And I hate to be antisocial, but my throat hurts too much for this conversation."

"I'm sorry. Text me what you need to feel better and I'll drop it off."

"You don't have to. The house mom is bringing me drinks and soup and popsicles."

I considered that, but fully planned to bring her more treats anyway.

"Luca? This seems like a sign."

The way she said it told me it was significant, but it took me a minute to realize what she meant. "A sign? No, Giada, it's strep throat. It's a virus."

"It's bacterial, not viral," she corrected.

"Well, whatever. It's not a sign from God. It's just normal, run of the mill human germs. And I'm pretty sure it's basically an outbreak this time of year. God can't possibly be punishing that many people at once. I haven't slept with all of them."

She mustered a laugh at that, then said, "Ow."

"Get some rest baby, I love you," I clicked to disconnect the call. After my last class, I left campus to pick up some goodies for Giada— Italian soup, some of her favorite raspberry candies, and a tub of store-bought gelato.

I snuck into the dorm while most of the students were at dinner, poking my head just inside her door to confirm she was awake. Giada rolled slowly towards the door and smiled, then pulled the sheet over her head.

"You shouldn't be here, Luca. I'm super contagious and I look like crap."

I set my goodies on her desk, shut the door behind me and sat on the foot of her bed, tugging the blanket down so I could see her face. Her hair was mussed and she wasn't wearing makeup, but she still looked beautiful.

"Your cheeks are pink but you look gorgeous as always," I said, smoothing the hair off her forehead.

"I'm going to make you sick."

"I don't get sick. But if I did, I'd welcome the break from class."

She groaned. "I still feel awful. They said the medicine would kick in, but…"

I stood to show her what I brought. "I'm sure the house mom got you some chicken noodle soup, but what you really need is pastina. I tapped the Styrofoam bowl with my finger."

"Is that just Italian for chicken noodle soup?"

I shrugged. "It's tiny noodles in a broth. Similar, but better. I also brought gelato, some bread to go with the soup, and a few other snacks. Anything sound good now?"

"Gelato."

I handed her the carton and a spoon, then sat on the floor beside her bed and started going through her backpack. "Should I start with math or science?"

"You're not doing my homework, Luca."

"Math or science," I repeated, my tone fierce.

"Science."

I rifled through her backpack to find the right textbook and then she handed me her iPad, cued up to the assignment. Having taken the same class the year before, I expected to breeze through her work. The assignment took me a good twenty minutes, but then I finished. I stashed the rest of the gelato in the freezer in the common room, then moved on to her math. I gazed up from the textbook to see Giada staring at me.

"You okay?"

She nodded.

"You didn't mean that stuff you said earlier, right? You don't actually think God is punishing you for what we did, do you?"

"I don't know. Will you stop doing my homework if I say yes?"

"I'll do your homework either way. And we don't have to do…*that* again if you don't want to."

"But…I do want to. So, that's the problem."

I was relieved by her response, but didn't really understand.

"Even if we don't do it again, it's still a sin for me to want to. And all the other stuff we do is a sin, too. But I knew all of that going into it and I did it anyway, so it's not like anything has changed."

"Okaaaaay…"

"In my mind, before we…you know, I was thinking it would be mostly for you. I mean, I wanted to, but maybe a little just because I felt like I owed you."

I cringed, grateful she couldn't see my expression.

"I didn't really think I'd like it. And I was assuming once I tried it and saw what it was about, I probably wouldn't want to do it again, or at least not very often."

She paused, and I knew I should say something, but I had no idea what to say.

"But I did like it."

"You did?"

"A lot. And now I keep thinking about it more, and wanting to do it more, and so I hardly think I can justify it as something I'm just doing for you. You know?"

I chuckled and turned towards her. "Honestly? No. You lost me there. But what I'm hoping I'm hearing correctly is that you enjoyed being with me last weekend as much as I enjoyed it and that you think we should try it again as soon as you're feeling better."

Giada made an adorable face and I think she might have blushed, but it was hard to tell since her cheeks were already bright red. "I guess that was the gist," she said.

"It's a deal," I said.

"But I'm not convinced we aren't going to hell," she added.

I pressed my lips against her forehead, wincing to find it was still so hot. "I promise to keep you company there just like I do on Earth," I teased.

There was a knock and a click at the door and I twisted back to face the door just as Ms. Carazo stuck her head in.

She glared straight at me and flung her hands in the air.

I rose to my feet slowly, keeping Giada's math book in my hands.

"Mr. Marino. First off, this is the girl's dorm. As a senior, you know the rules very well and I'm positive you know you don't belong in here. Second of all, this poor girl is sick. And contagious. She needs her rest and she's supposed to be quarantined."

I shrugged apologetically. "I'm so sorry, Ms. Carazo. I had loaned Giada my math book and, well, you know me and academics, I sure couldn't go another day without this baby. But now that I have it, I'll be on my way…"

Her glare didn't lighten, but she also didn't stop me, so I scurried into the hall. If she filed a report with the dean later, I'd just deny having been on the floor. I waited until I was outside and then texted Giada.

"Get some sleep, my princess. I'll finish your math and text it to you tomorrow."

"I love you," came her simple response.

CHAPTER 20

Luca

With Giada still recovering, I wasn't too angry when Lodovico called and said he needed Alessio and I to babysit some goods overnight. I didn't let him know that, though.

"We both have school," I reminded him as he drove us to the warehouse on the outskirts of town. "We need to sleep. And we need time to study."

"We'll call you both in sick tomorrow. Don't be such a baby. This is an easy job, and it's beneath you. This is the type of shit most guys have to do all the time when they're starting out. Your papà just wants you to be able to say you did it once."

Alessio insisted we stop for food, and I enjoyed watching Lodovico's grimace as he listened to Alessio's order. Despite his love of fast food, Alessio was a vegetarian. He ordered his burgers without the meat. I'd thought it was weird at first too, but now it just made me smile.

By the time Lodovico dropped us off at the dock, it was

nearing midnight. He greeted the guys we were replacing, then showed us to our post.

"So what do we do again?" Alessio asked cheekily.

Lodovico lowered his gaze. "Stay here till someone comes to relieve you, probably around seven or eight. You can take turns walking the perimeter along here while the other one warms up in the stall there. If you see anything suspicious, call me. If someone tries to touch our shit, call me. Whatever you do, don't fall asleep. And don't wake me up unless you absolutely have to."

He turned and started back up the pier.

"What if we have to pee?" Alessio called after him.

Lodovico pointed to the ocean without turning.

We listened to the rumble of his engine and a minute later, we were alone.

"Something feels off about this," I said, gazing around. "This reminds me of the places my papà used to have guys drive me so they could beat the shit out of me."

Alessio gazed around us then rubbed his hands together and blew on them to warm them. "Did you do anything to piss him off lately?"

"Probably."

Alessio kept looking around. "See any cameras?"

I joined him in doing a more thorough search. We weren't able to find any, but then he motioned for me to follow him towards the shed. We backed up against it and then I pretended to show Alessio something on my phone. He reached into his jacket and a minute later, I felt something cold slide against my lower back.

"You brought two?" I asked, eyes wide, the moment I realized what he'd given me.

Alessio nodded. "Friends don't let friends perform shady guard duty unarmed," he replied.

I laughed, then ducked into the shed to adjust the placement of the gun. We traded places after about fifteen minutes, then both of us hung out together on the dock. The night air was cold as fuck, but there was no breeze, so once I adjusted, the temperature was tolerable.

Besides, Alessio was good company. We hadn't had this much time to just talk since summer, really. I told him about my night with Giada. He told me about school, his mom, and his sister. His mom hadn't fully accepted he wasn't headed to college, so he'd sent out a few applications, and he'd even received a couple acceptance letters. We swapped stories about the what-ifs, playing out the hypotheticals in the imaginary world where we were just regular guys headed to college in the fall.

"A hundred bucks says you'd turn into one of those douchey frat boys within a semester," Alessio said, offering me a box of Nerds.

I shook my head, then watched as he tossed about a hundred little candies directly into his mouth. "You can't bet on a hypothetical. How will you ever collect?"

Alessio smirked. "It's not about the money, amico. I just wanted to make a point that you're totally the type."

"Whatever. I'm going to do another lap." I headed off towards the south end of the pier, not entirely sure what I was looking for, but certain I was warmer—and less likely to fall asleep—if I kept moving. The rhythmic sloshing of the water against the dock grew softer as I walked further away, but then I could've sworn I heard a different sound. I stopped, craning my neck as if that would help me hear better. It was like a shuffling, or scuffle of sorts.

I had just decided to walk back to Alessio to ask him about the sound, when I heard a distinct grunt.

I swore and took off jogging. The second I rounded the corner, I saw two guys where Alessio had been seated.

I skidded to a stop. I needed to formulate a plan, not run at them half-cocked. I started to reach for the gun, certain that whoever they were, they'd back off Alessio if I threatened to shoot.

But before I could reach the gun, someone yanked my arm hard, then cracked something against my head. I stumbled backwards as flashes of light flooded my field of vision. Whoever held my arm used it to swivel me towards them, and then a fist slammed into my jaw. I stumbled backwards right as another fist landed a hit against my temple.

The second hit cleared my vision. There was just one guy in front of me, and I came at him with everything I had, pounding at him with years of pent-up fury. I channeled all of my anger at my papà, all of my guilt over the shit he made me do, and all of my uncertainty over the future, and I threw it into punch after punch.

I had the guy on his back within a minute, then heard Alessio scream my name. I turned just as another guy took a swing at the back of my head with some sort of metal bar. I ducked, then kicked the guy in the balls.

When he crouched over, I yanked the bar from his hands and smashed him with it until he was lying on the ground, unmoving, right next to his buddy. The lights only illuminated the area directly above us, so I couldn't tell how many guys might be waiting around the corner or what we were up against. I needed to go help Alessio, but I couldn't risk finding even more men about to pop out of the woodworks. I grabbed my phone and dialed Lodovico.

The second he answered, I roared into the phone. "Need backup. Now!"

Then I rushed towards Alessio. He was conscious, but bleeding, and his injuries seemed to far surpass my own. I wondered why he hadn't tried to use his gun, and then I saw it, in the distance, teetering on the edge of the pier.

Damn.

"Alessio!" I shouted, more to get the guys to turn away from him for a minute then to get his attention. My tactic worked to distract one guy, but Alessio was too far gone to deliver much of an effective hit.

I was almost close enough to join the fight when one of the guys whipped out a blade. I couldn't tell if he was going to cut Alessio or just going to try to hold him hostage, but I wasn't taking that chance.

The deafening explosion from the gun pierced the silence of the night before I even fully registered the weight of the weapon in my hands. Time seemed to slow as I waited for some consequence of my action. After an eternity, knife guy screamed, dropped the knife, then fell backwards, clutching his shoulder.

The other guy took off running. I chased him down, slamming the gun into the back of his head and then punching him until I couldn't feel my hands anymore. When a hand tugged my bicep, trying to pry me off the guy, I swatted at it, not even realizing it was my friend until he shouted my name.

I slumped back onto the dock beside Alessio, panting and shaking.

Neither of us said anything for a full minute.

As always, it was Alessio who broke the silence. "Damn dude. You have reflexes like a cat."

I turned to him, confused.

"You just shot a guy for me. Like, no hesitation."

I peered over to where the man was sprawled on the dock. "I thought he was going to stab you."

Alessio nodded. "Yeah. Thanks."

I wiped my nose on my sleeve, then grimaced to see my jacket coated in blood. I reached for my phone and dialed Lodovico again. "Where the fuck are you?" I asked.

He rattled off some other names and said they were closer but that he would be there in ten minutes. I disconnected and pushed to my feet, swaying a bit.

"You should probably sit. If you pass out into the water, I

don't think I can save you. Pretty sure we both have a concussion," Alessio said.

"I think I broke my fucking hand," I mumbled, heading towards the guy I'd shot. "I just need to see if he's dead." I got closer, and nudged him with the tip of my boot. He groaned, and relief flooded me.

"Grazie a Dio," I breathed. And then I slumped back down.

Giada

*L*uca missed two days of school. He texted and said he got banged up in a car accident but that he was totally fine and just milking it for some extra time off. I tried to video chat with him, but the connection was weak, so I didn't actually see him until he returned to campus Thursday night.

I spotted him ambling across the lawn towards his dorm. He wasn't limping, but he did walk stiffly, like his entire body ached. I flew out of the dining hall, eager to grab his attention before he made it much farther.

"Luca!" I called. "Luca!"

He stopped, and slowly turned. I scurried to catch up, then gasped as his eyes rose to meet mine. His right eye was swollen and a blackish blue bruise highlighted the cheekbone beneath it. His lip was cut open, and he had stitches on his forehead just beneath his hairline.

"Jesus," I breathed, reaching a hand towards his face. I stroked his unharmed cheek, keeping my touch light. "Luca, this looks awful. You made it sound like it was no big deal, but—"

"It looks worse than it feels," he interrupted, clasping my fingers in his own hand.

My eyes dropped to his fist as it wrapped around my hand.

Cuts split open his swollen knuckles. I glanced at his other hand, which was secured in tight bandages.

"So your hands and your head took the brunt of it?" I asked. "Were you in the passenger's seat?"

Luca licked his lips and glanced to the side. Seeing no one around, he walked us towards a bench. I sat, then cringed as I watched him clearly in pain as he sat.

"We had to tell the school it was a car accident. They're looking for any excuse to suspend me, and it's too close to graduation."

"So you were fighting?" I confirmed.

"No," he said. "Well, yes, but not in the way you're thinking. I was out with a friend. Wrong place, wrong time, I guess. I don't know. And we were jumped. These guys just attacked us. Maybe it was a mugging, but they didn't have guns and didn't steal anything. They just started hitting us. So yeah, we hit back."

"Is your friend okay?"

Luca nodded. "He has a concussion. Honestly probably a little worse off than me, but we'll both be fine."

I chose my next words carefully. "I thought you said you were done fighting."

Judging from Luca's scowl, I'd said the wrong thing. "I might be dead if I hadn't fought back. I'm almost positive my friend would be. Is that what you want?"

"Obviously not, but if just seems like you get into a lot of trouble when you're with this friend."

Luca shuffled his feet in the dirt where the grass had been worn bare. "I should probably go ice my face. I'd hate to get any scars."

He stood and I followed suit. I hesitate, unsure of how to kiss him with his lips all mangled and bruised, then settled for pressing a soft kiss to his cheek. As he walked back to his dorm, I settled back onto the bench, alone with my guilt. He'd been honest with me about the bruises, with zero hesitation. What more had I wanted?

CHAPTER 21

Giada

I'd apologized to Luca for my weird reaction, he'd said it was fine. Then, life had gone on like normal. Well, except it wasn't exactly normal. Valentine's Day was fast approaching and whenever I asked Luca what we were doing, he'd simply tell me that he had a surprise planned. So, I bought him a gorgeous Fendi wallet and wedged a thoughtful love note inside, then waited for my surprise.

A week later, I'd all but forgotten about the holiday altogether. Really, it was taking all of my effort not to fall asleep during English when one of the school secretaries, Ms. Jen, popped into the classroom. Everyone appreciated the disruption as we all tried to guess which student might have done something bad enough to justify a trip to the headmaster's office. She whispered something to my teacher, who then turned to me.

"Giada, can you go with Ms. Jen?" she asked kindly.

I felt my face blanch. I'd never really been in trouble, not at this school anyway. And I didn't actually think I'd done anything bad lately, at least not that they knew about.

"Bring all your things, sweetheart," Ms. Jen said, her tone uncharacteristically kind.

Palms damp, I gathered my notebooks, not even bothering to shove them into my backpack before following her into the hall. Now that everyone was staring, I just wanted to get out of there as fast as I could. I started down the hall, assuming we were headed to the office, but Ms. Jen stopped walking.

"Giada, your father called to let us know there's been a family emergency and you need to return home for the weekend. He asked that we have you pack a bag immediately and tell you he'll have a car waiting in front for you," she said, her hand gently on my arm.

I felt sick. I couldn't focus, couldn't think straight at all. I fumbled in my pocket for my phone, staring at the screen. "No one called me. I don't…"

"Sweetie, they called us in the office. He said everyone was fine, but you need to pack quickly and meet him outside your dorm."

"He's picking me up himself? Not a driver?" I couldn't remember the last time my father had driven. That couldn't be a good sign.

"No, well…" Now Ms. Jen looked flustered. "I don't know, actually. I forgot to ask the name. I can call back if you'd like, he gave me a number to reach him at today. Or, it's just…in light of the circumstances, we can approve it for you to just go with whomever he's sent. I mean, provided it's someone you know and trust."

"It's fine," I said, shaking my head. "It's probably my usual driver. I should pack."

She looked relieved, not even batting an eye at the fact that I had a usual driver. That was more common than not at elite boarding schools.

"Do you need any help packing?" she offered.

"No."

She watched me head towards the side door, the closest to my dorm, then went towards the front, presumably to return to the office. As I pushed outside, I winced, the frigid air hitting my face. I didn't stop to put on my coat because I didn't want to waste time. My dorm was only three minutes away if I walked briskly.

I heard a noise to the side, but dismissed it as the wind. I wiped my eyes, surprised to see I'd already started crying. *Crap.* Maybe I should look for my dad before packing up.

"Giada!"

This time the voice was too loud to be mistaken for wind. I swiveled around, coming face to face with Luca. He was grinning widely, but his expression changed drastically once he saw me.

"Baby, what's wrong?" he asked, pulling me into his arms. Everything about him was so warm and comforting, including his thick winter coat.

"The school said my dad called, and there's some emergency, and I don't know what, and..." I shook my head, aware I wasn't making any sense. "I have to go pack. I'm going home for the weekend."

"No, no, no, Giada," he gripped my biceps and pulled back, swearing in Italian. "There's no emergency. Everyone's fine."

"No, he called the school, and..."

"That was me, Giada. I had a friend call the school and pretend to be your dad. I wanted to take you away for this weekend. I promise your family is fine."

I took a moment, replaying his words in my mind and allowing myself to fully process them. "There's no family emergency?"

"No," he confirmed.

"Your friend called the school and told them that?"

"Yes."

"Which friend?"

"Alessio. He doesn't go here, but..."

I started hitting his chest and stomach before he finished his sentence. "You asshole! I was terrified! I thought someone had died!"

Luca cringed and let me wail on him for a minute before grabbing my hands and squeezing them. "I'm sorry, baby. I'm so sorry. I didn't think." He leaned closer, his chocolate eyes pleading with me. "Everyone is fine. Just breathe."

I concentrated on his face and did what he said, letting my chest fill with oxygen then exhaling the stress.

"You can be mad at me later, but pretty please go pack now so they don't get suspicious," he said.

"But who's picking me up then?" I asked, still not understanding.

"Me. And pack warm clothes. We are going skiing. That's my Valentine's surprise."

"I don't ski."

"I'll teach you," he promised. "Go pack!"

Luca

Once Giada got over the fact that I'd lied to the school and worried her about her family, she seemed on board with my plan. She was definitely suspicious though, even making me call Alessio to hear his impression of her father. The ski resort was only a two hour drive, but since it was gorgeous weather for skiing, the place was packed. I'd banked on that, though, and planned for us to rent snowshoes and explore the resort that way.

The resort was idyllic, with sprawling hills dotted with evergreen trees. And when we checked into the room, Giada's eyes widened with glee. "Is this a hot tub?" she asked, flinging open the door to the patio.

I grinned. "If you forgot your suit…" I began.

She narrowed her eyes and thwacked me. "I didn't. I brought this gorgeous one-piece that I inherited from my grandmother, and…"

I pulled her into my arms and tickled her until giggling replaced her talking. The tickling of course led to kissing, and that led to me wondering why I'd planned on us doing anything outside the room. Really, I could've spent the entire weekend in bed with Giada and been perfectly happy. We didn't even need such a nice bed.

Still, I was determined to be the perfect gentleman. The closer I got to graduation and the dismal rest of my life, the more I panicked. I had so little time left. We had so little time left. I just wanted to have fun and enjoy being young and free while I could. And there was no one better at enjoying life than Giada.

The snowshoe adventure was a flop. Well, it was a blast, but neither of us ever got the hang of the goofy shoes and we made it less than a quarter mile past the resort parking lot before we decided to just make out in the woods and then tromp back to the resort for warmer socks. And by the time we got to dinner, we were both so famished that we spent the first ten minutes wolfing our food and barely talking.

"I love that you eat," I said, not realizing I'd spoken aloud until she paused, mid-bite, and smiled at me, her cheeks blushing red.

"Umm thanks?" she said, trying hard not to laugh.

"Oh come on, you know what I mean. My mom picks at everything that isn't lettuce and you know she'd be so much happier if she could just polish off a bowl of pasta. And half the girls at school are like that too."

Giada peered down at her plate, which wasn't completely clean, but close. She still had a few more green beans and a bite of lemon chicken to finish. I hadn't meant to make her self-conscious, and I really hoped she still split dessert with me. But as she stared at me with those sparkly eyes, I wasn't so sure.

"You say the most charming things, Luca Marino," she said, pinching a green bean between her fingers, then laughing away my weird comment.

We finished off the night in front of the fire in our room. Since it was our first night alone together since our first time together, I wasn't sure what to expect. I hoped Giada hadn't really believed her strep throat was a sign from God, but she hadn't expressly said if she was willing to continue to forsake her plan to wait for marriage.

To my great relief, she was. Even better, I didn't feel like I was pressuring her. I wasn't even the one to bring it up. Giada insisted I opened the present she bought me the second we got back to the room. It was a designer wallet that had to have cost her close to five hundred dollars, and inside one pocket she'd wedged a thoughtful love note. She'd filled each of the credit card slots with foil-wrapped condoms.

My breath caught in my throat as I realized what she'd done, and then I snapped the wallet shut, as if some hidden spy would see the contents of the wallet. Across from me, Giada bit her bottom lip, smiling shyly.

"We don't have to it you don't want," she said.

She squealed as I tackled her, kissing her until our kisses turned to much, much more.

The next day, the plan was to ski and then surprise Giada with a horse-drawn carriage ride in the evening. Part of me was to ditch the plan and take advantage of the private room, making love to Giada the entire day, but the other part of me realized we'd have time for that and the activities I'd paid for us to do as well. And as I fell asleep with Giada curled up in my arms, I knew I'd have a good day either way.

Giada

$\mathcal{M}$y phone buzzed just as we returned to the room after the most romantic day ever. Luca had attempted to teach me to ski, and then we'd ventured around the resort property on an actual horse-drawn carriage.

My eyes lowered to my phone, where a text from Matteo read, "Call me NOW."

"Shit," I mumbled, clicking the phone icon right as Luca crept up behind me, winding his arms around my waist and resting his chin on my shoulder. "I have to call my brother," I told him.

The phone began to ring as Luca growled into my ear and took fake nibbles out of my neck. He knew I was ticklish so of course that made me start to giggle.

"Shh," I snapped, squirming out of his arms just as Matteo answered.

"Hey Matteo, what's up?" I asked, giggling.

"Giada? Jesus, where are you?"

"Why? What's wrong?"

He blew out an agitated sigh. "Your school called. They wanted to talk with Dad but when I said he wasn't available, they said they were just checking that you were okay. They said they realized they were given a new number to contact your parents during the family emergency and just wanted to call the one on record to confirm everything was okay."

"Crap." I dropped to the chair beside the bed, shooing Luca away when he asked what was wrong. I switched my call over to speaker phone so he'd keep quiet and so I wouldn't have to recap the whole conversation for him later. "What did you tell them?"

"I said you were fine and the other number they had was probably the best way to reach Dad."

"Oh thank God," I said, exhaling the tension. "Thank you, Matteo. You are the best. I should go now, but…"

"Not a chance, Princess. Where are you? If you don't come clean, I'm telling Dad now."

"I went skiing with friends. I'm only like two hours from campus. I'll be back at school tomorrow morning."

"Are you kidding? You snuck off campus to go skiing? Do you even know how to ski?"

I cringed. I was a terrible skier. "Not really, but it's good to try new things. Anyway, I'm perfectly safe and I really appreciate you covering for me."

Matteo was quiet for a moment, but right then Luca sneezed loudly.

"What friends?" Matteo asked, newly suspicious.

"A group of us," I replied quickly, glaring at Luca.

"All girls?"

"Of course!"

My brother sighed. "Look, I don't want to rat you out to Dad and get you in trouble, but there's a reason he's always so paranoid. I don't think you're safe sneaking off for the weekend with a bunch of girls. You're too young to—"

"She's with me," Luca interjected loudly.

Matteo went silent. I glared at Luca.

"Luca?" my brother asked after a weighted pause.

"Yeah. I'm here and I'll make sure she's completely safe, so you don't need to worry."

I could hear my brother breathing, but the longer he went without speaking, the more nervous he got.

"Can you put Giada back on?" he finally asked.

I snatched the phone and switched off speaker, shooting Luca another mean look. "It's me, Matteo. Look, I'm fine. Luca's here, so you don't need to worry, but it's not what you think."

My brother laughed, as did Luca. "It's not what I think, huh? My little sister isn't alone in a hotel room with her boyfriend and expecting me to cover for her?"

I sighed. There was no winning with him today. "Fine, either tell on me or don't, Matteo, but don't act like you have any legit concerns about my safety."

"Angelo would kill Luca if he knew you guys were alone."

Matteo wasn't wrong. "That's why *he* isn't my favorite brother," I said. "Come on. I'll owe you."

Matteo groaned, so I knew I had him. "Fine, but text me the minute you're back on campus. And I swear if this somehow comes back on me..."

"It won't, it won't. You're the best. Thank you, Matteo!"

I hung up before he could say another word. Luca raised an eyebrow as though confirming it was all good, but instead of simply answering, I chucked a pillow at him.

"Ow! What was that for?"

"You told my other brother you were here with me. In what alternate universe was that a good idea?"

He chuckled, prompting me to pummel him with a second pillow.

Luca grunted and caught the pillow. "He wasn't worried about your virtue or reputation. He was worried something would happen to you and your father would find out that he knew you were unprotected. Now he knows I'm with you and since your dad trusts me, it's fine."

He clasped his hands firmly around mine so I couldn't throw anything else at him. "Remember when your dad asked me to watch you? He trusts me. Matteo knows that, and you should, too. Now stop wasting our last night alone!"

I gritted my teeth, but decided he was right. I could be mad at him once we returned to campus. Right now, we had a private jacuzzi tub, a plush bed, and nearly fifteen hours until check-out, during which we could take full advantage of both.

CHAPTER 22

Luca

The next three months flew by. My relationship with Giada had gotten very serious very fast. But so had my involvement with the family business.

I was living a double life.

The more entrenched I became in everything with my papà, the more apparent it was that I couldn't just opt out of the family business. I also started to realize that my work was not just a job. The mafia was an all-consuming lifestyle.

On the surface, the work didn't appear to conflict with my relationship with Giada. Papà would be thrilled if I'd settle down with Giada, but I wasn't so sure it was the right choice for me. Or for her.

If I had to carry out the horrific acts that I knew I was going to have to execute, I didn't think I could commit to being a loyal and dutiful fiancé or husband, especially not at nineteen. And despite my papà's claims that Giada would be accommodating of my work given her background, she wouldn't.

Papà was wrong about her. Giada was blissfully oblivious to

her family's activities. She was too naïve, no, too innocent, for any of that. She saw the best in everyone and ignored everything else.

It wasn't that I thought I could do better. Truly, I couldn't imagine ever finding a more beautiful woman than Giada, or one that was more fun, or more caring. Giada was absolutely perfect. And every minute I spent with her, I felt a little lighter, a little less doomed.

Giada was the light to my darkness. That, I was sure of.

But what was I to her?

And how was that fair?

"I could do a fashion internship in Italy," Giada said, jolting me from my thoughts.

"What?" I gazed down at her. She was laying with her head in my lap, her legs stretched out perpendicular to mine. Her plaid skirt had ridden up at the waist when she sat, so far more than the permitted three inches of thigh was showing. I reached my fingers down, tickling the line where her creamy flesh met the thick material.

She giggled, her head bopping against my groin, then she swatted my hand away. "Serious discussion, signore." She turned her face to mine, grinning proudly at the successful use of one of the most basic words in the Italian language.

God, she was adorable. I leaned down to kiss her, struggling to reach until I lifted her the last inch to meet me. Like most of our conversations over the last few weeks, this discussion had turned to the topic of what Giada would do after she graduated so that she could be closer to me.

We'd already planned out the details of our long-distance relationship for the next year, while Giada finished her high school studies. But as graduation loomed closer, she'd started to panic and second-guess the plans. Now, Giada was determined to come up with alternate plans for the year. Her parents had vetoed her request to transfer to a school in Italy and she couldn't possibly be emancipated, so her options appeared to be limited.

"So it's settled then," she said, taking my silence for agreement. "I'll look for a fashion design internship in Milan."

"Since when can you sew?"

"Well…yeah. Sewing isn't exactly my strong suit, but maybe they can teach me."

"Amore, Milan is nowhere close to Palermo. It's literally a fifteen hour drive, plus a ferry ride."

She sighed. "Why would I drive? And why are we comparing drive time to flights? It's a lot closer than Connecticut."

"You don't speak Italian. Who is going to hire you if you don't speak the language?"

"You could teach me."

I laughed so hard that I coughed. "Baby, I leave in two weeks. I couldn't teach you if I had all year." That was the truth. I'd tried— and failed— many times.

"Thanks for the vote of confidence," she said, mopey.

"Giada, I just want you to be realistic. You need to live your life, not revolve everything around me. If you're unhappy because of me, I'll hate it."

She seemed to consider that. "I'm going to be miserable spending a whole year here without you."

I ran my fingers along her dark hair, smoothing the silky soft strands away from her beautiful face. Giada had the biggest, brownest eyes I'd ever seen, and when she gazed up at me, I swear they shimmered.

"It won't be a year. I'll come home to see you as much as I can. And you'll visit me lots." I smiled, picturing our adventures. "God, I cannot wait to show you Italy."

"I've seen Italy. Lots of times."

I shook my head. "Not with me you haven't, not really."

"Is it that different?"

"Is it that different?" I repeated with a scoff and an eye roll.

"Tesoro, it's not even the same country when you don't have a true Italian by your side."

She pursed her lips together as though she was considering my words, but I could tell from the glossing of her eyes that she was struggling not to cry. *Shit.* I was trying to cheer her up, not make her cry in the middle of the commons area.

I tugged on her armpits and lifted her up so I could wrap my arms around her. "If you're going to look so sad, I'll have to take you back to my room. I only know one thing that always cheers you up."

"That does not cheer me up."

It absolutely did, one hundred percent of the time, but I wasn't about to argue with her now. "Well, it would cheer me up."

The slightest hint of a smile crossed her lips. "You're not even sad."

"Of course I am! I want nothing more than to spend the summer right like this." I paused. "But every time we're apart, that'll only make it better when we are together." I kissed the side of her head, inhaling the tantalizingly sweet fragrance of her hair.

"Do you promise we'll come back here together someday after we both graduate?" she asked after a lengthy pause.

I frowned. "Why would we come back after we graduate? Isn't the point of graduating so you don't have to go to school?"

Giada's smile made my stomach feel warm and gooey. "We could come back for your ten-year reunion."

"That isn't exactly my scene. Maybe we wait and come back for your ten year reunion," I suggested as an alternative.

"You'd do that?" She sounded surprised.

I nodded.

"You think we'll still be together?"

"I know we will." I pressed another kiss to her head, hoping this one calmed her.

"Will you write me while you're gone?" she asked after another minute of silence;.

I felt my eyebrow shoot up. "Like a letter? You know I'm just going to Italy and not on a time machine back to the early nineteen-hundreds. Is my phone broken in this scenario? And my texting?"

She pulled back enough to punch me in the shoulder. "I want a real love letter. Something I can crumple up in my underwear drawer and read in secret whenever I miss you."

"Ahh, so it needs to be in English I assume? Because all of my past love letter writing experiences were in Italian, so…"

Giada knocked into my arm again, but now she was smiling so I knew I'd distracted her.

"Tell me more about this underwear drawer," I whispered, my lips so close to her ear that as soon as she finished laughing I could kiss its adorable curves then move along to her cheek.

Giada

Every morning in May, my alarm reminded me of a ticking time bomb when it woke me. I was acutely aware of the finite number of moments stretching out before Luca and me where we were both together, as students, on campus. Soon, everything would change.

I wasn't scared of the change, no matter how much Blair or other possibly well-meaning classmates managed to bring up examples of past couples who'd promised to stay together after graduation and hadn't. No, I had faith. I'd prayed about my relationship with Luca before getting physical with him, and I'd prayed about it since. I trusted that God had put me in Luca's life for a reason, and vice versa. Whatever troubles the next year brought, I knew I wouldn't be alone in facing them.

Besides that, I trusted Luca. He wasn't the selfish, callous player that he'd once been. Maybe, he never had been. Luca loved me, and he'd never cheat on me, or do anything else to hurt me, whether we were living on separate sides of the lawn, or separate sides of the Atlantic Ocean.

But just because I wasn't worried didn't mean I wasn't sad. I loved talking to Luca, loved the sound of his voice and hearing him laugh. But there was something different about being near him. Just one touch from Luca had the power to calm me, to reassure me that all was right in the world. Catching a glimpse of his smile from across the hall between classes was enough to power me through a tricky history test, and one kiss from him could make me forget why I wanted to strangle whoever kept leaving toothpaste all over the sink in the shared bathroom.

What would I do without him next year?

I couldn't ignore the silent countdown that seemed to be looming over us, either. Every time we kissed, I mentally clocked it as one less to go. When we snuck off campus to fool around in his car, I wondered if it was the last time I'd get to see him all flustered and aroused. When Luca promised we'd spend one more night alone together after graduation, and I looked forward to that like I did Christmas.

But in the meantime, I wanted Luca to enjoy his last few weeks of school. So like any good girlfriend, I tagged along to all the fun Senior outings, helped throw a fabulous graduation beach party, and even sat through a painfully awkward brunch with Luca's parents the morning of the graduation ceremony.

I'd assured him I wouldn't be offended if he wanted time alone with his parents on his big day, but Luca said his parents really wanted to get to know me better. So, I'd dragged myself out of bed early, dressed in the jacquard floral knee-length sheath dress I'd bought for the occasion, and styled my hair to match the modest, yet sophisticated look I was aiming for.

I'd met Luca's parents before, but they'd never been very chatty around me, at least not in English. The brunch was no different. Camilla and Salvatore both greeted me in English and offered the traditional air kiss on either side of my face. Luca pulled out my chair, grinned at me, then held my hand under the table. His father asked me a couple questions in English while we looked over the menu, and then once we'd ordered, the conversation shifted entirely to Italian.

I tried to follow along, aided in part by Luca translating a few key points, but mostly I just picked at my food and tried to ignore the way his mother was scowling at me. I plastered a smile on my face and thought happy thoughts. Today was about Luca, and I wasn't going to let him see a single sign of annoyance on my part, even if his mother was grating on my last nerve.

Luca

My parents practically forced Giada to come to brunch and then ignored her the entire time, going out of their way to speak in Italian in front of her. After the meal, I drove Giada back to campus and apologized for their behavior, but she acted like it was the most enjoyable meal of her life.

"Amore, they're jerks and they were rude. You don't have to pretend you didn't notice," I said, running my fingers along her forearm.

"That tickles," she said, offering me her first true smile in over an hour. "Anyway, not being able to understand what anyone was saying just gave me more time to daydream about how handsome you're going to look waltzing across that stage to get your diploma."

She leaned forward and pressed a quick kiss to my lips before pulling back. I tried to follow her, hoping for a longer kiss, but she was already reaching for her door.

"Your dad said they'd be here early," she reminded me, apparently worried we'd get caught.

"They're going by the hotel to freshen up," I said, as if I had any idea what that expression meant. "We have at least a half hour to make out."

Giada giggled, but we compromised with fifteen minutes. Then we each walked back to our dorms. My parents texted when they arrived, and as predicted, my papà wanted to talk to me. I grabbed my cap and gown, then met him behind the library.

He greeted me with a broad smile that a casual onlooker would likely mistake for pride. He patted me on the back, then motioned to a nearby bench. We sat.

"That Giada seems great," he said.

His words were so far from what I'd expected that I nearly fell off the bench. My papà must have registered the confusion on my face, since he continued.

"She's polite, smart, seems to have a good head on her shoulders, not to mention gorgeous." My papà paused and looked at me.

I nodded in agreement.

"But she still has one year of school left," he said, as if this were news to me.

I didn't even deign that statement with a nod.

"Well, I know you mentioned before that you plan to keep seeing her, but those long-distance relationships don't have the best track records at your age. If you really want to secure your future together, you need something else."

"Like what?" I asked.

"You ask her to marry you." He paused, likely waiting for the horror to disappear from my face. "A girl like Giada would never go back on an engagement."

"She's seventeen. I hardly think she's gonna jump at a marriage proposal."

My papà thumbed his chin like the villain in some bad superhero flick. "You'd be surprised what young girls agree to when you're persuasive. Besides, women like men who can buy them nice things. Jewelry, shoes, clothes, handbags… you can give her things other boys her age can't."

I started to point out that Giada wasn't shallow like that, except, well, she kind of was. Not in a bad way, just that she liked nice stuff for sure. But it wasn't like she needed me to buy it for her. She was spoiled enough by her own father. "Yeah, well, even if that were the case, I'm not sure I'm up for it anyway. You gonna buy me nice things to get me on board?"

My papà chuckled. "If you lock down the Conti girl, I'd buy you anything you want."

My mind flitted to the poster of a Maserati that hung in my childhood room back home. I suspected he was exaggerating though and that wasn't the sort of present he meant. It didn't matter anyway. This was ridiculous. "You can't seriously think I'd have any clue who I want to marry at eighteen. Maybe I'll meet some nice Italian girl this summer. I figure you'd like that better anyway."

He shook his head. "Italian girls have nothing to offer your business. But the daughter of the head of the most prominent family in Connecticut…"

I opened my lips, then closed them. I'd asked him before about Giada's father and he wasn't too vocal. I'd have to ask Tomasso. And even if Giada's father was some hot shot, how would that help anything? Giada clearly wasn't involved. She was oblivious.

I raised my hands as if surrendering to the cops. "It doesn't matter. I'm not proposing to anyone anytime soon."

"What are you afraid of?"

Was he seriously that dense? "I don't know, maybe picking my wife when I'm still a teenager and then spending the next fifty years wishing I was with someone else. This isn't the middle ages. People don't just settle down at eighteen. I'd expect you of all people to encourage me to take my time, date more women, and figure out exactly what I want in a wife before rushing into something stupid."

His eyebrows furrowed in contrast to his broadening smile. "Luca, I'm not asking you to stop dating women. You could date every woman in Italy for all I care. In fact, I encourage it. You're young and you need to blow off some steam so you can focus on your work. Once you marry the Conti girl, you can still keep dating whoever you want. I won't tell."

My papà leaned forward as he spoke the last sentence and I struggled not to wince at the stench of cigar rolling off his breath. It was so strong that it momentarily distracted me from what I thought he was saying.

"You want me to marry Giada and then date other women?"

My papà shrugged. "Everyone does it. It's not like she could leave you anyway. Why do you think your mother and I live on separate continents half the time?" He chuckled sardonically.

I dragged my hand through my hair. "I've got to go line up for the ceremony."

He patted me on the back and sauntered off.

I tried to clear my mind, but nothing I did helped release any of the tension until all us graduates marched onto the lawn. We were seated on the stage, facing the audience, and the first person I spotted was Giada. The second our eyes locked, I felt my lips quirk up in a smile. Yeah, it sucked that I was graduating and leaving this idyllic place before her, but this wouldn't be the first time we'd been apart. We'd be fine.

Giada and I were meant to be, and we could get through anything. I had nearly two weeks to spend with her before I had to jet off to Italy. Then, she'd come visit me for three weeks over the summer. I could manage a quick visit before her classes started, and would be back for Homecoming. Giada already told me her family was coming to Italy for Thanksgiving, and then I could surely come see her over Christmas.

Then, I could work out a plan for second semester, and Giada could figure out what she was going to do when she finished school. By the time she graduated, we'd both know for sure if we were destined to be together forever. I wouldn't mind proposing once she was eighteen and I was twenty, but there wouldn't even be a rush. We'd be masters of the long-distance relationship by then. We could enjoy a long engagement and know it didn't even matter. We'd have the rest of our lives to be happy together.

God, I was stupid.

CHAPTER 23

Part III- Giada's Senior Year

Luca

I kept my promises to Giada, and summer went according to plan. Well, at least the parts that concerned her. My papà, still seemingly convinced that I might propose to Giada before she finished high school, was oddly accommodating of me taking time away from the business to either visit her or to entertain her when she visited me.

Alessio was less supportive. He didn't mind me hanging out with Giada or missing work; his issue was more with the way I spent my free time when Giada wasn't around. Despite my genetics, and despite plenty of opportunity, I didn't cheat on Giada. I occasionally flirted with other girls, but that was the extent of it. I could see how Alessio found that pathetic. I also realized it made me a bit boring.

The truth was, I was still struggling to solve my double life dilemma. Was I Luca, the idyllic boyfriend to the sweet, Catholic girl who volunteered for children's hospitals and prayed the rosary for fun? Or was I Luca, the heir to the evil empire of the notorious mobster who had a penchant for tormenting people just to teach them a lesson?

I tried to explain my identity crisis to Alessio, but he brushed it off. He said we weren't supposed to be just one person. Then he'd tell me all those different pieces made me a whole person.

I fell right into his trap. "Things with lots of pieces are broken," I told him.

"Non sei rotto, Luca," he said. *You're not broken.*

I sighed, then wondered how Alessio balanced the various sides of his persona. From what I could tell, he was content to entertain himself with a woman—or two—for a night. But I didn't think Alessio would ever be truly happy in a relationship with a woman. And yet he didn't seem to have some existential crisis over the fact that he couldn't openly be himself, at least not without risking the wrath of my homophobic papà.

Alessio and I were slated to spend a solid three weeks in the U.S. around the time of my alma mater's homecoming, but I hadn't told Giada the length of my trip. It wasn't that I didn't want to see her—I ached to see her. I'd never been so desperate to be with another person, live and in the flesh.

But that was the problem. We were busy the entire time, and with the type of shit my papà would likely have us doing, I knew I'd need a buffer between work and spending time with Giada.

By this point, I was a pro at lying to her. I told her I had to spend a couple days at home before coming to campus, but omitted the specifics about how many days. Our last night in New York, Alessio and I tagged along with Iacopo on one of his debt collection errands. I'd forgotten how unhinged Iacopo could be, and by the time I pulled through the familiar gates of the prep school, I was so ready for a break.

Giada rushed to greet me the moment she spotted my car in

the visitor's lot. The game wouldn't start for hours, but she'd planned for us to tailgate with her friends before the game. She had also planned for us to head to the Sullivan Farm after the game. We wouldn't be alone for hours.

Giada picked up steam as she neared me, slamming into me with enough force to propel me backwards into the side of my car. I caught her in my arms, shifting to support her weight as she wrapped her legs around my waist. She kissed me hard on the lips then pulled back, grinning widely.

"Buongiorno," she said, her accent on point even if the level of formality was not.

"Ciao bella," I replied, eagerly waiting to see if she'd learned anything else.

She had not, but that was fine. Better than fine, really. As long as Giada only understood English, Italian could remain my secret code, used for any nefarious purposes I so desired, without her ever knowing any better.

"I missed you so much," she said, slowly shimmying back to the ground.

"So much that you planned for us to spend every minute surrounded by other people?" I countered.

She scowled. "Yes, because I miss seeing you and spending time with you, not just…" Giada stopped talking instead of uttering any indecent words.

"Me too," I said, reaching for her hand and pulling her to me for another kiss. "Now, catch me up. How are your classes? Who is dating who? What's the latest drama?"

We walked hand in hand to the massive courtyard beyond the football field where the tailgate was being set up. A DJ played music, alumni staffed various booths with carnival-style games and prizes, and a few tents gave out food and drinks. Being immersed in all the wholesome traditions felt good. I didn't leave Giada's side for a moment, and work didn't even cross my mind.

For once, I just lived in the moment, pretending I was a normal teen enjoying a tailgate and football game with his girlfriend.

Our team lost the game, which was disappointing, but not surprising. We were known for our gorgeous campus, upscale housing, and varied academic offerings, not our sports teams.

We drove to Sullivan Farm after the game, pausing only for Giada to grab her backpack from her room.

"What's in the bag?" I asked as she climbed into the passenger seat beside me.

Giada's eyes twinkled with mischief. "My overnight stuff. Elise promised to cover for me tonight."

My heart thudded at the realization of what she was saying. "So you can stay out all night tonight?"

"And tomorrow."

Now I couldn't stop myself from grinning.

"You have a hotel room locally, right?" Giada asked. "I was going to ask, to make sure you weren't just like crashing with a friend, but I wanted it to be a surprise, and—"

I squeezed her hand to cut off her rambling. "I have a hotel room. It'll be just the two of us."

I gazed at her just in time to see her adorably shy smile.

The party at the farm was fine, but I couldn't wait to get out of there. All I could think about was being alone with Giada. She, on the other hand, seemed determined to stay as long as possible.

"Dance with me!" she begged.

"Isn't that the point of tomorrow?"

Giada pouted, so I joined her for one song, then stepped back and watched as she and her roommate danced together. Watching them spin around to the side of the massive campfire reminded me of the first night I'd really acknowledged my crush on Giada, over two years prior. She'd been so carefree, and so fucking oblivious to how sexy she looked dancing around in that little white gown. Tonight she wore a fiery orange dress, but otherwise, not much had changed. She was still carefree, and still too hot for her own damn good.

She didn't get drunk tonight either, which I appreciated, since the plans I'd envisioned required her to be conscious.

After what felt like an eternity, Giada finally strode back to me, reminding me of a lioness prowling towards her next meal.

"How do you make orange look good?" I asked as she neared.

She smirked. "Grazie."

"Oh, so you did learn other words."

Now she blushed, then flung her arms around my neck. "Not really, but I'm hoping to make up for my lack of language skills with extreme talent in other areas."

My laugh came out as a low rumble in my chest. Giada rose to her toes, pressing her lips to mine.

"Are you ready to go yet? I feel like I've been patient enough," I said between kisses.

"I suppose," she replied.

We said our goodbyes and made it to the hotel in record time. We barely made it through the door to our room before Giada launched herself at me, kissing me in the way I'd wanted her to all night.

I wanted to focus on the feeling of her in my arms, and the taste of her on my lips, but as she kissed me, a different sensation overtook me.

It was the smell of smoke. I hadn't noticed it at the farm, maybe because we'd all been completely enveloped in it. But now, it was inescapable.

The odor clung to Giada's hair, assaulting my senses the moment I drew close. I stiffened, instantly seeing Iacopo and the distant, uncaring look in his eyes as he held the lighter to the guy's hair. At first, I'd thought he was just trying to scare him, and yeah, singeing off a chunk of hair was a great way to do that. But then he'd moved to the man's arm. Iacopo had held the lighter in one spot just long enough to elicit a high pitched howl from the man, then he'd simply shifted it to another spot. Iacopo hadn't quit until the guy's entire arm was dotted with burns.

As far as torture went, I supposed it wasn't the worst. The guy hadn't lost any limbs, just had some scars. But the smell of that first chunk of burning hair stuck with me and even now, four days later, my stomach roiled at the memory.

I shoved Giada back harder than I meant and brushed past her to the bathroom.

By the middle of the night, I'd managed to pull my shit together, or so I thought. Giada fell asleep curled against me, her body arching towards me even in sleep as if she trusted me. And why wouldn't she? She had no idea that I literally hurt people for a living. She inhaled and exhaled peacefully, with no fucking clue that a complete monster lay beside her.

I thought about how much easier it was already, some of the shit my papà asked me to do. I still couldn't stomach it all, and maybe I never would be able to, but I'd changed already. Everyone had noticed.

Well, everyone who knew the real me, and not the nice guy persona I wore like a fucking mask for Giada. I wondered if she'd invite me to church with her Sunday before I left town. Would the holy water sizzle the moment I set foot in the sanctuary? Would the communion bread turn to rock in my throat if I dared partake? I nearly chuckled at the thought, and then somehow, I fell asleep.

My nights had been dreamless since summer, as far as I could tell. But for some reason, not tonight. The second I drifted off, I went back to the docks, that night Alessio and I were attacked. We never had figured out what had happened. He still believed we'd been set up, that my papà was testing us. I was less certain. It didn't matter anyway, at this point.

The cold air seeped into my skin and I shivered, but the Luca in my dream was drowsy, too. I didn't know what was about to happen, didn't pay attention to the warning signs. I ignored the little prickles of danger on my skin, maybe just assumed they were goosebumps from the cold. I started to drift off, jolting awake when I heard a noise. Something brushed against my shoulder and I flew into action.

I flipped over, tackling my enemy, my hands at his throat before he could even get in one good hit.

And then my eyes focused and I saw Giada's mess of brown hair beneath me. I yanked my hands back, nearly choking on my own breath, as her eyes popped open. Her expression bore a mixture of confused drowsiness.

I pressed my lips to hers before she could say anything or ask any questions I couldn't answer. My heart was beating too fast for me to think, let alone talk, and I could barely catch my breath.

Cazzo.

I could've really hurt her. And as always, she had no fucking clue.

⁂

Giada

*H*omecoming was everything I'd imagined and more. Luca was the most handsome man at the dance, obviously, and we looked stunning together. I'd chosen a fitted red dress with sequins and a gorgeous cutout bow design on the back. Luca had coordinated a pocket square and bowtie to match my dress. I'd curled my hair, leaving it all down across my shoulders, but after an hour of dancing, I'd twisted it into an updo solely so I could feel Luca's breath on my neck as we danced.

We'd spent the previous night together, but it hadn't been exactly what I'd anticipated. We'd had a blast at the tailgate, game, and after party. I'd been worried that there might be some awkwardness, but there hadn't been. From the moment Luca had arrived, it had been just like he'd never left. We got along perfectly and everything felt easy and natural.

Well, easy and natural until we were alone in his hotel room. Then, it was like some switch had been flipped. We started making out and all of a sudden, Luca had knocked me to the side and run off. He'd stayed in the bathroom for nearly ten minutes, and then when he came back, he insisted we both shower. We ended up making out in the shower and then everything seemed mostly normal after that, but it was all just so weird.

I'd talked about it with Elise today when we were getting ready for the dance. Her theory was that he was worried about performance issues, like since it had been so long, he thought he might finish too fast and panicked. I wanted to believe that was the explanation, but that didn't explain his face. Right before he'd run off, Luca had looked angry. Not aroused, not in love, and definitely not happy.

No, he'd been furious, and maybe a little bit scared or disgusted.

Still, we had one more night to spend together and I was determined to make it the best night ever. The whole long-distance thing hadn't been bad so far. Granted, we'd barely made it into October, but still, that was a decent chunk of the year. We'd be together tons over the holidays and then hopefully spring semester would fly by.

Even though he hated to dance, Luca indulged me and stayed on the dance floor until I said I was ready to head out. We stopped by the after party at one of the local's homes, and we stayed long enough to each have two drinks. I figured the alcohol might relax us both so things could go better tonight, although if Elise was right, we shouldn't have any issues tonight anyway.

Back at the hotel, I was more hesitant in approaching Luca. "Do you want to talk for a while? Or I could shower?" I suggested, realizing suddenly that maybe something about me had repulsed him.

Luca wrinkled his nose as if embarrassed, then crooked a finger for me to come closer. I obeyed.

"I'm sorry about last night. I was…I don't know, off. Maybe jet lag? I wanted to spend time with you but then I was worried about keeping you up all night and ruining the dance for you today if you were too tired, and I hadn't really anticipated getting to spend both nights together so my brain was all jumbled and I just started overthinking everything," he rambled.

I nodded, as if any of that had made sense.

Luca reached for my hand, entwining his fingers around mine. We both gazed at our fingers and I couldn't help but notice how well our hands fit together. Everything about us fit so well. We had looked so good in the photos, had been so in sync on the dance floor, and always just fit together like two pieces of a puzzle. Clearly, I was stupid to worry when everything about our relationship was such a perfect match.

Luca raised our joined hands to his lips and ran his lips along my knuckles, sending shivers down my spine. "I just want to make the most of tonight," he said. "Can we do that?"

I nodded, then shivered as his hand traced along the warm skin of my back, tugging the zipper of my dress lower and lower.

"Ti amo Tesoro," he whispered, swiveling me so my back was to him. He kissed the side of my neck while nudging my dress to the ground and unfastening my strapless bra. His hands massaged my torso before settling on my breasts and I gazed up.

Before us stood a floor length mirror. Even our reflections were a perfect match, with Luca's hands just covering my breasts. He smirked at me in the mirror.

"Why are you still dressed?" I challenged.

CHAPTER 24

Luca

I spent the entire flight home debating my next step, and I'd come up with only one option.

So, once I'd settled back into my normal routine in Italy, I found myself seated at my desk, staring at my phone, my chest filled with dread. I wiped my damp forehead, but it was futile. Moisture coated my palms as much, if not more, than my forehead. It was ridiculous for me to be this nervous. I hadn't been this scared when Iacopo nearly singed off a man's fingers. That should probably tell me something.

I briefly considered the possibility she wouldn't answer. It would be both a blessing and a curse to be able to delay. But there was no point, not really. It wasn't like anything would happen in a couple of hours that would seal our fates any differently. The fact remained that I couldn't be the person I needed to be with Giada in my life. I'd always feel guilty, always torn, if hers was the voice on my shoulder judging my every move. And she didn't need me. She needed goodness and light, not... a life of organized crime.

"Hey Luca," she answered, her voice as clear as if she were in the room next to me. "I didn't think I'd hear from you today. It's gotta be late for you. Or, early?"

My eyes dipped to the clock on my phone. It was just after two a.m. Late, but not unseasonably so, particularly for my line of work.

"How are you?" she asked.

Pangs of remorse hit me. She was so oblivious to what was about to happen. She was so, happy. The moment I spoke up, I'd ruin that. She'd be miserable, at least for some time, and she'd hate me, probably forever.

"Luca?"

The sweet way her voice curled around the letters of my name gave me pause.

"It is late, but I figured we should talk," I said, delaying the inevitable.

"Well, you know I always like hearing your voice."

Me too, Giada, me too.

"How was your day?" she continued.

I blew out a sigh. "Long. Stressful. It, um, well, working for my papà is more, I don't know, everything, than I'd expected."

"I'm sorry." She sounded sincere.

Maybe I was wrong. Maybe she could understand what it was like for me.

"Elise and Max broke up."

I frowned, trying to remember whether I'd even known they'd been dating. Giada's roommate went through guys so quickly it was hard to keep up. But I thought about my day, all the shit I'd been through. Then I thought about her day. She's probably spent forever on her makeup and clothes, daydreamed through class, then gossiped with her friends at lunch. Now that it had to be nearing dinner time on campus, the most pressing thing on Giada's mind was probably who she'd sit next to at dinner, or where they'd go shopping this weekend.

We had nothing in common. She would never understand my life.

"I actually wanted to talk with you about that," I finally said, not realizing until I'd spoken that she was still talking.

"About Elise?"

"No, about…" I sighed. I wasn't usually flustered around her. Of course, I wasn't usually about to break her heart, either. "I want you to have fun this year," I said.

"I know you do babe. And I—"

"Giada, can you let me finish?" I interrupted. She didn't speak, so I interpreted that as a yes. "I want you to do all the fun senior year things this year. I'm so glad I was able to get back there for homecoming, but it's naïve for us to think I'll be able to travel internationally every time there's some social event you need a date for. I don't want you to miss out, and I don't want to constantly let you down."

"You won't, Luca. I trust you."

I paused, not having expected that. I wasn't even sure what trust had to do with it, but maybe that was the point. Maybe that was the problem. "You shouldn't," I said. "I'm not a good person and I don't even know that I want to be. My world isn't all butterflies and rainbows. I'm not like you. I can't just ignore all of the unpleasant shit in the world and pretend everything is fine."

"O-kay…" she drew out the word in a way that told me she was struggling not to snap back at me, but I wished she would. If she'd yell, it would be a lot easier. I'd rather her hate me than just be hurt by me.

"I just think you'll be happier without me. We were stupid to think long distance would work."

The sound of her breathing was the only clue that she was still there.

"Giada?" I said when the silence was too tenuous to endure longer.

"Yeah?"

"Did you hear me?"

She breathed a bitter laugh. "I honestly don't know. I can't tell if you want to pick a fight or if you just want reassurance or if you're trying to break up with me, but—"

"I think we should break up." My words echoed back into my ear, but this time, I didn't dare rush her response.

More than a full minute passed before she spoke. "Luca, I won't pretend to know how your day was or what has you so stressed out lately. I only know what you tell me and clearly, you're not telling everything." She paused again, and I heard her take a deep, steadying breath. "What I do know though is that I care about you. I meant all the things I said to you. I'm okay with missing out on some of the fun things this year or showing up to dances without a date."

"You shouldn't be, Giada. You shouldn't have to miss anything because of me."

"We knew this year would be hard, but you told me we would make it work. You promised."

"I was naïve. We both were. It was wishful thinking."

"People make long distance work all the time, Luca."

"Yeah, if it's like Rhode Island to New York, maybe. Not Rhode Island to Italy. And not when we're teenagers. You've got your whole life ahead of you, Giada. You don't need to give up your senior year just to prove to yourself that you can make this work."

"You told me you loved me." Her voice was so void of emotion that it pained me. I wanted to tell her that I'd meant it, that I still did love her, that I always would. But for what? That would only make her more determined.

So instead, I said nothing.

"You said we'd be together forever, Luca. Do you remember that?"

"I'm sorry," I whispered.

"Seriously? You're sorry? Luca, I gave up my…" she began the sentence yelling, then quickly shushed herself. "I gave up every-thing for you." Now Giada sounded truly disgusted, whether we me or herself, I wasn't sure.

"I don't know what you want me to say, Giada."

"What I want you to say? I want you to say this is all a big joke, that you're not actually breaking up with me on a fucking phone call after promising me we'd grow old together. I want you to convince me you didn't just take advantage of me so that I'd…"

"Look, I said I'm sorry. That's the best I can do. I already told you, I'm not a good person. So you shouldn't be surprised when I don't act like one."

"Fuck you, Luca!" Giada snapped into the phone so hard that I actually flinched. "I hate you. And you are going to regret this," she said, disconnecting the call.

I already did.

I tossed back two of the sleeping pills Alessio had given me, washed them down with a grappa, then forced my mind to stay blank until sleep overtook me. Thanks to the alcohol I'd ingested before the call, plus the drugs, I fell into a dreamless sleep. When I woke, anger and restless energy flooded my veins.

I wolfed a cappuccino and croissant for breakfast, then spent two hours at the gym. I was due to meet Lodovico and the guys at the club around one to go over some paperwork, but I headed that way early thinking I'd grab lunch on the way.

Instead, I busied myself with another unofficial errand for my papà en route to the club.

I figured I looked bad by the time I reached Argento, but I couldn't be sure. I didn't have a mirror. I wiped my nose on my sleeve, grimacing at the sight of blood.

Well, *whatever*. My knuckles and hands were all bloodied and raw anyway, so I supposed it was only fair that I got a nosebleed out of the mess. Honestly though, the couple of hits they'd taken on me made me feel a lot better than the dozens of hits I'd gotten in on them, which made no sense.

And in the end, I still felt like shit. Maybe slightly better than I had after leaving the gym, but I supposed the moral of the story was that using a human as a punching bag didn't do much more for my mood than using an actual punching bag.

Live and learn, right?

The bell above the entrance to Argento chimed as I nudged the door open with my foot. I planned to make a beeline for the bathroom to clean myself up a little before seeing any of the guys, but Iacopo and Lodovico were right there at the entrance. They turned to me as I walked in, and both their jaws dropped.

They appeared to be in the middle of haggling with the jackasses that tried to rip us off over our produce deliveries every week and frankly, I just didn't get it. We had such a low tolerance for poor business practices in every other area of the company that I never understood why we put up with so much crap from the guys that did little more than bring the damn lemons and limes we used for cocktails. It was infuriating.

Lodovico and Iacopo were still staring at me, but the two produce guys were both still yammering away about why they were raising their prices yet again. The noise was echoing, thanks to my damn hangover.

Without thinking about it a moment longer, I'd pulled my knife from my pocket, flipped it open, and tossed it just above the main guy's head. The blade pierced the wall directly behind him with a dull thunk.

Thankfully, they both shut up.

"Prices stay the same from now on, or next time I don't miss. Understand?" I said.

The men both gazed from me to Lodovico, then back to me. After a long moment, they nodded their agreement, spoke with Lodovico, then left.

Iacopo rushed over to me, grabbed my elbow, and tugged me to a table, sitting me down.

"What happened to you?" he asked, at the same time as Lodovico roared.

"What the hell, Luca?"

I rolled my eyes. "They were annoying and you both know it. You're welcome."

Lodovico reached for my palms, turning them over in his hand. He touched my left hand and pulled back, his own finger now bleeding. "Is this glass?"

I gazed down at my hand, then did vaguely recall smashing through the car window when the earlier fight initially broke out. *Fuck.* That would probably hurt in the morning.

"I took care of another problem for you on my way in this morning," I said, just as the door chimed again. We all turned to see Alessio walk in. He took one look at me, slid his sunglasses on top of his head, then stopped dead in his tracks, eyes wide.

"You were alone?" Iacopo asked, his voice thick with shock as he correctly interpreted Alessio's expression to indicate complete obliviousness to my morning activities.

"We don't do everything together," I lied. Although, maybe now it wouldn't be a lie. I'd been quite independent so far that day. Perhaps it was a new trend. "Anyway, those guys that were always hanging around the dock? I took care of it. They won't be a problem anymore."

Iacopo looked impressed, but Lodovico sunk further into his chair and rubbed his forehead like I was giving him a migraine. My papà had been complaining about those guys for weeks though, and how they were always doing shady drug deals and selling knock off designer items right by the docks. He worried it would bring the wrong kind of attention to our business.

"Your papà wanted us to get his friend in the police department involved, Luca, not kill them." Lodovico said.

I shrugged. "Pretty sure I didn't kill anyone." That was a lie, too. I was positive they were fine. They'd all scampered off to their cars like little fucking babies after I came after them. "And now you can save your favor with the police for another time. You're welcome."

Iacopo and Lodovico exchanged a glance then turned to Alessio. "Sal will be here any minute. Get him out of here. Take him home, get him cleaned up, and then call one of us if you think anything might need stitches. The last thing Sal wants is for his pretty boy to get scars."

I rolled my eyes so hard I about fell out of my chair. Then I marched over to the bar, poured myself a double of whiskey, then downed it in one sip.

"Ooookay," Alessio said, retrieving my keys from my pocket then yanking me towards the door by my shirt. "Guess I'm driving."

"Don't you have your own car?"

"Yep, and you're not riding in it. You are covered in blood and you smell like you did twelve rounds in the boxing ring before whatever crime spree you decided to go on."

I blew out a sigh. "Yeah, I kind of did, actually."

He helped me into the passenger seat of my own car, then started the engine before talking.

"You want to tell me what's bothering you, or do we need to rough up a few more people before you feel better anyway?" he asked.

"I could kill half of Rome with my bare hands and still feel like shit," I replied.

Alessio sucked in a breath. After a moment, he turned to me. "Is Giada okay?"

A dozen different answers flooded my brain. On the one hand, she should be okay, now that I wasn't in her life. On the other hand, she was probably at least a little depressed at the moment over the breakup. But then the real, depressing truth of it all was that it wasn't even my business anymore. *She* wasn't my business anymore.

"I don't know," I finally said. "We broke up."

For once, Alessio had nothing to say.

Giada

I skipped dinner that night, and breakfast the next morning. I feigned a migraine to get out of classes, then spent the weekend in bed, crying. I tried to replay it all, tried to figure out where we'd gone wrong. Was it something I'd said or done over homecoming? Had he always planned to break up with me?

I alternated between wanting to hate Luca and wanting him back. I missed talking to him, missed seeing him, missed touching him.

Luca texted me the morning after dumping me. "I'm sorry," was all he wrote.

I growled at my phone, then screamed into my pillow. Elise asked what was wrong, so I handed her my phone.

"What does that even mean?" I asked. "What the fuck, Luca?"

She dropped the phone on the bed beside me. "He's a jerk and you are going to have a fabulous senior year without him."

My phone buzzed again, and as I went to read his response, I saw that Elise had actually texted "WTF Luca" in response to his last message. *Oops.*

"I didn't mean to hurt you," he wrote. "I do love you, but you are better off without me. Your year would've been ruined if we were trying to do the long distance thing."

"I don't need you telling me what's best for me," I replied, my fingers punching my phone screen.

I paused, but there were no little dots signaling that he was going to reply.

"I'm not going to wait for you," I added. "I'm going to date other guys and by the time you realize your mistake, it'll be too late."

"I want you to be happy," he said.

I groaned and chucked my phone across the room. "Prick!"

After that, Elise and the girls kept me busy, plus with the holidays approaching, I didn't have tons of time to mope anyway. Before I knew it, I was back home for Thanksgiving break. I thought the time at home would help me recover, then I could go back to school with a fresh, Luca-free perspective on life.

Except my first morning home, Angelo burst into my room and questioned why I wasn't packing.

"Packing for what?"

"Italy," he said, as though annoyed with me for even asking.

"I'm not going to Italy."

He rolled his eyes. "The whole family is. We're spending Thanksgiving at the villa in Palermo. Even grandma will be there. You've known this for months."

"Oh I am definitely not going to Palermo."

My brother frowned at me. "Matteo mentioned you and Luca were having some squabble. Is that why you don't want to go?"

"It isn't a squabble. We broke up."

He shrugged. "Well, maybe you'll get back together when you see him. His family is headed down to Palermo too."

"I'm not going to see him."

"There's no way dad will let you out of this trip."

"He would if he knew what Luca did to me," I retorted.

That caught Angelo's attention. "What did he do?" he asked, suddenly very interested.

I briefly toyed with the truth. Sure, it would be mortifying to tell my brother that my virtue was completely destroyed, but it might be satisfying to watch him murder Luca with his bare hands. Or would it?

"What. Did. He. Do?" Angelo repeated through gritted teeth.

"Nothing," I mumbled. "Never mind."

"Did Luca Marino hurt you?" Angelo rubbed his hands together like he was already warming up for the fight.

"Yes, dummy. He broke up with me. That hurts. So no way am I going to set foot in his stupid country ever again."

My brother rolled his eyes.

Unfortunately, Angelo was right that my parents didn't accept heartbreak as a legitimate reason to boycott the family vacation. My mom pretended to be on my side, but kept emphasizing how important it was to my grandma that I came. Then she tried to tell me our airline tickets weren't refundable.

"I'm sure we could just get a voucher for me to go visit grandma another time," I said.

"You will travel with the family," my father commanded, puffing his chest like a caveman.

"You can't make me," I retorted.

But four hours later, I was wedged between my brothers in the back of an SUV headed for the airport. At that point, I was nearly as appalled by the idea of spending time with my horrid family as the idea of seeing Luca. And they were not going to win. They couldn't literally force me onto a plane out of the country. That was kidnapping. Maybe even human trafficking.

I popped my earbuds into my ears as we waited in the terminal. I debated sneaking away once we arrived in Italy and flying back home. Surely I could put the ticket on my dad's credit card and be in the air before anyone noticed.

Then, I realized there was an easier way.

Just then, my mom tapped my leg and gestured at my ear buds.

"What?" I grumbled.

"I'm sorry about dragging you along on this trip. It's important to your father that we all stick together. And you know he does a lot of business with Luca's family, so he just needs reassurance that whatever happened with you two won't impact the business."

She paused as if I was supposed to profess my love or gratitude for her.

"We can go shopping when we get there," she promised.

"Sure."

When they announced that boarding would begin for our flight soon, my mom went to the bathroom. She asked if I needed to go, but I insisted I didn't. The moment she returned, I said I'd changed my mind. The entire family scowled at me.

"I had all that coffee earlier," I explained. "But I didn't have to go yet when Mom went. It will only take me a minute."

My father looked like he was about to stab me, but Matteo shrugged.

"I'll go too," my brother offered.

We both started towards the bathroom. I clutched my carryon tightly, then started into the women's.

"Wait for me right here, okay?" Matteo said, gesturing to the area outside the bathroom.

"K," I replied. I stepped inside the bathroom, counted to five, then peered out. Matteo was gone, so I took off sprinting. I made it out of the airport in under five minutes and had hailed a cab one minute after that.

"Where to?" the cabbie asked.

I cringed. "I'm not sure yet. Head towards Bridgeport for now." I ignored his judgmental stare in the rearview then pulled out my phone.

"I won't be meeting you outside the bathroom. I told you guys I wasn't going to Italy but nobody listened," I texted to Matteo.

"Wtf. Where are you?" his reply was instant, but before I could type anything, he called. I rejected the call.

"I already left the airport. Just get on the damn plane and we'll talk later. Sorry if dad blames you."

I spent the next ten minutes panicking about where to go, then asked the driver to take me to the mall. I couldn't go home right away. If my family tried to stay back and catch a later flight, that was the first place they'd look. I couldn't risk being dragged away now. So, I'd spend some time at the mall, then when I was certain they'd actually left the country, I'd catch a different ride home.

Unfortunately, right as I climbed out of the cab, fumbling with money to pay for the ride, a familiar car pulled up right behind us. I panicked, thinking it might be my brother, but then Enzo stood up.

Instinctively, I took a step back. "I'm not going to Italy," I said, my eyes locked on Enzo but my hand still gripping the top of the car door.

Lorenzo raised his hands defensively and slowly approached the cab. "I know. It's too late anyway. They already left." He took another step closer.

"Miss, is everything okay?" the cab driver asked me.

I didn't answer. I wasn't sure.

Lorenzo reached in his pocket and held out a wad of cash to the driver. "She's underage, and a runaway," he said. "You can call the cops if you want, but if you drive her anywhere else, I'll have to call the cops and give them your license number."

I scowled at Enzo, but shut the car door just in time for the driver to pull away from the curb.

"Did you follow me?" I asked.

"No. I tracked your phone. And I'm serious. Your family left without you. They're pissed, but gone."

"Do they expect me to catch the next flight?"

He shook his head. "No. Your dad asked what I was doing and then just assumed you could tag along with me." He sounded bitter, but I wasn't sure why.

I still didn't move.

"Get in the car, Giada."

Against my better judgment, I did.

CHAPTER 25

Luca

Alessio proved himself to be worthy of the role of second-in-command and best friend over the first few days after the breakup. He cleaned up my wounds, let me wallow, and helped me drown my sorrows in alcohol. Then, he distracted me. Alessio kept me busy with countless work projects that I knew couldn't actually have been intended for us during the day, then he dragged me out to various night clubs once we finished all of our official tasks.

Neither of us could pretend I wasn't still a mess, but I at least felt like someday, I might be normal again. I didn't have time to think about Giada, anyway. When the calendar hit November fifteenth, my first thought was that the American Thanksgiving was coming up. My second thought was that I'd survived a full month since the breakup. I wouldn't pretend that month without Giada hadn't been miserable, but it would get easier. It had to.

Alessio apparently thought it was time for me to move on, too. When we reached the night club that night, he scanned the dance floor, then nodded in a direction of a woman. I followed his gaze. She looked about our age, and yeah, she was hot.

Her espresso-colored hair cascaded hallway down her back, drawing my eyes to her perky butt and long, toned legs. Her skimpy black dress reminded me more of a negligee than an actual dress, but she wore it well. I wasn't about to complain. I couldn't get a good view of her face from this distance, but I wasn't sure that mattered either.

"Her name's Chiara," Alessio said.

I frowned. "You know her?"

He shook his head. "Not really. Iacopo's son dated her sister Concetta, or something like that. All I know is she's single, and she looked like your type."

I clenched my abs at the notion that I might have a type, as opposed to just a solitary person who was right for me.

"It's been a month. Time to get back on that horse," he said. "And from the looks of that dress, you won't have to go easy on this horse. Pretty sure you won't be her first rider." Alessio snorted at his own joke.

I winced, regretting having told him Giada was a virgin. Now that secret felt like a betrayal of her trust more than it had at the time.

"I don't need Iacopo finding girls for me," I insisted.

"Okay, then go pick someone else. I'll wait."

I scowled, then let my eyes roam around the room. Alessio was right though. Chiara was by far the hottest girl in the club. "Fine. I'm going to the bar. You want anything?" I didn't wait for his answer.

I sauntered up to the bar, stepped confidently around Chiara, and ordered a negroni for myself. As I waited for the bartender to prepare my drink, I turned. Up close, Chiara was just as pretty as from a distance. Her dark eyes and thick lips bore more makeup than I'd prefer on a woman, but it suited her fine. Besides, with tits like hers, I could overlook just about anything.

She cleared her throat and I realized she'd caught me staring.

"Ciao bella," I said, playing it off casually. *Hello, beautiful.*

She offered a half smile. "Do I know you?" she asked, her accent distinctly native.

"Not yet, but you should," I replied, extending my hand. "Luca Marino."

"Chiara Gambino."

"Piacere," I said. *It's a pleasure.* "Can I get you a drink?"

She lifted her still-full martini glass and shook her head. Her friend whispered something to her, then wandered off. The bartender handed me my drink, and I invited Chiara to join me at the end of the bar to chat.

We made small talk for the better part of an hour, moving on to a second, then third round of drinks. Chiara was receptive to my charm, and she was definitely flirting back. By the start of my third drink, I'd lost track of the number of times she'd stroked my chest, rest her palm on my upper thigh, or squeezed my bicep. I placed my hand on her leg a couple of times, but that was about it. I knew the time had come for me to seal the deal, but all I could think was that I was tired, and that Thanksgiving was this week.

Unless their plans had changed, the Conti family would be in Italy for Thanksgiving. And the last I'd heard, my papà was supposed to meet with Marco Conti. Most likely, that meant I'd be on the hook for at least one meal with the entire Conti family.

I nudged Chiara's palm off my lap and reached for my phone, pretending it had just buzzed with a message. I gazed at the blank screen for a moment, swore under my breath, then peered up at her, my most convincing expression of disappointment on my face.

"I'm so sorry, but I've got this work emergency. Could I get your number?"

She stared at me for so long that I half expected her to refuse, but then she handed me her phone. "Program your number in here. I'll call you," she said.

I quirked a brow, but did as she said. I just hoped I didn't have to change my fucking number now.

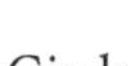

Giada

An hour later, Enzo parked the car in front of a charming Cape Cod-style house with beige bricks and muted green shutters. He popped the trunk, climbed out of the car, and then opened my door, motioning for me to get up.

"Where are we?" I asked.

"My house."

I stood slowly, confused. Enzo had lived at our pool house for as long as I could remember. He grabbed his bags and mind from the trunk, then nodded for me to follow.

"Where I grew up," he clarified. "My mom lives here alone now."

My next question was why we were there, but it was a short walk and he'd already knocked on the front door before I spoke it aloud.

A brunette in her mid-fifties answered the door. Judging from her big smile and even bigger hair, she was Italian. Aside from that, I didn't see a huge resemblance to Enzo.

"Lorenzo," she greeted him, "Mio topolino! How are you?" she squeezed his face and kissed both of his cheeks before pulling him inside and turning her attention to me.

"Giada, it's so nice to see you. I'm Carmella. It's been…oh gosh over a decade since we last met so I'm sure you don't recognize me." She offered me the traditional kiss on both cheeks also, then held me at arm's length. "God, they weren't kidding. You are gorgeous!"

I was really curious who "they" were and why they were commenting on my appearance to Lorenzo's mom, but instead I just mumbled a polite "nice to meet you."

"We'll have to catch up later," she promised. "Anyway, I only need to work the first half of my shift and then a coworker can come cover for the rest, but you both make yourselves right at home. If I'd had more notice, I would've left you some dinner, but I think we have the ingredients for a mostaccioli if you two want to cook." Carmella winked at her son, then brushed past us and left.

I lingered in the entryway, confused, while Enzo disappeared down the hall to the right. I took in my surroundings, observing that it felt like a completely normal, cozy home. Homier than any house I'd been inside for ages, actually.

"You coming?" Enzo called.

My eyes landed on the beige carpet. "Should I take my shoes off?"

His head appeared around the corner. "No, it's fine. Come on. I'll give you the tour."

Enzo led me to the right, where there was a dining room. I could see through it to the kitchen. He paused as we reached a narrow staircase. "The living room, bathroom, and laundry room were the other direction." At the top of the stairs, there was a small landing, with one room to the left and two rooms off to the right. "This is my sister's old room, and where you'll be staying, and this is where I'll be," he said, pointing to the two rooms on the right. He walked into each room and dumped the bags on the bed then returned to where I stood, dazed.

"I don't understand. Why are we here?"

His exasperated eye roll caught me off guard. Usually he was beyond respectful and patient with me. "You said you're not going home. And you're not going to Italy. So... where else do you propose we go?"

Hmm. He made a good point. "I have friends. Or a hotel?"

He laughed. "You think your father will let you stay at a hotel with me?"

Of course I didn't think that. But I also didn't think he'd agree to this. "Wait, does he know I'm here?"

"Of course. And he's fine with it as long as I keep an eye on you at all times. For some reason, he's afraid you'll run off." He gritted his teeth as he spoke the last part.

Now I was the one rolling my eyes.

"Come on. Are you hungry?"

I shrugged, which thankfully he interpreted as a yes.

I followed him into the kitchen as he began to pull ingredients from the cabinets. "I don't know how to cook mostaccioli," I said.

Enzo laughed again. "You don't think I know that?" He filled a pot with water and stuck it on the stove, then washed his hands. I watched as he cooked pasta in the pot, browned ground beef in a skillet, and stirred the remaining ingredients in a separate bowl.

"I had no idea you could cook," I said.

"There's a lot you don't know about me. Can you preheat the oven?"

I slid off the counter stool and stared at the oven, finally selecting the correct button for bake. "375 okay?"

"Sure." He pulled out a cutting board and knife, then unwrapped a loaf of bread. "Can you slice this without hurting yourself?"

I flipped my middle finger in his face and then set about the task. Once I'd sliced the bread, he mixed some herbs into a small bowl, added a softened stick of butter, and stirred it all together. Then he spread the herbed butter onto each slice of bread before putting it in the oven beneath the pasta dish.

Neither of us said much as we prepared the food. We separated to both unpack and settle into our rooms, then returned to the kitchen after. Right as we finished cleaning up, his mom returned.

"Oh it smells wonderful," she mused. "I so miss having you at home, mio topolino." She kissed her son on the top of the head before ruffling my hair and heading out of the room.

"She always showers after work," he explained.

I nodded. "Topolino?"

Enzo blushed a little. "It's an Italian thing. It means 'little mouse.'" He sat on a stool beside me and scrolled through something on his phone. I'd left my phone in my purse, certain all it contained were dozens of threatening texts and voice mails from every member of my immediate family. I stood and wandered around the room, meandering into the dining room and studying each of the framed photos on the wall. It was easy to tell which pictures were Enzo. He looked exactly the same as a child.

"Is this your sister?" I asked, even though it obviously had to be. The same blonde was in every picture with him and his mother.

Enzo came up behind me, startling me with his sudden proximity. "Yes. Bella."

"She's pretty. You guys grew up here?"

"Uh huh."

"Where is she now?"

"New Jersey. She's married and has a baby. You'll get to meet her tomorrow night."

"I don't mean to interrupt your family time," I said.

"Not much alternative, is there?" he replied. "I'm in charge of you until your parents are back."

His mom came up behind him and bopped his head before turning to me. "You're not interrupting anything. The more the merrier. Bella will love you." She swiveled back to the kitchen and began collecting plates to set the table.

"I can do that," I offered, certain I'd do it wrong but relatively hopeful she wouldn't care.

Carmella carried the casserole onto the table, wedging a serving spoon in the corner. Enzo brought out a bowl with salad and a basket containing the bread I'd sliced. He made one more trip and returned with a glass of water for each of us.

"Have a seat and please serve yourself first, sweetheart," Carmella instructed me.

Famished, I did as she said. Enzo sat beside me and began piling food on his plate as well. Carmella returned with wine glasses and a bottle of red wine. "Could you say grace, dear?" she asked Enzo.

He cringed.

"I will," I volunteered, launching into a short traditional before-meal prayer.

"Thank you," Carmella said with a warm smile. "Dig in."

I started with the pasta, practically groaning in delight as the flavors of my first bite hit my tongue. It smelled great, but it tasted fantastic. I quickly devoured another bite while Carmella poured wine for everyone.

Just as I peered up at my glass, Enzo snatched it, dumping its contents into his own. "She's seventeen, ma," he snapped.

Carmella gazed at me. "She looks older. And it isn't like she's going to go drive anywhere, is she?"

He scowled at his mom but she poured a smaller serving of wine into my glass.

I waited until she looked away to sip the wine, smirking at Enzo as I did so. He rolled his eyes and turned back to his food.

"This is actually really good," I said.

Enzo thanked me.

"I used to hope maybe he'd be a chef when he grew up," Carmella confessed. "I think he would've gotten bored pretty quickly though."

She asked me about my interests and then asked how my family was doing. After more small talk, we'd all finished eating. Enzo carried all of the dishes back into the kitchen while his mom and I talked, but I couldn't help but notice that his phone kept buzzing. And each time it did, Enzo looked more stressed.

I excused myself from the table and joined him in the kitchen. "Is that my dad?" I asked, suddenly feeling guilty that I hadn't checked my own phone.

"No. Not everything is about you," he snapped.

My mouth fell open. Enzo had never used a sharp tone with me, and I really didn't know what to say.

"I'm sorry," he said. "I'm just stressed. Ma, I'll do the dishes in a few. I need to make a call first."

He raised his phone to his ear and I heard a woman answer before he even made it out of the kitchen. She had a high pitched voice and seemed annoyed with him.

"Kristin, I'm sorry but I can't make it. I told you, something came up," he said, speed walking towards the front door. "It's not like that, but…"

I watched as he paced anxiously on the front porch, dragging his fingers through his hair. Then I startled as his mom came up behind me.

"It's always something, isn't it?" she asked, gesturing to her son.

I shrugged. I didn't really know Enzo well enough to answer that. And I was still stinging from his comment.

"Could you dry?" she asked, handing me a dishtowel.

I nodded, realizing the small kitchen lacked a dishwasher.

"Do you have a boyfriend?" she asked me, giving her wine glass a final rinse before handing it to me to dry.

"I, uh, no." I paused, the question having caught me off guard. Everyone else in the world seemed to know that already. I was surprised Enzo hadn't told her. "I had a boyfriend, but he's older and he moved to Italy after he graduated. We tried the long-distance thing and it wasn't working, so we broke up. Well, I mean, he broke up with me."

"Sorry to hear that. I'd imagine it would be hard, living in different countries, especially at your age."

"He said we were going to get married," I said bitterly. "And then he dumped me."

Carmella made a face and shook her head. "Well, his loss, I'd say. And your gain. A girl like you—you don't want to be tied down so young. You have so many adventures in your future I bet."

"It's hard to have many adventures when my father requires I have a chaperone at all times."

Carmella turned to me, her expression sympathetic. Then she shrugged. "Well, take your chaperone on your adventures. He can handle it. It'll be good for him, really."

I wasn't sure what to say to that, so I continued with my sob story. "My family is in Italy now, visiting my ex-boyfriend's family. That's why I'm not going."

"Understandable."

We washed and dried a few more dishes in silence. Then Carmella turned to me again. "Bella had a serious boyfriend all through college and she was so sure she was going to marry him. But they broke up her last semester and one of her lab study partners asked her out on a date. He's the guy she ended up marrying."

She shook her head. "You girls spend so much time doing all of the things everyone expects you to do that you don't really have a chance to figure out what you want until you're a little older. Boys tend to figure it out sooner since they never think of anyone but themselves, anyway."

A small laugh escaped my lips at that.

"Trust me when I say you'll meet some other boys and then, if you're really supposed to be with your ex-boyfriend, you'll know it."

She shut off the faucet and wrapped aluminum foil over the remaining pasta right as Enzo returned. She suggested we all watch a movie, so we did. About halfway through, she excused herself for bed.

It felt weird sitting on the couch beside Enzo, nothing but a bowl of popcorn between us. We'd spent a lot of time in close proximity over the past year, but usually in a car. I'd never really considered him a confidant or friend. But now, it seemed that was a possibility.

He'd changed clothes after dinner, swapping out his slacks and button down for dark grey sweatpants and a black tee shirt. I wished I could snap a picture for my roommate Elise, because she already thought he was ridiculously hot and if she saw him in this outfit, she'd probably die. But I couldn't figure out a tactful way to ask if I could photograph him. Instead, I went for another equally awkward question.

"Who's Kristin?"

He turned slowly to face me. "A girl."

"Yeah. Figured that much. I guess I was asking if she was, like your girlfriend or something. It's none of my business though. Sorry." I shoved a handful of popcorn into my mouth as if to show I truly didn't care.

"Um, no. I'm not trying to be evasive. I just don't really know. I guess I thought we were dating, but now she's pissed."

"Because you had to cancel plans with her to babysit me?"

Enzo stretched his arms above his head, revealing a sliver of bare skin beneath his tee shirt. "Yeah."

"Sorry. I ruin everything."

"It's not your fault. She's… I don't know. A normal girl would just let it go. She's somehow convinced that I'm cheating on her."

"With who?" I asked, trying to imagine how Enzo would possibly have time for another woman with how much time he spent doing shit for my dad. "You spend all your time with me lately."

He chuckled and cleared his throat. "She thinks I'm with you."

"You are." I still didn't get it.

"No, I told her I'm with you, but she thinks you and I are involved romantically."

"Oh." I cringed. "I could tell her that isn't the case?"

"Yeah, something tells me that won't help."

"You could tell her I'm not your type."

He laughed.

"Why is that funny?"

Enzo grabbed his phone off the coffee table and scrolled down for a moment before tilting the screen to me. It was a picture of a pretty girl with long, dark brown hair and big brown eyes. "That's Kristin," he said.

"She's gorgeous."

He scrolled back to another picture and showed me. It was a different girl, but she was also an attractive brunette with similar features. "That's Chloe, the girl I dated before Kristin."

"Also pretty. What's your point?"

Enzo made a face. "You are my type, and Kristin knows that."

I considered his words for a moment. I did share a lot of the same features as all of his girlfriends, but it didn't seem like that mattered so much.

"I mean, obviously I would never date a teenager. And you'd think Kristin would get that, but all she sees when she looks at you is…" his eyes scanned me as he motioned vaguely up and down my body.

Again, I wasn't sure what to do with that comment. "Having a type is a lot more than just how someone looks. Personality matters too. What type of woman—like her character—do you usually go for?"

He laughed again. "Apparently, controlling bitch is my type. Maybe I should let you talk to Kristin then. She'd never believe I'd be into the whole sweet and innocent thing you have going on. She'd spend five minutes with you and realize you're way too nice for me."

"You think I'm nice?" I reached for my soda, but realized it was empty.

"You want another?" he offered.

I shook my head. He took a swig of his beer, then returned to my initial question.

"I think you're *too* nice."

"That's not possible."

He raised an eyebrow, challenging me.

"Nice girls don't barge into your family time and screw up everything with your girlfriend."

Enzo's brows furrowed. "You're here because your family tried to drag you to a different country to spend time with the guy that just broke your heart. A less nice girl would not have handled this whole ordeal this way. But you...you didn't get revenge on Luca and you didn't sabotage your family's trip. Shoot, you probably won't even hold it against them that they still went after everything he did to you."

When he phrased it that way, my simple refusal to join them on the trip didn't seem so rebellious. But he was painting Luca as the villain when I wasn't sure he was. "Luca didn't *do* anything to me. We just broke up. It happens. The long-distance thing wasn't working."

Enzo stared at me in complete disbelief. "You're really not mad?"

I shrugged and blew out a sigh. "At him? What's the point? He loves me, or he did anyway. He didn't have a choice about going to Italy."

"He's known for years he had to go to Italy when he graduated. Was the plan always to break up when he moved away?"

"No, but—"

"Let me guess. He made a bunch of promises. He told you it would work. He'd call more, he'd visit more, and it would all be fine."

I mean, Luca had said all of that, and more, but I didn't see what that had to do with anything.

"And then after he got what he wanted, he told you it wasn't working," Enzo continued.

Now I didn't follow. "What did he want?"

Enzo stared pointedly.

"Seriously, I don't follow."

He rolled his eyes. "Giada, everyone knows how much the Church means to you, and you weren't exactly subtle about your whole plan to stay abstinent until marriage."

I swallowed the lump growing in my throat, feeling all the blood rush to my face. "Wait, are you saying Luca told you when we…"

"No, he didn't have to tell me. It was obvious, the way you were with him. And you went away with him for the weekend. Did you really think I didn't know about that? How much do you think I suck at my job?"

"Just because we went away for the weekend doesn't mean…" I began, but there was no point in arguing. He was right. I did have sex with Luca. "Are you saying he broke up with me because I slept with him?"

"No. But I am saying Luca had to have known you guys wouldn't survive this year. Or the next four. But he didn't tell you that because he knew the only way he stood a chance at getting you in bed was by convincing you that you guys would be together forever." Enzo paused, scooping a handful of popcorn into his mouth while waiting for me to process his words.

"Let me guess," Enzo continued. "Luca reasoned that if you're going to get married someday anyway, it's not really breaking the rules to sleep together first."

I leaned forward and thrust my head into my hands. "Oh, God," I mumbled. Of course everything Enzo said made perfect sense, but why hadn't it occurred to me before? I mean, technically it had been my idea—not that I'd ever tell Enzo that—but still. *Ugh.* Somehow Luca had managed to convince me that he was doing me a favor by breaking up with me, that he just didn't like seeing me not enjoy my senior year because I was sitting around waiting for him.

"I am such an idiot," I said, still covering my face.

"You're not an idiot," Enzo said, rubbing my back.

I peered up at him. "You just finished telling me I fell for the oldest trick in the book. How does that not make me an idiot?"

"You see the best in people, Giada. That's never a bad thing. And Luca is a master manipulator."

I excused myself to go up to bed after that, but it took me forever to fall asleep. Like every night, I spent way too long crying over Luca. Except tonight, I had to concentrate on crying quietly. My room was connected to Enzo's via the bathroom, and the last thing I wanted was for him to overhear me sobbing.

When I awoke though, I felt oddly well rested. I tugged a zip-up hoodie over my tee shirt, confirmed my pajama pants were decent enough, then went downstairs in search of coffee. Luckily, there was a full pot in the kitchen. I helped myself, then glanced into the living room. Enzo hadn't been in his room, but he also wasn't anywhere downstairs. That seemed odd. I was about to retreat upstairs when Carmella came down.

"Good morning, sweetheart. Did you sleep okay?"

I nodded and smiled.

"Can I get you anything for breakfast?"

"Not just yet. Thanks though." I needed to be fully caffeinated before I thought about food.

"Well, I was about to bake some cookies for when Bella comes. Want to help?"

That actually sounded great. Much better than crying in the shower, which had been my only other plan for the morning. We made small talk as we baked and had just begun rolling the dough into balls when Enzo returned.

He waltzed into the kitchen wearing athletic shorts, a sweatshirt, and ear buds. He looked and smelled like he'd been exercising. He brushed past us to fill a glass of water for himself.

"Morning," he greeted me.

"How was your run?" his mother asked.

"You run?" I asked.

"It was good," he told his mother. Then he just shook his head at me. "I've run nearly every day of the last decade."

He stole a bite of cookie dough from the bowl and popped it into his mouth right before his mom swatted his hand. "You'll get salmonella," she said.

"Worth it," he retorted. "I'm going to shower. Please make sure our guest eats something other than coffee."

CHAPTER 26

Giada

*L*orenzo's sister was just as kind as her brother and mom. I'd expected to feel lonely on Thanksgiving without any of my actual family, or at least like the odd man out, but instead, I'd ended up feeling oddly at-home. We all helped with the cooking, and the meal turned out delicious.

After dinner, we'd all gone to the theater and watched some ridiculous holiday action movie. My first thought was that I couldn't imagine my family ever going to a movie like that as a group. My second thought was how depressing it felt to sit through any movie in a theater without a date.

No sooner had that thought crossed my mind than Enzo's hand had reached across my lap. He was offering me Junior Mints, not an actual hand to hold, but the gesture was comforting anyway. I glanced over at him and out eyes met.

He frowned, then mouthed "you okay?"

I nodded and tried to focus on the movie, but then the thought that he was looking out for me just made me start to feel even sadder. Like, why couldn't Luca care about me the way

Enzo did? Would there ever be a guy who actually cared about me and wasn't just using me for sex?

I felt tears start to well up in my eyes right as Enzo shifted. He swung an arm over my seat and angled me towards him, wrapping his arm around me so my head was resting on his shoulder. The position felt oddly intimate, but also comforting. I couldn't cry about Luca when I was tucked under the wing of another man.

After the movie, Enzo insisted on moving to the couch for the night so his sister and her husband and baby could have his room. I offered to let Bella have her own room, but they claimed Enzo's room was better for the baby anyway. I wasn't sure about that, but decided not to protest. They stayed until Saturday afternoon. Enzo accompanied me to church, and then Sunday he drove me home. I packed all my stuff, then Enzo shuttled me right back to school.

"You're sure you won't get into too much trouble?" I asked for what had to be the tenth time as we neared campus. My parents had told me I needed to be at the house waiting for them when their flight got in that afternoon. But presumably, they just wanted to lecture me before letting Enzo drive me back. My preference was to postpone the lecture till Christmas break, when I'd be home again anyway.

"Don't worry about me. I can handle your dad," Enzo reassured me. "Besides, he owes me. I babysat his only daughter during my entire vacation."

I cringed, but his hand reached out over the dash and patted my thigh before I could feel too bad.

"I'm kidding. It's fine."

He helped me with my bags when we pulled up to the entrance to my dorm, then he grinned at me.

"I'm sorry I ruined your holiday," I said.

Enzo shook his head. "You really didn't." He extended his arms, and I couldn't resist the chance for one more hug. He released me promptly, then spoke again. "Will you do me a favor though? Date some guys at school. Like, just keep it casual. No more marriage plans. And don't talk to Luca."

I smiled and nodded. "It's not like I have a choice on that last part. He dumped me. He's not exactly begging for forgiveness."

"Yet," Enzo mumbled. "Alright, well, take care."

I waved, then watched him drive off before rushing inside to catch up Elise on everything.

Luca

The day after I blew of Chiara, I had a dinner meeting with my papà. I'd been so focused on working my question about the Conti's impending visit into the conversation that I hadn't even thought to ask what the purpose for the meeting was. Luckily, he didn't make me wait. For once, Papà was proud of me.

He said his guys had commented on how efficient and decisive I'd been lately. Iacopo said I reminded him of my papà which, apparently was a compliment. Lodovico agreed, rambling about how the timid Luca of early days was gone and had been replaced with a ruthless leader.

I cringed, barely even meeting Alessio's eye, certain none of these were actually true praises. But then came the real insult.

"It seems I was wrong. I thought the Conti girl was good for you, that a match with you two would be good for business and therefore good for us all," my papà began. "But thank God you knew better. You've grown into the man we need you to be since you cut her loose. You were the only one who realized she was holding you back."

I opened my mouth to protest, but Papà kept going, rambling about how Giada had been my weakness. I'd lost all my appetite by the time the main course came out, and then it only got worse.

"We're supposed to have dinner with the Conti's tomorrow, but Marco told me his daughter refused to get on the plane. Apparently she ran off at the airport, so she's not even with them," my papà explained.

"What?"

"Marco can't even control his own daughter," he repeated with a chuckle. Everyone at the table—except me—laughed.

"Wait, so Giada isn't even in Italy?"

"No."

"Is she coming later?"

My papà shook his head again. "No, apparently she's spending the week at her driver's house. Some kid named Lorenzo?"

My stomach churned. I turned to Alessio. He kept his gaze on his plate, which was a good sign for me to keep my mouth shut too.

Before I could say something I'd regret, my phone buzzed. I glanced down and noted the unknown number. I almost never answered calls when I didn't know who was calling but I needed a break from the table more than anything.

I excused myself and hurried to the hall.

"Pronto," I said, holding my phone to my ear.

"Did you get that urgent work wrapped up Luca?" a familiar voice purred in my ear.

"Chiara," I said, already feeling my lips tug into a grin.

"Of course. Expecting someone else?"

"Nope."

"So, about that work?"

"Yeah. I got that resolved, but I'm just finishing up a work dinner now. If I gave you an address, would you be able to meet me there in, say, two hours?"

There was a pause, and I briefly prayed, but whether I wanted her to agree or reject me, I wasn't sure.

"I have a better idea. What if I text you my address, and you just come here after your work dinner? I'm more in the mood to stay in tonight anyway."

I exhaled through clenched teeth. "It's a date."

I disconnected, then grinned as the text with her address came through right as I returned to the table.

Giada wanted to blow off Thanksgiving with her family? No problem. I had other plans anyway.

CHAPTER 27

Giada

When I returned to school, I tried to follow Enzo's advice about dating, but we'd reached that precarious time right before final exams. No one was focused on first dates. Besides, even the guys who'd willingly flirt with me in class didn't seem willing to take it a step further and ask me out. I even garnered the nerve to invite Will, a guy from my literature class, out to a movie with me, but he somehow turned it into some big group thing and I ended up cancelling anyway.

"Maybe they don't realize I'm single," I mused, flopping down on my bed while Elise sorted her laundry.

She made a face. I would've brushed it off as something related to the socks in her hand, but they were clean, and I could smell the fresh linen fragrance from where I lay.

"What?" I prodded.

Elise sighed and chucked the socks into her drawer. "Literally everyone heard when you and Luca broke up. Even the teachers were talking about it. But guys don't want to risk getting on Luca's bad side by asking you out."

"That's ridiculous. Luca doesn't even go here anymore so who cares about his bad side? Also why would Luca care anyway? He dumped me."

Elise crawled onto the bed beside me. "I say this in the nicest way possible, but Luca can be a little scary. I know he was harmless, but he had a reputation is all. And you have to admit you guys were a little intense. Maybe people just assume you're getting back together right after graduation."

My stomach clenched at the thought. "We're not."

Elise quirked a brow as if maybe I were wrong and for a moment, I actually hated her. She knew I resented my urge to wait for him, to just forgive the shitty way he'd up and quit after swearing he wouldn't and to just assume that someday he would come crawling back. I didn't need her encouraging my delusions.

"Okay, well, how about that hot driver of yours? He seemed more than willing to brave the ire of Luca Marino."

I giggled at Elise's dramatic tone, but shook my head. "He's like three and a half years older. When I'm eighteen, he'll be almost twenty-two."

She shrugged.

I supposed the age difference wasn't that big in the long-run, even if it seemed pretty significant now. So I pointed out the other issue. "He thinks of me like a little sister."

"You've got all of winter break to change that," she said.

I chucked a pillow at her, but really, it wasn't a terrible idea. Well, except that the next day, my mom called and told me my grandma had a stroke and was moving in with us until she recovered.

I got along okay with my grandma, but hearing that she'd nearly died after I blew off my last chance to visit her in Italy churned up some huge feelings of guilt. How could I have been so self-absorbed that I almost missed saying goodbye to my own grandmother—all because of a dumb boy?

I needed to seriously reevaluate my priorities. I'd been

granted a second chance and I wasn't going to waste it pining after boys. I was going to focus on being the person I should be.

Luca

*I*taly was gorgeous at Natale. The entire country transformed into a series of charming towns that looked just like the idyllic villages out of every Christmas movie. I couldn't stop thinking about how Giada would've loved it. And every time I thought of her, I felt like an asshole all over again. She'd probably moved on by now anyway. I sure had.

Life was good.

I was killing it at work—well, not literally, or not yet anyway. I'd really leaned into the whole ruthless reputation and decided the guys were right. Everything in our line of work was easier once you had a reputation. People were starting to know who I was, and in turn, learned not to mess with me. But it would only stay that way as long as they knew I wouldn't go easy on them if they crossed me.

Chiara was fun. She was no Giada, and that was a good thing. She didn't pressure me to go to church or ask questions about bruises on my knuckles. Actually, Chiara didn't ask me much of anything. My relationship with Chiara was primarily physical. We met up for sex, and the occasional drink, generally pre-or post-sex. We talked some, but never about anything serious. She didn't ask about my work, and I didn't get the impression she cared.

I considered the possibility that I'd be up for more with Chiara eventually, but neither of us pushed it. She was hot and managed not to get on my nerves, which was more than I could say for most women I'd talked to post-Giada. Alessio was convinced that my parents would love Chiara, and that she was the kind of girl I needed on my arm to make it in our world. I didn't necessarily disagree with him, but I also didn't care enough to think about it much.

I started carrying a gun when I was working. I'd kept up my training and gotten really good, at least according to Tomasso. It wasn't as common for guys to carry over in Italy as back in the U.S., but I wouldn't be in Italy forever. My papà had already started talking about me eventually taking over the U.S. portion of his business. He predicted I'd be dividing my time equally between the two countries in another couple of years, so Lodovico said I should get used to the gun stuff now.

When I wasn't working or hooking up with Chiara, I hit the gym. A lot. Mostly boxing, but some running and lifting. I'd learned that the more exhausted my body was, the less my mind wandered. And everyone agreed that a focused Luca was a powerful Luca. The fifteen pounds of muscle I put on wasn't a bad look, either. I no longer felt like a teenager, so it made sense that I no longer resemble one, either.

Alessio and I also managed to make some new friends. First we met Giovanni, then a month later, Thomas. Giovanni's uncle had worked with my papà back in the day, but he and Thomas both would have to prove themselves to all of us before they'd be fully welcomed into the folds. Still, I'd learned to trust my instincts. I was a good judge of character and I was confident those two would someday join Alessio and I in both our work and social endeavors. I'd grown comfortable with my papà's men, but I still wanted some of my own choosing, too.

By the end of February, I'd settled into a decent routine. A sustainable one, I thought. I still thought of Giada on occasion, and she still played a starring role in my dreams, when I had them. But she was no longer a constant weight on my mind at the time my papà mentioned the funeral.

"Ilaria Conti has died," my papà announced one morning at

breakfast, setting the newspaper down on the table as if he'd read the news there and not via text message hours before.

My mother gazed up, horrified, then began to mumble random sayings in Italian.

Alessio quirked a brow and peered at me. He'd been the one to tell me when Ilaria Conti had a stroke back in early December and moved in with her son all the way over in Connecticut. At the time, I'd wondered how Giada would fare, spending her entire winter break under the same roof as her Italian grandma, but I'd decided she probably loved it. Giada always appreciated the hustle and bustle of a busy house, and she loved her family every bit as much as I disdained mine.

"We must pay our respects." Mamma asked.

"I know, but I can't possibly get away this week. The funeral is in Connecticut." Papà shook his head as if that were ridiculous.

"But she was Italian!" my mom agreed.

Alessio and I exchanged a look, both of us probably realizing that someone as old as Ilaria likely had no friends left on either continent anyway.

My papà turned to me. "Luca, you will go in my stead. Explain why I can't be there. Pay our respects."

I opened my mouth to protest, but he shushed me with a firm hand to the air. It wasn't up for discussion. I was going to see Giada again, whether I was ready or not.

CHAPTER 28

Luca

Giada appeared to have aged years in the four months since I'd seen her last. Then, she was a teenager. Now she looked like a woman. She wore a sleek and sophisticated black dress that fell just above her knees. A thin black satin ribbon that encircled her ribs and formed a bow just under her right breast was the only embellishment. The straps along her shoulders were modest, but still showed off her shoulders and drew my eyes to her collarbone. *God* how I missed kissing her there. And the way she'd squirm against me whenever my breath hit the side of her neck…

I suppressed a groan and forced myself to look away for a moment, but my self-restraint didn't last long.

Her hair reached almost to her waist. I wondered how it was even possible for hair to grow that quickly, but then I realized it was straight now, and that, were she wearing it in her normal wavy style, it probably would appear an inch or two shorter. Her jewelry and makeup was simpler than normal, as were her shoes. Everything about her looked mature, dignified, and respectful.

Until she turned and caught me staring at her.

I quickly looked away, but didn't wait long enough before glancing back. Giada's eyes narrowed at me and she stuck out her tongue.

Right. So maybe not so mature.

Alessio snickered beside me, clearly having seen it all, and then Lodovico reached over and subtly smacked each of us on the back of the head. While I didn't think my punishment was merited, I tried to focus more on the service anyway.

When mass ended, we all went to the cemetery for what felt like another service that lasted hours. I remembered my papà's instructions and stayed alert and studied the faces. As far as I could tell, everyone from the Conti family was here. Roughly one quarter of our crew was present too, and the second in command from one of the bigger NYC families had come to show their respect, too. I didn't think Ilaria Conti was that big of a deal, but her husband had been. And until Marco figured out who had ordered the hit on his father years before, everyone was determined to make sure he knew they hadn't been involved.

After an eternity, the priest stopped talking. People close to Ilaria lined up to toss some dirt on the casket. Giada took her turn, then stepped out of the way. I was about to take my chance and go talk to Giada, but a woman I didn't recognize came forward to comfort her. I watched as the woman said something which prompted Giada to nod, and then they embraced. It was a long, familiar hug, not the type you'd share with some random stranger expressing condolences. I turned to Alessio, but before I could even ask if he knew the woman, he shrugged, silently answering my question.

As the hug ended, Giada's driver, Lorenzo, came up and joined them. He patted the woman on the back, then she turned to him, stroked one cheek, and kissed his other cheek. It was such an obviously maternal move that I was near certain the woman was Lorenzo's mother. I understood why she was here—her son worked for Marco, and if I recalled my Conti family history well, her husband was actually killed in the same hit that took out Marco's dad, Giuseppi.

But why would she know Giada?

The woman walked off, leaving Lorenzo and Giada alone. I again contemplated making my move to talk to her, but then Giada threw her arms around Lorenzo. I couldn't tell if she was crying or not, but even if he was only comforting her, it made my stomach churn to watch him rub her back soothingly as she pressed her face against his chest. The embrace went on for way too long, and it was then that I remembered. When Giada boycotted the family trip to Italy over Thanksgiving, she'd spent the week with Lorenzo instead.

Were they actually dating now? That would explain the painfully long embrace.

Alessio clearly thought so, too, since he tried to reassure me. "Everybody hugs at funerals. She's just upset and he's the nearest warm body. Nothing else going on there," he said.

I nodded, swallowing the lump in my throat. "Yeah," I agreed.

But even if I'd been convinced, I would've thought otherwise when they finally split apart, only for Lorenzo to offer his hand to Giada. As they walked away from crowd hand in hand, my lunch practically came back up. I watched as he handed her a bottle of water then took it back after she sipped.

I swore in Italian, causing Alessio to chuckle.

"Literally everyone here speaks Italian, you know?" he reminded me.

"Giada doesn't," I replied, even though she was out of earshot anyway and way too focused on her new boytoy to even notice I was still there. They'd sat down in chairs back over by the gravestone.

"What if we head out, you call up Chiara, and then we join up with the rest of the funeral crew later?" Alessio suggested, clearly uneasy with my increasing tension.

"I just need to talk to her," I said. Talking with Chiara was not going to take my mind off things. Besides, we didn't have the sort of relationship where we chatted on the phone.

"Watch my back," I joked, starting off towards Giada.

She was deep in some discussion with Lorenzo when I approached, but he noticed me coming. Giada turned to me, probably having picked up on the concern in Lorenzo's eyes. Lorenzo rose to his feet, as if suddenly back on duty.

"It's not a good time," he said, his expression stern.

I shot him a look, and was about to tell him that I just needed to talk with her, but Giada beat me to it.

"Enzo, it's fine," she said, patting his waist in an overly familiar way.

My stomach roiled at the gesture and the nickname.

Lorenzo stared at me for another moment, then nodded and walked off. I dropped into the seat he'd vacated.

"I'm really sorry about your grandmother," I said.

"Thank you."

I paused, trying to think of something else nice to say about her. But I really hadn't known her well, and frankly all old people seemed largely indistinguishable to me.

"At least she and your grandpa are together again," I said. If her grandpa was anything like my papà, I didn't imagine he'd ended up in heaven, but I was banking on Giada thinking otherwise.

Luckily, she forced a smile, so it had been the right thing to say.

"So…are you dating your driver now?" I asked. I was painfully aware it was a tacky question for a funeral, but I needed to know. And I wasn't sure how long we'd have before we were interrupted.

Giada's smile widened, morphing into a genuine expression of amusement. "You broke up with me," she reminded me. "I told you I wasn't going to wait for you and you said okay."

I didn't exactly think those were my words, but it seemed beside the point. "So?"

"You don't get to be jealous when I move on. This was your choice."

Yeah, like I'd really had any choice in the matter. "He's too old for you. He's an adult."

"Technically, you're an adult," she retorted.

Lorenzo was at least two years older than me. It was different. She had to know that. "Your dad is okay with you mixing with the help?"

She glanced over to where Lorenzo now stood, adjacent to her father but still watching us, ready to pounce if I tried anything.

"I'm not dating Enzo. I don't even know what made you think that. We're just friends."

The relief was palpable, but I couldn't just let this all slide. "He's not your friend, Giada. His job is to protect you and to drive you places."

She sighed. "I guess I have pretty low standards for friends these days. I'm supposed to be enjoying the best year of my life and instead, my boyfriend dumped me and my grandma died and I'm probably not getting into either of my first two choices of college. Literally nothing is going according to plan. So yeah, I'm lonely and sad and totally fine with my father paying someone to be nice to me, especially when he was there for me when my only other option was to fly to a foreign country and spend a week with the boy that betrayed me and broke my heart."

Giada paused to catch her breath, but before I could think of anything to say, she continued. "And you don't get to march over here and act all jealous and boss me around."

"I'm sorry," I said.

Giada gazed up at me. Her brown, doe eyes were still glossy but clear, and she had only the slightest smudge of black from her makeup under her lashes. She was so beautiful up close that it was hard to breathe.

"For what?" she asked.

I swallowed. "For all of it. I'm sorry you lost your grandma. I'm sorry about the school stuff. I'm sorry I hurt you. I'm really sorry you've been lonely and sad. That wasn't my intention. I figured you'd have ten new boyfriends by now." I paused, realizing she still might. "And I'm sorry for being jealous. Seeing you in person…it reminds me how beautiful you are and how happy I was with you. I miss being your best friend. I miss having you love me."

My words fell into the silent chasm between us. The silence stretched on for an eternity before she finally reached her hand over and placed it on top of mine.

"Me too, Luca," she said.

The way she looked at me made my chest ache. I was tempted to take it all back, to beg her to take me back, to promise I'd figure out some way for us to be together.

But then Lorenzo returned, and with one glance from him, the spell was broken. Giada pulled back her hand, flashed me a fake smile, and asked if she'd see me back at the house. I nodded, and she walked off with her driver.

Giada

*E*nzo walked me to the car, but I knew we weren't leaving until Matteo joined us. Still, he climbed into the driver's seat and adjusted the mirror so he could see me. "Are you alright?"

I knew he was asking about Luca, and not my grandma. And the truth was, I wasn't sure. "I think so. He's going to be at the house though."

"I can keep him away from you if you want," he offered.

I smiled at the image of Luca and Enzo playing some sort of monkey in the middle type game. "He said he misses me."

Enzo snorted. "I'm sure he does. He's got to be kicking himself for ending it when he did."

"You think so?"

He turned to speak to me face to face. "I'm positive. He's never going to find another girl like you."

I knew Enzo was just flattering me since I was so sad, but it worked. I needed the ego boost. I gazed out the window, watching as my brother slowly waved goodbye to each person even though he'd see most of them in another hour at the house. I loved Matteo, but he could talk like a little old church lady. We might be waiting a while.

"Giada?" Enzo waited until I was looking at him to continue. "Can I give you some advice? Don't go back to Luca, not yet anyway. I have a feeling your father is going to have some strong opinions about the kind of man you end up with, or even the ones you date when you're a little older. So for now, you should do what you want. Date the guys you like."

"Yeah, you've mentioned that, but no one will date me at school. Apparently Luca scared them all off."

Enzo snorted.

"It's not funny."

"No, you're right. I guess I just think it's also not surprising. Well, keep trying. But worst case scenario, you'll get a fresh start at college."

"I don't want to miss prom."

"I'm sure you'll have dozens of offers for prom, and if not, I'll personally find you a date," he offered.

I rolled my eyes. "Yeah, and that doesn't make me seem super pathetic."

"Giada, you couldn't be pathetic if you tried."

I had some questions about what he'd said, but of course then

Matteo joined us, climbing in the car completely oblivious to the heavy moment he'd interrupted.

"Are we off?" my brother asked. "Or are we waiting for Angelo?"

"Nope, we're cleared for takeoff," Enzo replied, navigating the car onto the drive.

I didn't end up talking with Luca at the house. He was there, but he stuck mostly with some of his own family and friends I didn't really recognize. I saw him talk with my parents for a bit, then with my brothers, but he didn't approach me again. And that was fine by me.

Enzo was right. I needed space.

CHAPTER 29

Luca

Alessio and I made it through the funeral then went straight back to Papa's club, 4ᵗʰ and Main. As a Sunday, the crowds would peak early evening, then dwindle by ten pm.

Iacopo sighed when he saw us. "Lodovico told me you'd end up here after seeing your girl."

"Ex," Alessio corrected.

Iacopo chuckled and began packing up his stuff. "If you're both here, I'm heading out. Tony will close up tonight and Christopher is handling security, so just let them know if there's any issues. Stay off the main floor if you're drinking anything since you are not of age in this country."

I rolled my eyes at the stupid reminder. My papà would never let the kind of cop who would protest underaged drinking into his club. But *whatever*.

"A guy is coming with a payment. If he's not here by ten, call me. It should be ten k. Count the money and lock it in the safe. If we're short tomorrow, it's on you."

I nodded. "Night," I mumbled.

He started out of the office and then poked his head back in. "If you sample the girls, use protection. The last thing your papà needs right now is one of his best girls getting fat with some dumb teen's lovechild."

Alessio and I both flipped him the bird, he cackled, and he left.

We waited less than a minute before Alessio trekked out to the bar to get us some drinks. As instructed, we consumed them inside my papà's private office, and then we went to the floor to watch the girls.

Starr was on stage, giving her best performance despite a small, bored-looking audience facing her. Another group of men occupied the bar, but they were talking, not even watching the girls. I couldn't wrap my mind around that logic. Was it normal to actually reach a point in life where you got bored of watching women dance around in a thong and stickers?

Starr crawled off the stage and directly onto my lap.

"Hello pretty boy," she purred, taking my soda out of my hand and setting it on the table beside her. "Your daddy told me you're single again."

"Yeah, shocking," I mumbled, sucking in a breath as she gyrated against the fly of my jeans. Her breasts bobbed along with the movement, nearly smacking me in the face as she moved.

"Meet me in the back after my set and I'll cheer you up," she promised.

I wedged my hand into my pocket and pulled out a crumpled twenty. "Sorry, Starr but this is all I have today."

"Oh stop, you know your money is no good here. I wanted you to talk to Lodovico about something. You can do that, right?"

"I can talk, but he might not listen."

Starr smiled. "That's all I'm asking." She grabbed my hand and guided it to her thong, helping me tuck my "no good" money against her flesh. Then she stood up and moved on to the next poor chap.

I reached for my drink just as a hand tapped my shoulder. It was Christopher, one of the random employees I didn't know too well.

"Bouncer says there's a guy here to see you."

"Alright." I glanced around for Alessio, but he was nowhere to be seen. I supposed it was good that he'd already found some private entertainment for the night. I took my drink with me and asked Christopher to bring the guy back to the office. I walked on ahead, then saw he brought two men.

I shook my head at Christopher. "Only one of them is coming in here," I said. I reached under the desk to confirm the Glock was still there where it should be, then motioned for the guy to come in and shut the door behind him.

"I was told to give this to Iacopo," he said, his eyes darting around the office like he was high on something.

"Well, I'm telling you to give it to me. He left early. Is it all there?"

His nod looked more like a twitch.

I reached for the bag and he pulled back.

"I'm not sure I should give it to you. I don't even know you."

"I don't think you want to know me, but I'm Luca. And I was sort of in the middle of something out there, so if you keep me much longer, the total is going up by a hundred. Do you hear me?"

The guy slid the bag across the desk and turned to leave.

"Stop," I said. "Unzip the bag and line it up."

He did as I'd asked, and I quickly counted it. I glanced closely at a few random bills just to confirm they looked real, then counted a second time. Everything seemed in order, so I handed him the empty bag.

"You can go," I said. I locked the money in the safe after he left, then went to look for Starr. She was at the bar fending off advances from a drunk guy asking for a free birthday dance.

I rolled my eyes, but before I had to say anything, Alessio reappeared.

"There's no freebies, and you've had enough to drink," he said to the guy. "Head on out front and Christopher here will call you a cab." He pulled the guy to his feet and nudged him towards the door before turning to me.

"Everything go okay in the office?"

"Yep."

"Sorry, I was…" his cheeks flushed.

"Yeah. No worries," I said with a laugh.

Starr nodded her head towards the back hall and I followed her to one of the private rooms. It was the only room that didn't have cameras, the one that only family could access. What happened in that room truly stayed in that room.

Starr didn't waste any time. She locked the door, tugged my shirt free from my pants, then skimmed her hands up my bare stomach.

"Has anyone ever told you that you look hot when you dress up?" she said, her tongue lapping at the edge of my ear.

"I was at a funeral," I said.

She pulled back and grimaced. "Oh. Sorry." Starr gathered her long copper hair between her hands, then twisted a band around it. "So how much cheering up do you need, exactly?" she asked, nudging me backwards until I hit the edge of the sofa.

I sat, and she climbed onto my lap, her strong thighs on both sides of mine.

I reached my hands up to cup her gorgeous tits. They were totally fake, but I didn't mind. They were humongous and perky and accented with shimmering stickers covering her nipples.

"I didn't even know the deceased," I admitted. I dipped my nose into her cleavage, briefly fantasizing about death by suffocation.

Starr arched her back, pressing her breasts further into my face, then began to sway. After a minute, she slid off my lap and knelt on the floor between my knees. I handed her the small pillow from the edge of the couch and she paused, smiling.

"Always such a gentleman," she cooed, unbuckling my belt.

I settled back against the couch, willing my mind to think about anything except Giada. Starr unfastened my pants but didn't bother pulling them down. She stroked me for a moment, then replaced her hands with her breasts. The sensation as she moved up and down was pleasant, but the view was fucking fantastic. I breathed a happy sigh and let my head roll back against the back of the sofa.

I would've been happy to finish like that, but after a minute, she replaced her breasts with her mouth. She used her hand to guide me further into her mouth than I thought possible, then pulled away just before gagging. It was intense and different that anything anyone had ever done before, so exactly what I needed. My body responded quickly, and I reached for her arm and glanced around for a tissue.

"Hey, I'm gonna..." I began.

She groaned and took me further in her mouth, which instantly sent me over the edge. Starr showed no signs of struggle but just kept at it. She continued nearly a full minute longer than necessary, then pulled back, peered up at me and smiled.

"If your last girlfriend didn't drink up every last drop like a good little girl, she wasn't doing that right," Starr cooed in her singsong voice.

I nudged her out of the way and turned as I stood up, adjusting myself back into my pants.

I was glad she was nothing like Giada, and I didn't need the fucking reminder of it. I just needed to get home.

Starr reached for my wrist before I could leave.

"Tell Lodovico we need a new DJ. Michael sucks and I don't like the way he leers at me. It's creepy," she said.

I nodded, certain Lodovico would honor that request immediately. "Consider Michael gone," I said. "But you know, Lodovico wants you girls to be happy. He would've done it if you'd asked him yourself. You don't have to call in favors with me."

She winked and licked her lips. "Oh I know. Have a good night, pretty boy."

It didn't even occur to me until I was home and in bed that Chiara was the one I should've been thinking about when I was with Starr.

Giada

Second semester senior year was a whole different beast. College applications were done. Any grades that actually mattered had already been entered. Now, all that was left to do was enjoy the last few months of my high school career.

Still concerned that no one would actually ask me out, I invited Reed, a local from church, out on a date. He knew it was just as friends, but no one at school aside from Elise realized that. He came to campus to pick me up, and I made sure to brag about our romantic date all over campus. After that, guys were more willing to approach me.

I didn't want to get involved in another relationship again, not with graduation approaching so quickly, and I made sure everyone knew that. What I wanted was fun. Enzo was right. I'd wasted enough time being serious, I needed to enjoy my youth while it lasted.

Elise and I privately pledged to each date ten boys and kiss five before prom. No boyfriends, no commitments, just girls being girls. That famed Cyndi Lauper hit? It was my new theme song.

I wasn't going to let anything drag me down—even the news that Elise had been accepted into her first choice school…all the way out in Chicago. I'd finally gotten some good news on the college front and at least knew I'd be staying close to home and studying in New York.

I hadn't yet accepted an invitation to prom, but had a few options. Elise and I were headed to New York with my mom the next weekend to go shopping for prom dresses. I couldn't wait.

CHAPTER 30

Luca

I slept in the next day. Aside from a few random errands for my papà, the biggest task on my list was to meet Alessio at our favorite diner for a big, American breakfast. I dressed, combed my hair, and was about ready to head out, when I remembered my promise to Starr about the DJ.

I dialed Lodovico, not surprised when I got his voice mail. For once, I could safely share my entire message on the recording without having to worry about wiretaps or cops or the likes. I hung up and motioned to Alessio that I was ready to go. Lodovico called back right as we reached the car.

"Hey, I left you a message," I said.

"I got it. When were you with Starr?"

I tried to recall the timing. "I don't know. It wasn't late. Iacopo left, and she'd just finished her set. And then I left right after…" I stopped myself there. I didn't think Lodovico would disapprove necessarily, but I wasn't going to kiss and tell, or whatever. "I got home before midnight, so—"

Lodovico sighed loudly into the phone.

"Is everything okay?"

"Yeah, it's fine. Apparently some guy followed Starr to her car last night at the end of her shift and tried to attack her."

"Where was Christopher?" I asked, switching the phone to speaker so Alessio could hear.

"He was busy with some other shit. He got there and scared him off before he could do any major damage, but the guy got away."

"Is Starr okay?"

"She'll be fine. Bruised cheekbone. Won't be dancing tonight, but should be fine. She says it's the same guy that Alessio pulled off her earlier, so I figured if you had a better idea of what time it was, we could narrow down the credit card receipts."

"We're in the car. We'll be there in fifteen minutes," I said.

Once we made it to the club, we were able to ID the guy from the security camera footage at the bar. From there, we figured out his name, then address, in a matter of minutes. Knowing Alessio and I had a flight to catch the next day, Lodovico offered to deal with the guy himself, but I wanted to take care of it. Starr had been good to me, and I owed her.

The next afternoon, I felt Alessio's eyes on me the entire time during takeoff. I had hoped to sleep on the flight, but that would never happen with him staring at me.

"What?" I snapped, turning to him.

He seemed taken aback by my harsh tone. "Nothing."

"You've been staring at me for fifteen minutes. It's obviously something."

Alessio shrugged. "I was going to ask how you felt after seeing Giada at the funeral, but—"

"But what?"

He gave me a pointed stare.

I shrugged as if I had no clue what he was getting at.

"Seriously? You nearly killed a man for getting a little too aggressive with a stripper. I have a decent idea how you're feeling."

I shook my head and reached for a magazine. "That has nothing to do with Giada. He was a dirtbag who needed to learn to respect women."

Alessio stared for another minute, then nodded in agreement. "Okay. Yeah, you're right. Just checking that you're okay."

"I'm good. Great, actually."

"Good."

Giada

I tried to get excited about prom. Shopping with my mom and Elise was so much fun, and I really did adore the dress I chose. The Valentino gown was silk, with a lace overlay. Its rich violet color made me feel like true royalty and truly brought out the sparkle in my eyes and made my hair seem even glossier. The fit accentuated everything I loved about my figure, too.

The only downside of the dress was my acute awareness that Luca would never see it. While there were several girls at my school who would likely appreciate the value of the dress as a Valentino, aside from its obvious beauty, none of the guys knew anything about designers. Had Luca still been my date, he would've recognized the importance of my choice.

"You're going to have so much fun with Joel," Elise reassured me, almost as if sensing my skepticism.

I smiled. She'd started dating Cam, and Joel was one of Cam's best friends. So when Joel threw his hat into the ring as a possible prom date, I jumped at the chance. The four of us planned to share a limo with another couple, head to dinner as a group, then go to the dance. So, even if Joel didn't end up being my Prince

Charming, the night was guaranteed to be a blast because I'd spend it with Elise.

"And if you don't, we're going to hit up the party together, so no worries."

"I know," I said. I tried to sound convincing, but my mind had already started to wander. I'd made so many plans about prom back when I was still with Luca. I'd dreamed about prom with him like some girls fantasized about their wedding day. And now, no matter how magical the day was, it wouldn't be what I'd pictured.

CHAPTER 31

Giada

Despite Elise's best efforts, my senior prom was depressing.

Okay, it wasn't all bad. Elise and I had a blast getting our hair and nails done. We'd even gone to the spa for bikini waxes, even though there was no way anyone was seeing anything near my bikini line. We did our makeup with the other girls on our floor, then hit up a few different gorgeous spots on campus for a mini photo shoot before meeting up with our dates.

Once we joined the guys, we'd posed for more photos on the beach. Then we passed a flask around the limo while we drove to the restaurant. We dined on shrimp and steak, then squeezed back into the limo. Elise and I sang along to the music, and even stuck our heads out the sunroof, although only at stoplights so as not to completely ruin our hair.

Once we arrived at the dance, I kept thinking of the last year, when I'd attended Luca's prom with him. That had been one of the most romantic, happiest nights of my life. He had promised me we'd attend my prom together, no matter what. *No matter what*. That's what Luca had said.

And like the naïve idiot I was, I believed him.

Joel was nothing like Luca. He was a jock and a party boy. Nothing he did was controlled or calculated, and that made him a blast by all accounts. He was the center of attention, from his mystery flasks in the limo ride to his over-the-top dance moves during the official event.

I hadn't planned to drink anything at prom, but every time I started to think about Luca, Joel's flask distracted me. During every slow song, Joel held me and swayed to the beat of the music like the perfect man, but he didn't whisper Italian sweet nothings in my ear. Feeling his heart beat against mine didn't magically restore my faith in humanity or make me feel less alone in the world. I had no misgivings about Joel being my soulmate or us someday telling our grandkids about this dance together.

It just wasn't the same.

We'd each been nominated for prom court, but I was honestly relieved when I didn't win. Joel did, of course, and he made an adorable couple with Lana, the crowned queen. Joel basked in the momentary fame, shared the requisite dance with his queen, then came over to comfort me. It was probably the most thoughtful thing he'd done for me, aside from the fact that I really wasn't disappointed. Standing on that stage with anyone but Luca by my side would've been torture. I was happy to watch Joel from the crowd.

I assured him I was happy for him, and stuck around for a few more minutes just to make my point. Then I excused myself to the restroom. We were only staying for a few more songs anyway, and I needed a moment to myself before heading to the after-party. The giant ballroom packed with happy people totally in love with their dance partners was stifling.

I anticipated the night air having cooled, but I didn't bother to collect my coat. Head down, I wrapped my hands over my bare arms and scurried towards the exit. Two minutes of cool, fresh air would be all I'd need. Then I could return to Joel, enjoy my night, and figure out a way out of what he was expecting to come next. Truth be told, when he'd invited me, I had planned to fool around with him. Not because I really wanted to, but because something about the awareness that Luca had been my only partner made me hate myself.

But now I realized how ridiculous that was. I'd made an exception for Luca because I loved him, I'd seen a future for us, no matter how naively, and because I couldn't not be with him. If I was going to be with someone else before marriage, it was going to have to be someone else I felt that strongly about.

Or else I'd need to be a lot drunker.

My eyes were on my feet, so it shouldn't have shocked me when I ran into someone. I grunted as we collided, then noticed the expensive-looking leather shoes I'd nearly trampled. Even when he pressed his hands to my biceps to steady me, I hadn't planned to look up, only to apologize.

But then he spoke. It was a single word, but that was all it took.

"Princess." His voice was deep and smooth, but barely above a whisper.

I gazed up slowly, certain I was hallucinating.

But no. There stood Luca Marino.

I drank in the sight of him, fully expecting the mirage to fade then disappear any moment. His dark hair was longer than when I'd seen him last—at the funeral—and he seemed bigger. Not so much taller, I supposed, as stronger. Maybe he just had better posture from his increased confidence. He wore a grey suit tailored to fit him perfectly, and I knew without even touching him that it was finely woven from high thread-count Italian wool. He wore a simple black shirt beneath it, and two gold chains instead of a necktie.

I didn't say anything. For the first time in my life, I was literally speechless. And either Luca truly was an illusion, or my uncharacteristic silence caught him off guard.

He eventually dropped his hands from my arms, then gazed into my eyes. I couldn't help but stare back. Everything about his buttery eyes entranced me. Suddenly aware that I was dizzy, I drew in a deep breath, but that only made things worse, as now the scent of his familiar cologne flooded my nostrils.

"Tesoro?" he finally said, and even though I didn't know what he was asking, I was sure I had the exact same question.

"I need air," I blurted out after another lengthy moment of silent. I brushed past him and out into the cool night. I scurried around to the side of the building, feeling like Cinderella escaping the ball. When I stopped, I was panting and breathless, though I'd only run ten yards or so. I peered around me, half expecting to see other ghosts. When none appeared, I pinched my arm.

"Ow," I mumbled, just as the familiar apparition stepped around the corner.

His hands were in his pockets now, like he couldn't possibly be more relaxed.

"This is my senior prom," I said.

Luca nodded. "Yeah."

"Are you actually here?"

His eyes narrowed at my dumb question.

"I mean, why are you here?" I asked, now even more flustered.

"I told you I would be." Luca stepped forward cautiously, as though worried I'd hit him.

"That was last year. You told me a lot of things back then."

"I know." He bowed his head as though acknowledging his vast collection of broken promises. "I'll go if you want, but I… needed to see you, wanted to see what dress you chose."

I gazed down, temporarily having forgotten what dress I'd worn. It was an embroidered silk gown, with the bottom layer closely skimming my curves and pushing the limits of appropriate school dance attire but the lace overlay more than compensating by covering significantly more flesh.

Luca motioned for me to twirl around, so I did one slow rotation.

"It's a Valentino," I said awkwardly.

"It's perfect. You look stunning, and the gown seems like it was designed for you." He grinned. "And that shade of purple—it's the color of royalty, you know?"

"Thank you." The compliment, coming from Luca, meant more than when Joel had similarly praised my appearance, if only because Luca had a more sophisticated appreciation of fashion.

"So, um, Joel Aaronson?"

My palm slapped his cheek without any hesitation. Luca had no right to question me about my date. He stepped back and turned his face from the contact, but didn't retaliate or respond in any way.

"You're shivering," he said. In one large stride, he was closer, fully invading my personal space. His arms wrapped around me and offered instant warmth. It was almost too much. Another minute of his embrace and I might have suffocated.

"I need to go back to Joel," I said, pushing back.

"One dance," Luca countered.

"Here?"

Luca smiled, his forehead tilting towards me as he reached for my hands. As my breathing stilled, I realized I could still hear the music from the event. Luca clasped my right hand, then placed his other hand on my hip. We'd never danced like that before, both of us always having needed more contact. But somehow, this felt more proper, more fitting for the last dance with Luca.

When the song ended though, Luca didn't immediately let go.

"He's going to wonder where I went," I said, breaking free.

Luca dipped his head in acknowledgement of my statement.

I stepped around him and started towards the door, then

paused. I knew I was making a mistake before I even spoke, but I did it anyway.

"Luca? Can you wait for me? Maybe fifteen minutes?"

His lips curved into the slightest hint of a smile. "Take your time."

Luca

Seeing Giada was a mistake. From the moment the idea of surprising her at prom had popped into my head, I'd been certain nothing good could come of it. There were dozens of reasons I shouldn't go and none in favor, and yet I went anyway. I supposed my papà would say it was a weakness, my inability to do what needed to be done rather than what I wished to do.

Either way, I didn't care. Seeing Giada up close in a dress that somehow both revealed too much while also leaving more than enough to the imagination was worth every regret I'd have the next day.

I'd driven myself, not wanting to deal with the lectures from anyone else and also not willing to implicate anyone else in my dumb scheme to see Giada again. But I didn't want to wait in the car in case I missed her. So instead, I returned to the lobby. I stayed to the side so no one would recognize me, but I kept watch, hoping she'd return sooner rather than later.

She did. She caught my eye, then made her way to the coat check. I watched as Giada retrieved her coat from the attendant, and then she walked out the front door without waiting for me. I followed her into the parking lot, catching up as her gait slowed.

"I'm this way," I said, gesturing. "I drove myself."

I unlocked the car and held open her door. She climbed in, smoothing her dress around her. I hurried to the driver's seat, wanting to leave before she changed her mind. I started driving, having no destination in mind. I was curious what she'd told her date, but knew it wasn't my place to ask.

"Is this your car?" she asked.

"Yes." The engine on the new Audi wasn't noticeably better from my old car, but the stereo system and heated black leather seats were significantly more luxurious. "Where to?"

She shrugged and stared out the window. I had a brief but powerful urge to head to the highway, start driving to Florida or something where we could hide out for years. Instead, I drove her to the upscale hotel where I was staying, about twenty minutes away. I avoided the closer hotel, certain that would be where her classmates would head.

And when I pulled into the lot, handing my keys to the valet, I was confident in my choice. Giada was uncharacteristically quiet as we walked through the lobby and rode up in the elevator, but the moment I locked the door behind us, she turned to me.

"I'm not sleeping with you," she said.

"I'll drive you back to campus whenever you're ready," I promised, suppressing a smile when I noticed her eyes drifting down my body, lingering around my midsection in a way that contradicted her words. "Drink?"

She glanced at the contents of the mini bar, then pointed to the coffee maker. I brewed us each a cup, dumping sugar and cream into hers without asking.

"Thanks." Giada sipped tentatively, then paused, pressing her fingers against the side of her hair and wincing.

"Here," I offered, instantly sensing her discomfort from the array of pins securing her hair in place. I spent the next several minutes carefully dislodging each and every pin from her hair. When I was done, I unwrapped the band at the crown of her head, and gently wove my fingers between the sections of her hair until it fell in dramatic, loose waves.

"God," I murmured. "I still think of you often, but I forget how beautiful you are."

I scooted back to stare at her, intending to soak in the vision as long as she'd let me. Not surprisingly, she blushed shyly after a single minute, and rose to her feet. My stomach clenched at the thought that she might want to leave already, but instead she set down her coffee and reached for my hand.

"You owe me a real dance," she said.

I pulled her into my arms without hesitation, holding my phone behind her back until I could start some music. Once successful at that task, I dropped my phone onto the bed. She smiled at me, and then we danced. We swayed together to two different slow dances and then had fun with some more casual moves to the next two songs. When the fifth song came on, another slow dance, I rotated her so that her back was to me, and I linked my arms in front of her abdomen.

"I've missed dancing with you," I admitted.

She didn't reply, but she didn't have to. It was obvious from the way she leaned against me, sinking into my arms. She felt the exact same way.

After the song, she dropped onto the foot of the bed and gazed up at me.

"So, how have you been, Luca Marino?"

Talk about a loaded question. "I'm better now," I said, sitting beside her but careful to leave a decent amount of space between us. "I missed you."

Giada shook her head. "Nope. You don't get to dump me and then complain about missing me."

"I wasn't complaining…" I began, but she shot me a look that stopped the lie. "Did you have fun today?" I asked instead.

She turned to me, sucked her bottom lip between her teeth, and laughed shyly. Giada was so beautiful when she did that. I should've looked away, but instead I reached my hand out, casually dropping it over hers. Our connection was still so strong that even the slight touch send electric shock feelings through my core.

"How's your dad?" she asked, breaking the spell and looking away.

"He's a dick, same as always. Yours?"

She shrugged. "Haven't seen him since the funeral."

That didn't sound right. "You didn't go home for spring break?"

"No, Florida with friends."

"Wow." The Marco I knew would never allow that.

"Matteo and his friends came also," she added.

I chuckled. That explained it. I scooted off the bed and crouched down by the mini bar again. There was a selection of pantry items above the fridge section. I grabbed the Sour Patch Kids and tossed them to Giada before selecting a box of Junior Mints for myself.

"Are we going to a movie?"

"I'm betting you didn't eat much before the dance. You must be hungry."

"Ahh, so you're feeding me healthy snacks," she teased, picking through the candies until she had a handful of yellow ones. Those always had been her favorite, which was weird on its own. But it also struck me as funny how she always ate those first. Everyone else seemed to attack candy with their least favorite first, saving the best for last. When I'd asked Giada about her differing approach, she said life was short and she didn't want to risk not savoring the good parts.

We continued the awkward small talk while we snacked, and eventually, she'd relaxed enough to face me. Her dress wouldn't let her get too comfortable, but I scooped up her feet and dropped them in my lap. She raised an eyebrow but said nothing as I began to rub one foot, then the other.

"I said the part about how I won't sleep with you out loud, right?" she asked.

I laughed but nodded. "I didn't know how you'd react, honestly. I told my friend I was going to go see you and he tried to talk me out of it. He said it was a dumb idea."

"It was," she agreed. "Wait, you have friends now?"

I swatted her playfully before continuing with what I needed to say. "You've been on my mind a lot. I figured seeing you tonight might give me some closure."

"Closure," she repeated.

"I know nothing's changed. I'm still there, you're still here, and I'm still too jealous to watch you live your life and not get to be a part of it."

"I never said you couldn't be a part of my life. But you promised to be all of it and then said you wanted nothing to do with it."

I nodded. She was right. I hated seeing her with Joel. All of the things that she'd have to do to enjoy a normal life were the precise things that made me miserable and murderously jealous. "When I told you last year that I wanted to be with you tonight, I meant that. It wasn't just something I said," I told her. I paused, gazing deep into her shimmering espresso eyes. "I meant everything I told you when we were together."

Giada stared at me as though trying to gauge the truthfulness of my words. "You're saying there was no elaborate scheme to convince me we'd end up together just so I'd sleep with you?"

Her words hit me hard. My chest ached, and the minty filling of the candy suddenly felt too sweet on my teeth. I blew out a breath. "You didn't think that," I said, willing it to be true. I squeezed her feet harder until she made eye contact again. "You didn't, right?"

Giada shrugged.

I wanted to hug her, but I was scared to push her away just yet. "I'm sorry," I said instead, aware that my words were insufficient. "I never thought we'd break up. From the moment of our first kiss, I was positive you and I would end up together. I spent so much time convincing myself we could make it work after I graduated that it really never occurred to me that we shouldn't." I paused again. "Well, I mean, until it did. And that's when I told you."

She didn't say anything, but she dropped the rest of her candy on the bedspread beside her.

"I still think we'll end up together," I added.

Her eyebrows furrowed. "But not yet?"

"Not yet," I confirmed, certain my confession had now sealed the deal and she'd ask me to drive her back to school now.

"You wanted to interrupt my prom, spend the night with me, then head back to Italy as though it never happened?"

A chuckle escaped my lips. That was essentially the truth, but she seemed to miss the intention. "I just wanted to see you. I hadn't even planned to say anything, but then you looked so..." I gazed up at her. "Lonely."

Giada wrinkled her nose in an adorable expression of confusion. "You were just going to watch me and not say anything?"

I nodded.

"That's, like, stalker-level creepy."

I shrugged in response.

"I wanted to be at prom with you," she said after a long pause. "You were always supposed to be my senior prom date."

I nodded. "I'm sorry. I would've liked that too."

"When do you head back to Italy?"

"Tomorrow afternoon."

Silence filled the small room for what felt like an eternity.

Finally, her eyes locked on mine. "I don't want to waste our time then."

I froze.

I didn't dare move or even breathe. My heart might have even stopped for a moment.

Without breaking eye contact, Giada stood, taking my hand with her. I let her pull me to my feet, but still didn't want to assume anything. She slid her hands between my shirt and my jacket, resting her fingers on my hips. I shrugged out of the jacket, unsure why I'd even left it on this long. I draped it over the back of the chair then dipped my head. I placed my hand on her cheek, shivering at the smoothness of her skin, but then I stopped. I wasn't making another move until she confirmed what she wanted.

Luckily, I had to only wait a moment before she rose onto her toes, her fingers pressing into my sides. I closed the distance between us and kissed her, bringing my other hand to her face as well, holding her to me. This close, I was overwhelmed by Giada. She tasted like lemon candy and smelled like an exotic mixture of honeysuckle and vanilla. Her lips were even softer than I remembered, her hands even warmer.

I was so fully ensconced in the sensations of kissing her that I didn't notice her fingers fumbling with my pants until she'd unfastened the button.

A better man would have stopped her, but I skimmed my hand along her back, searching for her zipper. It took both hands to lower her zipper and I moved slowly, not wanting to snag the delicate fabric. Giada got my pants down first, so I stepped out of them before holding her hand so she could climb out of the dress. I walked it over to the closet, carefully hanging it on one of the wooden hangers provided by the hotel, then turned back to her.

She was laughing, but I knew she appreciated the thoughtfulness. It would be a crime to throw a Valentino gown on the floor. As I dared let my eyes roam down her body, my breath caught in my throat. She wore a nude, sleeveless bra and matching barely-there panties. To say she was a sight for sore eyes was an understatement.

She quirked an eyebrow, enjoying my appreciative gawking. Giada may have been shy sometimes, but she also knew exactly how good she looked naked and exactly what effect she had on me.

"Cat got your tongue?" she finally asked.

I shook my head. Giada gazed flirtatiously at me for another minute, then stepped forward and curled her fingers around the hem of my shirt. I yanked it up over my head right as her palm flattened against my stomach. Her other arm looped around my neck, dragging me down to her. Our mouths crashed together, and I swiveled her around and guided her onto the bed.

After we made love, we lay in bed, her head on my chest. It felt like old times, as we lay there talking and laughing. I wondered if Giada needed to get back to some after-party, or maybe even back to campus, but I figured she'd tell me if she did.

Eventually, she crawled out of bed and went into the bath-room. I expected her to reach for her dress then, but she didn't. Instead, she emerged a minute later, my toothbrush in her hand. "Can I use this?" she asked.

"Gross."

"You should probably take me back to campus then," she replied.

I leapt out of the bed and coated the toothbrush in minty paste and shoved it in her mouth before she could protest. She laughed, but brushed her teeth. Then she rinsed it and offered it to me. I accepted it and brushed quickly, eager to discover what she had planned next.

Instead, she just stood there, naked, waiting for confirmation.

"I want you to stay the night," I said.

Giada nodded and climbed back under the covers, grabbing something on her way.

I scooted in beside her, having forgotten how calming it was just to be near her. But then, she was moving. I craned my neck to see her and realized she was chewing.

"Are you eating candy after stealing my toothbrush?"

Giada laughed, then fed me a Sour Patch Kid. They weren't my favorite, but at this point, anything tasted heavenly when fed to me by her. We talked for hours, then fell asleep. When we woke, she climbed on top of me. In her sleepy state, it was clear she forgot about protection. I almost didn't speak up, reasoning that an unintended pregnancy might actually solve all of our problems. But then I realized how insane of a notion that was and I paused the action to reach for a condom.

We showered after we made love and then I helped her back into her fancy gown. I offered her a tee shirt to wear over it, but she assured me that her jacket was adequate.

The sun was coming up by the time I drove her back to her dorm. As we neared the massive gates welcoming us to the campus, the pit in my stomach grew. So much remained unsaid between us, but at the same time, it seemed we both knew there was no point.

Nothing had changed. She still loved me, and whether she believed it or not, I still loved her. But that didn't make us any better suited for each other. In another lifetime, maybe we could survive.

But in this one?

No way.

The villain never ended up with the princess. She'd find her happy-ever-after with some prince.

And me? I was destined to become the moral of the story.

CHAPTER 32

Giada

The dorms were empty when I returned. All of the seniors had permission to stay out the entire night, so when I unlocked the main entry doors with my ID card, I didn't need to sprint to my room. Instead, I slipped out of my delicate heels and slowly made my way down the hall, clutching the straps of my shoes in one hand and a wad of fabric from my dress in the other.

Alone in my room, I stripped to my undies then crawled under the covers. Dawn had already arrived and my brain was nearly as exhausted as my body, but I still didn't expect to sleep right away. I assumed I'd spend at least an hour or two overanalyzing every word Luca had spoken, every look he'd cast in my direction, and every touch he'd bestowed on my skin.

Instead, I felt oddly at peace. And then next thing I knew, my door swung open with an indelicate clang.

"Giada?" Elise's voice was so loud I wondered if she was still a bit drunk.

I sat up, rubbed my bleary eyes, and read the clock. Two P.M!

"Oh my God. When you said you weren't feeling well and were headed back to the dorm, I thought you were kidding. I'm like, the worst roommate ever. I should've come checked on you. Are you okay?" Elise plopped on the bed beside me, crushing my ankle.

I winced and tugged my foot free. "I told you to stay. I think I just drank too much or something. Or maybe the food didn't agree with me. It's fine. I had a great night until the end and then I was tired anyway." At that moment, a yawn erupted from deep in my soul, as if on cue.

"Do you need me to get you anything? Are you better now?"

I rubbed my eyes. "I'm good now. You should get some sleep. I want to hear all about your night, but maybe tomorrow? We could do lunch and then facials, my treat."

Elise leaned in and hugged me. "You are the best roommate ever." She stood and started towards her bed then paused, turning back to me. "How exactly did you leave things with Joel?"

From the half-cringe on her face, I suspected Joel had done exactly what I'd hoped he would and turned his attention immediately to Lana, the prom queen. I offered a reassuring smile to my roommate.

"I told him I wasn't feeling well and thought I'd had too much to drink or something. And I thanked him for an amazing evening and said I loved being friends with him but that we both knew he was way out of my league for anything more than friends. Then I told him he should try his luck with Lana."

"No!" she gushed.

I nodded, then shrugged.

"But he is soooo not out of your league."

I agreed, but it didn't matter. I didn't want to hurt the guy's feelings, and I definitely didn't want to stir up any drama that would interfere with my plans for an idyllic last month at school. But Joel wasn't Luca, and while maybe someday I could settle for a guy who wasn't Luca, today was not that day.

The next few weeks were a frenzy of excitement. I muddled through final exams, putting the expected bare minimum effort into my last semester, and I indulged in every single one of the senior traditions. By the time graduation weekend rolled around, I felt like I'd been at a week-long party, or maybe summer camp, not school. Exhaustion riddled my body, but in a good way, like after a long day at the beach with too much sunshine and salty air. I lived those weeks with no regrets, stacking up memories and documenting every moment so that Elise and I could compile our senior year scrapbooks together when she came to visit on my birthday.

When my parents and brothers arrived on campus for graduation, the mood shifted. Suddenly, everything felt more serious, more final. And as we flipped our tassels from one side of the mortarboard to the other during the ceremony, it hit me. High school was over. My childhood was over. This was truly the end of an era.

I said my goodbyes and left campus with my family that night. I stayed quiet the entire ride home, crushed by an almost unbearable sense of longing for the past that I'd only just experienced. It didn't help that my birthday was a week away. As the youngest of all of my friends, I was eager to finally turn eighteen, but there was also something depressingly final about officially reaching adulthood.

I was on the precipice of something; I just didn't know what. Everything was about to change, and for the first time in my life, I felt completely unprepared. I wasn't sure why I felt so hapless. I'd been here before. When my parents had abruptly forced me into a new boarding school, I'd known no one. I was starting over then, too, and it had turned out fine. I'd met Elise.

Then I'd met Luca.

But this was different. I'd barged onto campus full of resentment at my parents for upending my life and that negative energy had empowered me to be bold in a new, unfamiliar place.

Now I was making my own choices, ruling my own life. I didn't have anyone else to blame if things went wrong.

I had all summer to prepare for college, so I spent the week leading up to my birthday lounging by the pool. Or, more accurately put, wallowing by the pool. I couldn't stop thinking about Luca, how everything would be different if he'd just had enough faith to stick with our original plan. Maybe I'd still be headed to college in New York, but maybe not. Maybe I would've gone someplace in Italy. Maybe I would've actually gotten accepted to a fashion design program there. Now, I'd never know.

Elise kept telling me it was better this way, to start college with a completely fresh slate. She promised I'd fall in love so many times my head would spin, and she worried my new roommate would be even cooler than her. I appreciated her optimism, but I knew she was wrong. She was irreplaceable, and Luca was one of a kind. I just couldn't shake the feeling that, I wasn't quite eighteen and I'd already had—and lost— my one great love.

Luca

I didn't tell Alessio that I'd spent the night with Giada. For once, he hadn't accompanied me on the trip to the U.S., so that made the lie of omission easier, but it still didn't fully make sense. I wasn't even sure why I never told him. He wouldn't have judged me, wouldn't have told Chiara, and certainly wouldn't have told my papà. And Giada would never know I'd betrayed her trust.

But still, when Alessio asked about the trip, I'd shrugged and acted all nonchalant, like I hadn't wanted to freeze time when Giada had been curled up in my arms. I could tell he knew something was up, but in typically Alessio fashion, he gave me space.

By the end of the week, we were back in our normal routine,

anyway. My papà stopped sending us on dumb errands and let us have a little more authority at work. We started training Thomas and Giovanni. And we started to enjoy the good life.

I'd never been poor, but there was definitely something to be said about earning a big paycheck rather than just being born into it. I no longer felt sheepish about my fancy watches, designer jackets, or sportscars. Now, I deserved that shit. I worked hard and it showed.

Towards the end of May, my papà told me he'd paid for a full table at a local charity event. "Bring that girl you've been dating," he ordered.

That was the first direct confirmation I had that he even knew about Chiara, and I supposed the charity event was our first official date. I'd worried about appearing in public with her, since our time together up to that point had largely been spent in various states of undress.

I'd offered to buy her a dress, not-so-subtly reminding her that her attire needed to be more conservative than usual for the evening, but she'd declined.

"I'm not a child. I can dress myself, Luca," she'd snapped.

After that, I'd bought her a bracelet, figuring if it didn't match the dress she chose, at least it could function as an apology gift. Luckily, she accepted it as both an apology and an accessory for the evening. And she had managed to dress appropriately for the occasion, too.

It turned out that all of my worries for the evening had been unfounded. Chiara looked elegant in a navy blue gown, and she appeared at ease conversing with the other rich people at the event. She knew which forks went with which course, she didn't drink too much, and she kept her hands in an appropriate place when we danced. Perhaps the most alarming fact was that my parents both loved her, although that could've been just because she actually spoke Italian.

I excused myself towards the end of the evening to call Alessio and report that tidbit. He wasn't surprised, and asked if that wasn't a good thing.

"I don't know. Isn't it a red flag if my papà likes someone?" I asked.

"He likes me," Alessio replied.

That was true, although he didn't really know Alessio all that well. And I still had a weird feeling in my stomach whenever my mother introduced me and Chiara to someone as "mio filio e la sua ragazza". *My son and his girlfriend.* I barely knew Chiara. She couldn't actually be my girlfriend yet, could she?

That night, after we had sex, Chiara invited me to stay the night. She always did, and I always declined, claiming I had work in the morning. This time, I hesitated. I'd been a terrible sleeper lately. Maybe I'd actually sleep better with Chiara next to me. Or maybe we could just talk and get to know each other.

I hesitated, then agreed. She smiled and rolled onto me, placing her bony chin just below my breastbone. I shifted uncomfortably, then tried to distract myself. "My parents seemed to like you," I said after a moment, determined not to let her fall asleep in that position.

"Yeah? I'm glad. I mean, most parents do. They seemed great though."

I cringed, but said nothing. I hadn't told her about my relationship with my parents, and I didn't want to get into that now.

She lifted her head to look at me. "Seeing you with your dad was crazy though. He reminds me so much of you." She plopped her head back down. "You guys are just so much alike."

I nudged her head to the side, suddenly aware that I couldn't breathe in that position. Once free, I gasped for air, only for a wave of nausea to wash over me.

"You okay?" Chiara at least had the decency to look a little concerned.

I shook my head. "No, I actually feel a little off right now. I think I'm going to head home after all. I'll call you tomorrow."

I dressed in record time. The moment I got back to my apartment, I called Alessio. I told him everything—how the night had gone, what Chiara had said, and how I'd nearly run out in my underwear. He'd listened without interrupting until I stopped, then told me Lodovico mentioned needing someone to check up on something at the club in New York next week.

"I didn't mention it to you earlier because I wasn't sure if it was a good idea for you to be in town…" he paused, then said exactly what I'd been thinking. "Over her birthday. But why not? We'll go together. You could ignore her altogether. Or you could get some closure." He paused. "Or you could go see her and keep things open…"

I sighed, understanding exactly what he was hinting at. "I saw her when I was in town last time."

"Yeah. I figured as much."

"How?"

Alessio breathed a laugh. "I don't know, Luca. It's hard to explain, but you've got this look when you're thinking about her. I can just tell. And I knew it was prom. You had the date on your calendar until like a month before."

"Yes, when I deleted it because I didn't want you to think it was weird that I had my ex-girlfriend's prom on my calendar."

"It's not weird if you're planning to go."

"I wasn't planning to go."

"But you did go."

"Yeah."

"And?"

"I don't know."

"How'd she react?"

I considered that. "I'm not sure."

Alessio laughed. "Well, you weren't all bruised when you came back, so that's a good sign."

I wasn't sure if he was implying Giada would've beat me up or that I would've picked a random fight with a stranger if she'd rejected me, but either way, he was right. I had returned home unharmed.

"We spent the night together," I finally admitted.

"How was it?"

I squeezed my eyes shut. There weren't words adequate to describe my nights with Giada. Even if there were, I wouldn't waste them on Alessio. "How do you think?" I finally retorted.

"Did you tell her about Chiara?"

"Of course not."

"So go back for her birthday. She'll love it, and it'll be good for you."

I considered his suggestion. That was, in a way, the ideal solution. I'd have access to Giada whenever I needed her. I could get my Giada fix every month or so, then return to my normal life in Italy. No one would ever have to be the wiser. Even if my papà figured it out, he sure wouldn't care. He'd basically recommended I do that over a year ago anyway.

But I wasn't that shitty of a person. Not yet, anyway. Chiara might not see a difference between me and my papà, but I still did.

"I need sleep," I told Alessio.

I waited a few minutes and then texted him. "Book the tickets."

CHAPTER 33

Giada

The day before my eighteenth birthday began with a massive brunch with my entire family. Elise and I had dinner plans on my actual birthday, then the party with all our friends was slated for the day after that.

I'd just swallowed a bite of the most sinfully delicious cinnamon roll I'd ever tasted when my phone buzzed with a text. The message came from an unknown number, but I had no uncertainty about the sender's ID.

The text read, "Happy birthday eve, princess."

I gulped some orange juice, the cinnamon roll now having turned to a lump in my throat. A second text followed the first.

"I'm in town. I don't want to interrupt your birthday celebrations, but I have something for you. I can drop it off at the house if you don't want to see me, or I can meet you whenever it's convenient."

"Giada, no phones at the table!" my mom scolded.

"It's her brunch, she can do what she wants," my cousin said.

But I had already pushed away from the table, my chair

clanging noisily. "It's fine. I was headed to get more juice anyway."

I scurried into the kitchen, staring at my phone as if willing Luca to send a third message. He didn't, so before I could think better of it, I replied. "I can meet you later today. 4 o'clock?"

He agreed, and I listed the address of a coffee shop near town. I knew Enzo would drive me there without any suspicion.

"Juice?"

I nearly jumped out of my shoes as Angelo crept up behind me, the jug of orange juice in his hands. He refilled my cup, eying me like I was insane.

"Probably good you're having juice and not more coffee. You seem jumpy," he said.

"You shouldn't sneak up on people."

My brother quirked a brow. "No one was sneaking. I was literally standing here on my phone. One of my friends posted all these pictures from some charity thing in Italy. Lots of hot girls."

I cringed at the thought of my brother with any girl, then took the opportunity to tease him. "Wait, you have friends?"

He made a face, then kept scrolling on his phone. "I guess you probably don't want to see Luca's new girl," he said.

For once, it didn't sound like Angelo was trying to be a dick. As far as he knew, I'd gone out with plenty of guys since Luca. He probably thought I'd moved on. I briefly considered if he'd seen me texting Luca, but he couldn't have possibly from where he stood, and it wasn't like Luca had said his name anyway.

I tried to snatch the phone out of his hands but he lifted it out of my reach.

"Geez, hold on. I'll show you." Angelo clicked on something and then handed me the phone.

My breath caught in my throat at the first glimpse, but before Angelo could stop me, I snapped a screenshot and sent it to myself.

"Weirdo," he mumbled, yanking his phone back then returning to the dining room.

I stared down at the picture on my phone. Luca was devastatingly handsome in the photo, of course. He wore a tailored suit and everything about him looked expensive and mysterious. He wasn't smiling, but the girl on his arm was grinning widely enough for both of them. She was thin, with big boobs and excessively long legs. I begrudgingly admitted she was what most people would consider beautiful.

I instantly hated her. I texted the picture to Elise before returning to the table.

She wrote back right as I resumed eating. "Not your business. You broke up. For all you know, he's looking at pics of you and Joel right now. You don't get to be jealous."

I wrinkled my nose, but knew she was right.

"Giada, phone," my mom chided.

"My birthday, my rules," I said.

"Her hair looks like extensions tho," Elise texted. "And either way, you're way hotter."

I smiled and put away my phone.

Luca

I arrived at the café before Giada, ordered myself a plain black coffee and then settled on a vanilla latte for her. I grimaced as I watched the barista froth the milk. No matter how much time I spent in America, I'd never adjust to the American tradition of drinking milky coffee after noon. In Italy, a cappuccino or other creamy coffee drink was acceptable at breakfast, never later. Giada, on the other hand, liked her coffees how she liked her movies—sweet and void of substance.

"Ooh, trying something new," she teased, stepping up behind me right as I thanked the cashier for our finished drinks.

"Ha, ha," I replied. I handed her the latte, then pressed a kiss to her left cheek, then her right. "I got you vanilla If you prefer something else, I can—"

"No, this is good," she said. Giada led the way to a table in the corner. She sat against the wall, but I hated having my back to the door, so I scooted a chair to the adjacent corner by her and continued checking her out. She wore a ruffled, floral print skirt in bold colors that reminded me of the Mediterranean and a simple teal crop top. The outfit was sexy for sure, but on Giada somehow it also looked classy. Somehow, she always managed to look amazing without actually appearing to have put much effort into it.

She gazed up at me and I realized I'd been ogling her for too long. I needed to say something. I wanted to compliment her, but without giving her the wrong idea. "You look..." I paused, searching for the right word. "Well," I finally said, apparently having forgotten the English language altogether.

Giada bit back a smile. "Umm thanks? You look fantastic. I'd say Italy agrees with you." Her gaze was locked on my face at first, then traveled down my biceps.

Since I'd put on a fair amount of muscle since moving to Italy, the clothes I'd left behind in the States fit tighter. I'd known exactly how this short sleeved Polo accentuated my biceps and chest muscles when I'd chosen it for this meeting.

"You've been working out?" she asked.

I nodded. Then, already feeling flustered, I reached for the small gift bag I'd brought along and placed it on the table in front of her. Giada's face lit up like a child on Christmas, which was fitting, given the gift. She tapped her fingers together, then reached beneath the tissue paper and lifted up the delicate ornament.

"It's from that church we went to in Palermo, just the two of us," I explained. "They were selling these before Christmas at the craft fair, and I—"

"The church was selling salsa dancer ornaments?" she interrupted, rotating the ornament from side to side, smiling as she gazed at it.

The ornament portrayed a woman in a flowy red dress, so I understood why that had been her first thought. "I thought the same thing, but I believe it's actually an angel," I explained. "But it seemed kind of perfect since—"

"Since we learned to salsa dance right after we left that church," she finished, nodding. "Wow. Yeah. Thank you. I love it." Giada carefully placed the ornament back inside the gift bag then gazed up at me. "Why didn't you give this to me for Christmas?"

I chuckled, though it was an easy question. "I didn't see you over Christmas."

She raised an eyebrow.

"Well, and you hated me then."

"What makes you so confident I don't hate you now?"

I sipped my coffee and thought about that. "I don't know. You still should. I'm no good for you." I finally said, staring directly at her.

Giada turned away, gazing at the throng of people in line. After a minute, she sighed then faced me again. "Well, I didn't get you anything."

"It's not my birthday yet."

"This was clearly a Christmas present," she said, tapping the gift bag. "You didn't get me a birthday present, either."

I wrinkled my nose. "I still have a few hours."

"You never used to be a last minute guy."

I reached into my pocket and retrieved the charm bracelet I'd purchased before her prom. I hadn't wrapped it, and I almost hoped that made it seem like it was less expensive, or at least that I'd put less thought into it. Neither was true, of course. The bracelet was white gold, and bore her birthstone, along with a couple of diamond studded charms.

"Okay, I get the coffee cup and the nail polish and the pearl, but what is the fourth one?" she asked, pointing to a tiny colorful charm.

"Venetian glass," I explained. "Like the kind we used to find on the beach when we were kids." I didn't tell her that charm was custom made.

"Oh cool!" she exclaimed, draping the bracelet over her wrist, then extending her arm for me to fasten it.

"I left lots of space for you to get more charms, since your life is just beginning," I said.

Giada appeared to consider that, then leaned forward, rising off her seat. "Thank you," she said, before pressing her lips to my cheek. She lingered there, and her hand dropped to my thigh as she pulled back. My heart skipped a beat, but I said nothing.

We made awkward small talk for a while longer, and then I asked Giada what else she had planned for her birthday. She told me, but I noticed she didn't list anything taking place over the next twenty-four hours. I couldn't seriously be that lucky, could I?

If I was, it had to be a sign.

"Are you saying you don't have any plans for dinner?" I asked.

"I'm still full from brunch."

I masked my disappointment at her response. I had already started thinking of excuses to leave when she spoke again.

"If you wanted to hang out for a while, I'll probably be hungry again in a couple hours."

I looked over and our eyes locked. My heart thudded at the intensity of the stare from her sweet, sparkly brown eyes.

"Do you have a hotel room?" she asked. "Or—"

I nodded, even though I didn't. I'd brought an overnight bag with me in case things went well, but had planned on staying at my house if not. I pulled my phone out under the table and quickly texted Alessio. He could book the room online and send me the number and digital key before we even left the café. "Hang on, I need to send a message real fast," I said, typing quickly.

I glanced up after clicking send and saw Giada still staring at me. I noticed her hand hadn't left my thigh, either. "Do you want me to make reservations for dinner?"

"Takeout is fine."

"For your birthday?"

She nodded. "I just want to catch up." Giada paused, yanking back her hand. "I'm not necessarily staying overnight though. Or doing…anything. But I'd like to talk someplace more private."

"Okay. I can drive you home whenever you want."

Giada stood abruptly, carrying her purse and her gift bag, but leaving her empty coffee cup for me to dispose of. I followed her out of the café, then placed a hand on the small of her back and guided her towards my car.

It felt oddly risky, being out in the middle of the day with her, like anyone could see us. But then, so what if they did? We weren't doing anything wrong. Not yet, anyway. Not ever, really. We were both consenting adults.

I carried my bag up to the hotel room when we went, holding open the door for Giada to enter before me. She made her way immediately to the window where, surprisingly, we actually had a view of the port. Alessio had done well. Then she turned back to face me.

"I miss when things weren't so awkward between us," she admitted.

"Me too."

"Do you think we'll ever be able to go back to being friends?"

I wasn't sure how to answer that, so I didn't. It wasn't that we hadn't ever been friends, because we had, back when we were kids. But back then, Giada hadn't looked like she did now. Or at least, I hadn't noticed.

"You don't want to be my friend?" she guessed.

I shrugged. "I do, but I just don't know how to be friends with someone I'm attracted to."

That made her smile. "You're not attracted to your other friends?"

"I don't really have other friends."

Her smile widened. "Yeah, it is kind of distracting."

"What is?"

"The attraction thing."

"Oh? So you feel that too?" I asked.

Giada rolled her eyes. "Yeah, like you didn't pick that shirt on purpose. You know exactly what you look like." Her expression changed, softened somehow. "And I still remember exactly what you feel like."

"Feel like?"

Giada stepped closer and rest her fingertips against my chest, lightly against, then with more pressure. I gripped her hand and gently pried it away from my chest. She looked visibly dejected, until I lifted my shirt over my head. Then I reached for her hands and placed both of them on my chest.

She sucked in a breath right as all of my breath whooshed out of me. I supposed it was a little distracting. I let her grope me for a minute, then I stepped closer, pressing my hand into the bare small of her back. I hauled her firmly against me, certain she could feel every inch of my desire for her. Then, I captured her lips with my own.

We kissed for an eternity, or so it felt. I loved kissing Giada, and I hadn't thought that was odd until I'd met Chiara, and quicky discovered I didn't like kissing her at all. I felt the impact of Giada's kisses all over my body, in a weird way that both satisfied me and left me desperate for more.

I'd planned to follow Giada's lead, but my hands had a mind of their own, and soon tugged that tiny crop top up over her head. When she didn't protest that, I unfastened her bra, and it tumbled to the ground. I spent the next hour pleasuring Giada in every way I knew how, letting her reciprocate only once. Finally, once we should've both been fully sated, we made love.

My only thoughts in the moment were of her—how Giada felt moving against me, how beautiful she looked, how her skin tasted, how her soft moans sounded, even the faint, yet distinct, smell of her arousal…

But after, when Giada curled against me, her head against my chest, I thought of Chiara. Sex wasn't like this with her, and I wasn't sure it ever would be. What if Chiara wasn't the problem? What if it was me? What if I was destined to never have this sort of physical or emotional connection with anyone else ever again?

CHAPTER 34

Giada

Words couldn't describe how relaxed I felt by the time Luca and I had put our clothes back on and begun eating our dinners. We'd forgotten to ask for plates, so we took turns forking bites out of the various flimsy cartons. I'd suggested Thai food, and Luca had agreed without protest, even though I knew it wasn't his favorite. He dared me to eat one of the spicy peppers and I pretended to cram it into my mouth before pouncing on him and kissing him, leading to us both giggling. It felt like old times.

I could tell we were both getting full by how much we'd slowed down, and now I was comfortable enough to pry into Luca's personal life.

"Can I ask you a question?" I asked.

"Si, but I might not answer." His expression was playful.

"Who's Chiara?"

Luca's face fell.

I wanted to spare him the awkwardness of trying to come up

with an excuse, but I also needed to hear his full, unfiltered explanation.

"She's an Italian girl I've been dating. Why do you ask?"

"Angelo showed me a picture of the two of you."

Luca rolled his eyes. "I fucking hate that stronzo."

I wasn't sure exactly what name he'd just called my brother, but I figured it wasn't a compliment. I didn't normally defend Angelo either, but in this case, he wasn't exactly the bad guy. "We broke up seven months ago. He assumed I knew you'd moved on." I paused. "Besides, I dated other guys."

"Guys, plural?" Luca repeated. "More than just Joel?"

I nodded. "Nothing serious, but you told me not to wait for you."

"I know, but you don't always listen to me."

I smirked at his annoyance, then remembered the rest of my questions. "So, is this Chiara a girlfriend, or just—?"

Luca fidgeted with a carton before folding the top down, wiping his hands on a napkin, then placing the carton behind him. "I don't know. I don't consider her a girlfriend, but I'm not sure how she thinks of me. We only went out a couple times and I wouldn't say it's anything serious."

"Is it over now?"

He inhaled slowly. "It wasn't when I left, but we weren't ever exclusive, so…"

My stomach clenched involuntarily. I tried to stay calm, to act the way a mature adult would, but I couldn't. I'd literally just had sex with a guy who was now telling me he had a girlfriend back home. *I* was the other woman.

I pushed to my feet and began gathering the takeout cartons. Tears began to blur my eyes, but I kept tidying. Luca reached for my arm, but I swatted him away.

"Giada, come on, stop."

"No, Luca, it's fine. I'm just cleaning up, and then…"

He gripped my arm harder, yanking me to him. "Listen to me. You didn't do anything wrong."

"Something tells me your girlfriend would view things differently," I said, wiping my eyes on my arm.

"No, that's what I'm trying to tell you. It's not like that. I didn't cheat on her. We don't have that kind of relationship. We just go out sometimes. For all I know, she's with someone else this weekend too."

"Are you just saying that to make me feel better?" I asked.

He kissed the top of my head, still holding me to him like he thought I'd run if he loosened his grip. "You know I'd tell you anything if I thought it would spare you pain, but no. That's the truth."

"So I suppose you'll tell me you didn't sleep with her?"

"Giada, baby, come on."

"Well?" I wriggled in his arms so I could pull back enough to see his face.

Luca gazed down at me as he answered. "No, I'm not going to tell you that."

It took me a minute to piece together what he was admitting.

"I don't want to lie to you, so I'm not going to. I slept with Chiara before I knew her last name. I barely knew anything about her." He let go of me altogether and dropped onto the bed, apparently ready to let me run away if that was my choice. "I also fooled around with one of the strippers at a club."

I couldn't hide my disgust.

"Giada, I know you must think I don't care since I was the one who ended things, but that's not the case. I was a mess after we broke up. I still am. I did all sorts of crazy shit to try to get you out of my head, and I'm not proud of any of it, but…" He flung his hands in the air like he was giving up.

I gazed at him for a long moment, trying to gauge how I felt about his admission. Truly, it just raised more questions. "Why didn't you tell me this before?"

Luca scowled. "How would that be fair? It didn't seem right for me to dump you and then be like oh, don't worry, I'm miserable too. It was my decision. You didn't have any say in getting hurt."

I sat on the edge of the bed beside him. "I just assumed you moved on right away. You had your whole new fancy life in Italy and just started over without me."

"You really think you're that easy to get over?" Luca breathed a laugh. "No one in Italy can take your place."

"What about Chiara?"

Luca made a face like that was the dumbest question anyone had ever asked. And then he started rambling in Italian. Just when I started to wonder if he'd forgotten who he was talking to, forgotten that I could hardly understand a word of Italian, he stopped. He brushed my hair off my forehead and tucked it behind my ear.

"You are the only person I've ever called Amore or Tesoro," he said, his fingers lingering on the side of my face. "And I know this makes me sound like a jerk, but that really scares me. When I think about it, I can't imagine ever meeting someone else that I want to call that." Luca sighed, frowning. "What if it never feels right with someone else?"

I wasn't sure what to say to that. As a big believer in signs, my philosophy was that if something didn't feel right, it probably wasn't. Luca didn't think that way though, and it wouldn't help for me to just tell him to trust his instincts. Still, sitting beside him, listening to his words, it was hard to ignore the gist of what he was saying.

Luca, like me, was miserable on his own. And he definitely wasn't convinced that we weren't supposed to be together long-term. We were actually on the same page, for once. I just needed to get him to admit it. Well, and to be willing to have faith that we could survive a year of long distance. Surely I could transfer or study abroad after this year, and...

"I should probably get you home," Luca said, his deep voice penetrating my thoughts.

"Is that what you want?" I made no effort to conceal the hurt in my tone.

"No! But it's late, and I don't want you to get in trouble."

"I'm an adult. I don't have a curfew anymore," I said. We both giggled at the ridiculousness of that last notion.

"You're technically not an adult for another two and a half hours," Luca said, consulting his Panerai watch.

"I can't think of a better way to start my new year than with you," I said.

Luca leaned in slowly as if about to kiss me, then paused, close enough that I felt his warm breath on my lips. I realized he was waiting for permission, but it took me longer to remember why. Yes, he'd confessed that he was dating someone else. But we'd broken up before then, so it wasn't like he cheated on me.

Besides, what stood out to me most was the fact that he'd told me. Luca could've hidden so much about his life over in Italy, but instead, he trusted me with the truth.

I closed the last inch gap between us, relishing the softness of his lips against mine. Kissing Luca felt like coming home after a long, hard journey. Our mouths fit together like two pieces of a puzzle, and our tongues moved against each other in a practiced dance that left us both breathless and wanting more. I could've kissed Luca for hours.

In the end, I did just that.

By the time the clock struck twelve, officially commencing my birthday, I was wrapped up in Luca's strong arms under the thick cotton sheets. We'd ditched our clothes almost an hour before, but the heat of Luca's body kept me plenty warm.

"Happy birthday, amore," Luca whispered, his tongue tickling the side of my ear.

"You always have to be the first to say it, don't you?" I teased, my voice coming out breathy and wanton.

Luca merely grinned in response, moving slowly inside me as the pleasure mounted higher.

Luca

I hadn't meant to fall asleep, hadn't wanted to waste my limited time with Giada, but at some point, I had. When I awoke, light was streaming in through the gaps around the blinds. My arm ached from the prolonged immobility, but I didn't dare shift and risk waking Giada. Her hair tickled my cheek, but the delicious strawberry scent was so pleasant that I didn't mind.

Giada looked so peaceful when she slept. She reminded me of Sleeping Beauty, or some other princess under a spell of sorts. More than anything, she deserved some sort of heroic prince who could break the spell and make all her wishes come true.

I was not that prince. I doubted I ever would be, but what mattered was that I wasn't now. The prince of Giada's fairy tale wouldn't run off and fuck some Italian maiden two nights a week before seducing the princess on her birthday and then abandoning her again for another three months. The prince wouldn't beat the shit out of someone over a botched delivery of watches.

No, the prince was supposed to rescue the princess. And the one thing I knew for sure was that if Giada stayed with me, sooner or later she'd need rescuing from me, not by me.

My shoulder spasmed and I tried to slowly shimmy my arm free, but the movement woke Giada. She sighed and rolled towards me, smiling before her eyes even opened.

"Sorry," I mumbled. "My arm went numb."

She pressed a kiss to my bare chest in response, saying nothing for several moments. I started to wonder if she'd fallen back asleep when she spoke.

"I like starting my birthday out beside you," she said.

"Well, if we're getting technical, I wasn't so much beside you as inside—" I began.

She sat upright and swatted me with a pillow. "Luca!"

I grinned at the gorgeous pink color flooding her cheeks, then stretched my arm. "Do you need to be home now, or can I feed you first?"

"I always have time for food," she said.

The hotel didn't have room service, so I pulled on some clothes and went to the café we'd visited the prior day to pick up food. When I returned with coffee, juice, and pastries, Giada had already dressed and styled her hair.

I pouted, but she pointed to the clock.

"Isn't checkout at eleven?" she asked.

"I paid for late checkout. We have the room till one. Plenty of time for whatever the birthday girl desires."

"Birthday girl is famished," she said, reaching into the bag.

I was too, so we dug into the pastries. Giada told me more about the plans for her party while we ate, and then when we'd both had our fill, the conversation turned heavy.

"How long are you in town?"

"I leave Tuesday, but I have work in New York until then, so I'll be at the house in Staten Island."

Giada nodded. "And then what?"

I quirked a brow.

"When is your next trip?"

My abs tightened and I felt tension creeping into my jaw. "I don't know. Most of my work is still in Italy, and it tends to be pretty last minute when my papà asks me to come to the U.S."

Giada stared at me, her eyes searching my face. "I don't understand."

"What is there to understand?" I stood, and began gathering my stuff.

"It seemed like we were on the same page last night. You told me you don't feel the same way about other girls as you do me. Was that a lie?"

"No!"

"So why are you being all weird and stand-offish now?"

"I didn't realize I was."

She cocked her head to the side and propped her hand on her hip. "I'm just asking when you're going to visit. I know you have to work, and I don't expect you to have to be the only one to make adjustments here, but I've already committed to school. At least for the year, I can only travel on breaks." She paused. "Unless I defer a year, but—"

My heart pounded in my chest. "Giada, no. I think there's been a misunderstanding here. I don't…I mean, well, why would you defer?"

The pleading look in her sweet, puppy dog eyes nearly broke me. "So we can be together," she said, as if it were the most obvious thing in the world.

Shit. "Giada, nothing has changed with us. I thought you understood that. Yes, I miss what we had, and yes, I love being with you. But that doesn't mean we're right for each other."

Her bottom lip began to quiver. "You said you didn't think you'd ever find anyone else you'd want to call amore."

My chest tightened so severely that I wondered if I was actually having a heart attack. "Yeah, and I meant it. But Giada, it's been like six months. It's not like I've been searching for years."

Giada's expression turned cold. "Seriously?"

I finished shoving my stuff into my bag then turned back to face her. "Yes, seriously. We have our whole lives ahead of us. So yeah, I'm not ready to completely write off the chance of finding someone else. And what about you? You've dated like one other person. There's a whole world out there. You'll find someone better than me."

I thought my words were cruel enough to make my point, but Giada had a different take. She reached for my hand.

"I don't want someone better, Luca. I want you, and like you said, we're young. We have our whole lives to get better together." Her eyes pleaded with me with a suffocating intensity.

I shook my hand free of hers, but she kept talking.

"All I'm asking is that you have a little faith. Trust that we wouldn't both feel the way we do if we weren't meant to be together."

"I don't have faith in anything and I never will," I replied.

Suddenly parched, I reached for my bottle of juice and drained the last sips. I clutched the bottle in my hand, trying to control my breathing, trying to figure out how the fuck I let the night get this out of control. I was actually yelling at the sweetest person on the entire planet—on her literal birthday. If all the other shit I did didn't make me a monster, this sure did.

"You and I are different people, Giada. Don't you see that? I'll never understand why you want anything to do with me."

"Because I love you, Luca. And that means something. And I know you feel the same way, or you wouldn't keep coming back to me." She held up her wrist and jingled her bracelet in my face. "You wouldn't buy me thoughtful gifts like this if you didn't care."

I knocked her arm out of the way. "That's not even the point. You could do better. Do you get that? Did you hear the part about me and Chiara? Or me with the stripper? That's the kind of guy I am. Stop deluding yourself into thinking I'm something I'm not."

"Stop treating me like an idiot!" she shouted back. "I heard what you said about the other girls, and you know what I got from it? That you were willing to be honest with me, even when it was hard."

I couldn't hold back my laughter at that. "Okay, I was honest about that, but every day I do ten other things I can't tell you about. My whole life is a lie. I am not the nice guy you think I am."

"Bullshit, Luca. You get to choose who you are, just like the rest of us."

Something inside me snapped and I chucked the juice bottle at the wall. Giada startled at the explosive crash as the glass shattered into pieces all around her, but her eyes didn't budge from mine. I lunged forward, but she kept right on talking.

"You love to blame everything on your dad, but at the end of the day, you decide what kind of a man you are."

My palm was centimeters away from slapping her cheek when I stopped myself. I was shaking and my breath was ragged, but Giada didn't even fucking flinch. "You don't know what you're talking about," I finally growled, still looming over her.

"I know you won't hurt me," she said, only infuriating me more.

"That's where you're wrong," I said. "I almost just did."

"But you didn't."

My hands clenched into fists at my sides. "Someday I won't stop myself. I won't be able to. And I don't just mean hurt you like that. No amount of you saying I'm a good person will make it true. I'm just not. I do horrible things all the time. Eventually, I'll cheat on you or embarrass you or forget your birthday altogether. No matter what happens, I'll end up disappointing you."

"You already have," Giada whispered, maintaining a brief moment of eye contact before shoving me back enough so she could step out from between my body and the wall.

I peered down, feeling a sharp sting in my foot as a shard of glace sliced into my heel. I plucked out the fragment, then walked across the room to my shoes, leaving dots of blood in my wake. I thrust my feet into my shoes, wishing for the sake of the expensive Italian leather, that I was a sock person.

Giada watched as I reached for my bag, slid my phone and wallet back into my pocket, then moved towards the door. Right before I reached the handle, she spoke again.

"If you're not willing to try, there's nothing I can do. I can't save you if you'd rather drown," she said. "I meant everything I said to you last night, and I think you're making a huge mistake.

But I'm not going to keep setting myself up for disappointment."

I nodded once, even though I wasn't sure exactly what any of that meant for me. Thankfully, she clarified.

"I don't want to see you ever again. Don't call, text, write, or drop by unless you're ready to admit you're in control of your own choices. I don't want anything to do with you until you're willing to at least try to be a good person. That's the least I deserve."

I drew in a shaky breath. "You're right," I agreed. "I'm sorry about…everything." I opened the door and then gazed back at her one last time. "I hope the rest of your birthday is happy."

I got to my car in record time and made it to a nearby parking garage before I had to pull over. I couldn't catch my breath. I was panting like a dog, but getting dizzier and dizzier with every shallow inhale. After a few minutes, I gave up and texted Alessio.

"How fast can you get here?" I asked. Then I sent him the address.

CHAPTER 35

Giada

I watched through the window as Luca's car left the parking lot. Then, before I completely fell apart, I called the only person I could think of.

"Hello?" Enzo sounded thoroughly confused when he answered.

"Hey, am I catching you at a bad time?"

"No. I just wasn't expecting to hear from you today. I figured you had big plans and all," he paused, then added, "Happy birthday."

"Thank you. Listen, um, I needed a favor, but if you're busy or if you're with a girl or something…"

He laughed. "I'm alone, Giada. I'm on an errand for your father, actually. What do you need?"

I swallowed. "I need a drinking buddy who won't judge me or try to sleep with me."

A lengthy silence ensued.

"Enzo?"

"Yeah, um, I'm here. I just… um, it's like noon. On your birthday. Did something happen? Are you okay?"

"I'll be fine. But I really don't want to be alone today."

"Why would you be alone? Aren't you having a party?"

"That's Saturday. I was supposed to go out with Elise tonight, but if I tell her what I did…" I stopped myself. "I need to reschedule with her is all. Or at least have some buffer before I see her. Are you free?"

"Free for what?"

"To go out for drinks."

He chuckled softly. "Giada, you're underage. Even if I don't get arrested for taking a teenager out drinking, your father would literally murder me. So, that's a no from me."

I sighed. "I'm officially eighteen now. An adult. So I'm allowed to hang out with older men without anyone going to prison."

"Drinking age is twenty-one, Princess."

I grimaced. Of course I knew that, but for some reason I thought his concern was that someone would think we were dating. Of course not. "Right. Well, we can both pretend I don't have a fake ID and just get drunk at home."

"Your home or mine?" he asked, his tone extra snarky. "Oh wait…same place, and absolutely no way."

"A hotel?"

Now he outright laughed. "Is this a prank? I mean, you don't actually want your father to kill me, right?"

I had no response to that. Obviously he was exaggerating, but I wasn't sure that mattered.

"You're not supposed to say no to the birthday girl," I reminded him. I wasn't above begging. "How about I still go for drinks with Elise and you just pick us up early, before she can get on my case? And then you can talk me off a ledge and make sure I don't spend the last few hours of my birthday crying."

"Giada, what happened?"

"I don't want to get into it on the phone."

"Where are you?"

I cringed and rubbed my forehead. "A hotel room."

"What? With who? Where?"

"It doesn't matter. I'm alone now. I..." I stopped midsentence. Saying the word "alone" out loud, I truly felt its impact. I was alone, and probably would be till the end of time. I inhaled slowly, clenched my jaw, and focused all of my attention on not crying. But it was futile.

Before I knew it, I was sobbing.

"Which hotel, Giada? I'm on my way."

Enzo was nearly a half hour away. A rational woman would've used the time to clean herself or the room, but I just climbed under the covers and sobbed until I heard the knocking on the door.

I peered out the peephole, then unlocked the door. Enzo barely looked at me before brushing past, scanning the room.

"You're alone?" he asked.

My eyes followed his movement to his hip, where his hand rested against a handgun. "Yes. Jesus, Enzo. You don't need a gun!"

"What happened?" he asked.

I sniffled and ran my hand through my hair. I must have looked terrible, but the room was in worse condition.

He looked around the room again, his gaze stopping on the trail of blood for several beats before he peered back up at me. "You need to tell me what happened, Giada. My mind is going to some dark places, and—"

"Luca," I interrupted.

That shut him up.

"Luca was here."

Panic flooded his face as his hand drifted to his hair. "I didn't realize you were back together."

"We're not."

"But you..." he glanced at the clearly disheveled bed, the

empty miniature bottle of booze, and then, oh God, the condom wrapper we'd forgotten to throw out. Cringing, I slowly kicked it under the bed, even though it was obvious Enzo already seen it.

I shook my head, wanting to change his focus.

"Wait, did he force you to…"

It took me a moment to realize what he was thinking. "No, God. No. Okay, um, Luca was here last night, I mean, I was with him overnight. And yes, *that* happened, but everything was totally consensual, so you don't need to get all overprotective alpha male on me now."

"He didn't hurt you?" he asked, crouching down and pinching a tiny piece of glass between his thumb and forefinger, inspecting it like a detective.

"I…no. He was mad," I said.

Enzo's eyes flared.

"I mean, we fought. Like, argued. And he threw a bottle and it broke and then he stepped in the glass and I'm totally fine. He wouldn't hurt me. I mean he almost…" I stopped talking, sunk onto the foot of the bed, and rubbed my forehead. "I wanted to see him last night. It was my idea to stay the night."

A long silence passed between us. Then Enzo scratched his head, still wincing. "You spent the night with Luca but you're not back together with him?"

"Right."

Enzo blew out a breath. "Why am I here, Giada?"

That was an excellent question. It took me a moment to remember why. "Because now it's over for real between me and Luca. I told him this couldn't happen again, that he shouldn't call me the next time he's in town, and—"

"Wait, this happened before? You meeting up with him since the breakup?"

I debated lying, then quickly decided against it. The whole reason I'd chosen Lorenzo and not Elise to confide in was because he wouldn't judge me. Or at least I didn't think he would. "I spent the night with him after prom."

Enzo inspected the corner of the bed then sat down on the desk chair. "I thought you went to prom with some Jewish guy."

I wasn't completely sure Joel was Jewish, but that was irrelevant. "Yeah, but I left with Luca. We'd sort of left it that it was a one-time thing, but then he texted again yesterday because he was in town. He always likes wishing me happy birthday right at midnight…"

I paused as Enzo rolled his eyes, like that was the most ridiculous thing he'd ever heard.

"Anyway, so we got together last night to…celebrate early."

He snickered at my word choice, but let me continue.

"It was nice. Amazing, really, but…"

Now Enzo cringed. "I do not need details, Giada."

I blew out a sigh. "I'm not talking about the sex, although no complaints there. Not that I have anything to compare to, but—"

"How much caffeine have you had today?" he interrupted.

"Some," I admitted. "Now just let me talk. Anyway, I mean that being with Luca is amazing. Everything is just so easy with him."

"I'm sorry. Easy? Are we talking about the same guy? Luca Marino?"

I nodded.

"He's the least easy-going human alive."

"Stop. Interrupting." I glared. "Luca's different with me. We just work together really well. Everything is completely perfect and every time we get together for a night, I'm reminded of how perfect it is and how miserable I am without him. So this morning we got in a big fight because he isn't even willing to try the long distance thing. I told him not to call me ever again and that we weren't going to hook up again or see each other again."

"Okay."

"And I can't talk to Elise about all of this because she'll lecture me about letting a man use me for sex and then if I tell her I'm happy with him, she'll lecture me about telling him we shouldn't see each other. I'm already second guessing myself enough. And…"

Enzo scooted his chair closer and pressed his hand over mine. "Giada, take a breath. Look at me."

I did as he said.

"You're a smart girl. You are protecting yourself. You already dealt with the trauma of the breakup once, and every time you spend a night with him, it reopens that wound and you have to start healing all over again. You need to move on, and you can't do that when you're still involved with him."

"So you think I did the right thing?"

"Yes."

"And you think he's using me for sex?"

He laughed.

"I'm completely serious."

"Well, honestly, no. I don't. From everything you've said and every time I've seen you guys together, I think he really likes you. You guys had this connection and… I don't know, you both seem to enjoy being together. And don't take this the wrong way, but Luca doesn't need to use someone for sex. He has plenty of options and willing partners if all he wants is sex. He kept coming back to you because he wanted you."

I squeezed my eyes shut. "I'm so confused."

"Giada, you're eighteen. You have your whole life ahead of you. If there's such a thing as soul mates and Luca is yours, you'll end up with him. But you can't put your life on hold for the boy you started dating at fifteen. You need to experience the world, date other boys, practice being single for a while. Figure out what you like. Then if it's meant to be, it will be."

I inhaled slowly, letting his words wash over me then digesting them slowly. That was what I needed to remember. That was what I believed.

God put Luca in my path for a reason, and right now I couldn't tell if that was because Luca was supposed to be my husband or if Luca was just supposed to be some stepping stone towards some other part of my life. I needed to be patient and trust that I'd see the big picture eventually.

"I need to have faith," I finally said, still breathing deeply.

"Yes. Every princess gets her happily ever after."

Luca

Alessio made it in record time, but I'd managed to calm myself down by then anyway. When I saw his car pull into the garage, I jumped into the passenger seat.

"I need to make sure she gets home okay. Take me to the hotel," I said.

My friend frowned, but started driving while pointing out the numerous holes in my logic. I hadn't told him what had happened, but he could surely guess it hadn't ended well.

"You can't take her home if your car is still in a garage, and if you left in a huff, I'm guessing she doesn't want to go anywhere with you anyway. Is your plan to have me drive her home?" he asked.

"I don't know. I could call an Uber for her. I just want to make sure she's okay."

"Why wouldn't she be?" The question was pointed.

"Jesus, I didn't hurt her," I said. "But it's her birthday."

"Okay, so she's an adult. She can get her own ride home."

I blew out a sigh. Alessio parked in the back corner of the hotel lot. We were only about forty meters from the entrance, so I could see the door, but it was unlikely anyone exiting would notice us.

"Why don't we wait and watch from here?" he suggested.

"What if she already left?"

"Then you're worried for nothing."

I couldn't fight with his logic, so I just glared out the window. After a minute, I started to unload random details from the night. I told him how it started well, then how she thought we were getting back together. I even admitted how I felt with her, how it was so different than with Chiara.

"So why don't you get back together with her, Luca? You don't need to torture yourself."

I wanted to explain my reasoning in a way that Alessio would understand, in a way that wouldn't result in him just telling me I wasn't broken. Finally, I said, "I threw a bottle right by her head. And then, I almost slapped her."

I paused, and a twinge of a grimace crossed Alessio's face, but he said nothing.

"My hand was a fraction of an inch from her face before I stopped myself. Do you know what the worst part was? Giada didn't even flinch. She made no attempt to protect herself." I traced my fingers along the stubble covering my chin. "That's when I realized she'll never save herself from me. I'll completely destroy her and she'll let me do it."

Alessio opened his mouth to say something, but just then the entrance to the hotel swung open and out stepped Giada. She still wore the floral skirt and crop top from the day before, which I guessed shouldn't be surprising. She paused just outside the door and turned towards a man exiting behind her. He was tall, dark haired, and distinctly Italian. I figured out who he was right as he wrapped an arm around Giada's shoulder.

"She called Lorenzo?" Alessio asked.

I didn't answer, could barely even breathe with how jealous I felt. Seeing him touch her made me feel like my blood had heated a hundred degrees and my heart couldn't beat fast enough to compensate.

I watched as they stopped by a sedan. He reached for the

handle of the passenger door, then stopped, turning to her as she said something. I would've given anything to be able to hear their discussion over the next minute. Then, Giada rose on her toes and hugged him.

A noise escaped my throat, like a half-grunt, half-gag, and Alessio tapped the wheel anxiously.

Lorenzo opened the car door, waited while Giada sat, then closed the door. His gaze scanned the parking lot as he walked around the car, and I could've sworn he paused when we were directly in his line of sight. I couldn't be sure that he saw me, thanks to his dark sunglasses, but I would've bet on it.

He must not have told Giada though, as a moment later, they pulled out of the lot.

"They're not dating," Alessio reminded me after they were gone. "He's just her driver."

"I know." But that didn't make me any less jealous about the fact that Lorenzo got to spend time with her and take care of her. He got to see Giada smile, got to be a part of her normal, day-to-day life.

"Marco would never allow that. And he's too old for her anyway," Alessio continued, apparently sensing my skepticism.

I wasn't sure about either of those things. Lorenzo may be older than me, but barely, and in another couple of years, that age difference wouldn't matter much. I blew out a sigh, but still couldn't formulate words.

"The ball's in your court, Luca. You just have to decide what you want," Alessio said.

That set me off. I flung my hands in the air and turned to him. "Why does everyone keep saying shit like that to me? What choice do I have in any of this? I want to be with Giada, but I'm no good for her. I can't change that."

"Yeah, I'm sorry." Alessio sounded uncharacteristically serious. "I guess what I mean is figure out what you want, within the realm of your actual reality. Stop keeping Giada on your mental backburner. Tell yourself she's out of the picture for you for good and start enjoying what you've got. If you don't like Chiara that way, fine. There's a hundred more hot girls you haven't even sampled yet. And if you don't like any of them, you can start dating the ones on the mainland."

I cracked a smile at that.

"Giada and you had something special. You'll never forget that first true love. But your adventure is just beginning, Luca. Don't let the past hold you back."

I took a few deep breaths, then nodded. "Alright. Take me back to my car. We should get some work done.

Alessio shifted the car into drive, then looked at me. "You okay?"

"No," I said. "But maybe someday I will be."

The End… for Now

*T*hanks for reading! If you enjoyed this story, feel free to leave a review! Click Here to Review

ACKNOWLEDGMENTS

Thanks to all who are joining on the full journey of the Mafiosa Princess. This book is a response to everyone who wondered about the backstory of our main series characters.

If you're reading this in the middle of the rest of the series, be sure to check out the ninth book in the series. If you're starting with the prequels before starting Book 1 in the series, don't despair… our characters will find happiness again someday!

ABOUT THE AUTHOR

Liza Malloy writes contemporary romance and women's fiction. She's a sucker for alpha males, bad boys, dimples, and muscles, and she can't resist a man in uniform. Liza loves creating worlds where her heroine discovers her own strength and finds her Happily Ever After. When Liza isn't reading or writing torrid love stories, she's a practicing attorney. Her other passions include gummy bears, jelly beans, and the occasional marathon. She lives in the Midwest with her four daughters and her own Prince Charming.

Visit her website at https://authorlizamalloy.wixsite.com/lizamalloy

Join her email list at http://eepurl.com/gnuROD

ALSO BY LIZA MALLOY

Sixty Days for Love

For Love and Italian

Forbidden Ink

The Brothers' Band

The Brothers' Band: The Next Track

Hollywood Endings

Hollywood Beginnings

Supporting Roles

Legacy: The Awakening

Legacy: The Revelation

Legacy: The Reckoning

Mafiosa Princess

Mafiosa Princess: Sacrifice

Mafiosa Princess: Honor

Mafiosa Princess: Trust

Mafiosa Princess: Omertà

Mafiosa Princess: Loyalty

Mafiosa Princess: Faith

Mafiosa Princess: Family

Her Mafia Valentine (A Short Story)

Love All- A Steamy Sports Romance

The New Boyfriend (Kindle Vella)

Manic Love- A Billionaire Romance (Kindle Vella)

The Cowboy Assignment (Kindle Vella)

My So-Called Superpower (Kindle Vella)